Stacy Lynn Carroll

ISBN: 978-0-9908041-5-4

Library of Congress Control Number: 2015941521

To my readers: thank you! Without you I'm just another crazy person, responding to the characters in my head.

And to Errin, Tena, Kami, and Alysa. Long live Gilmore Nights!

Other books by author Stacy Lynn Carroll:

*The Princess Sisters*
*Frogs & Toads*
*My Name is Bryan*
*A Tale of Tails (children's)*

# *Chapter One*

"Snow, come on! We're gonna be late!"

"Just a second!" she yelled back down the stairs to
her cousins. They were impatiently waiting for Snow White
to be ready so they could get to the movie before any
previews started.

"Where is that shoe?" Snow White asked aloud as
she continued to frantically search her room. All the
contents of her closet were strewn about the floor. Her
bedroom resembled the aftermath of a tornado, yet she
remained shoeless. With one sneaker on, she hobbled across
the carpet to look under her bed for the hundredth time.
She groaned in frustration when it didn't magically appear.

Snow White got back to her feet and put her hands
on her hips as she looked around. Her eyes stopped on the
tall, six-drawer dresser. She charged forward. She yanked
each drawer free and dumped the clothes in a big pile at her
feet. Still no shoe. Dropping to her stomach, she scanned
underneath. She was about to give up when her eye caught
sight of what looked like a blue shoelace hanging down
from behind the dresser.

Jumping to her feet again, Snow White smashed her
face against the wall. Sure enough, her other sneaker was
wedged between the dresser and the wall. She grabbed the
edge of the white, painted wood and slid the dresser out
about a foot. The now empty dresser moved with relative
ease.

"How did you get back here?" she asked, extending her arm as far as she could to grab it. Her fingers closed around the object of triumph and she pulled it to freedom.

With the shoe gone, Snow White noticed a little white card lying on her floor behind the dresser. One last time, she extended her arm as far as she could and raked her fingers along the carpet. Her middle finger finally touched paper, and she slid it out slowly. She picked up the card and examined it carefully. She couldn't believe she had forgotten about this!

Snow White could hear a loud BEEP BEEP from Belle's car down in the parking lot. Cinderella's voice came up the stairs. "Do you need help? Belle, Aurora, and Ariel are in the car waiting."

"No thanks, I found it."

"Well, let's go then!"

"Actually..." Snow White frowned down at the little card. "Go ahead and go without me."

"Are you sure?"

"Yeah, I need to take care of something instead."

Snow White listened for the front door to close, and then she waited a minute longer until she heard Belle's car drive away. She held up the card and stared at it again:

*Noah Wilkins*
*District Attorney*

She remembered when he handed her the business card about four months ago and told her to call with any questions. Well, she had plenty of questions! And her mom wouldn't tell her anything about why the lawyer had come in the first place. Snow White decided it was time to take matters into her own hands.

With a racing heart and trembling fingers, Snow White pulled out her cell phone and began to dial.

"Noah Wilkins' office, this is Janette. How may I help you?"

Snow White opened her mouth to speak, but no words came. All thoughts vanished as she stared down at the card still clutched between her fingers.

"I…I think I have the wrong number," she said and quickly hung up. Snow White slumped down on the carpet. She picked up her shoe and hurled it across the room. It smashed into her wall on the opposite side, tearing a corner on her favorite movie poster. Snow White punched the tattered carpet until her knuckles burned red.

"Why can't I do this?" she yelled up at her ceiling. "This man is the key to getting some answers!"

Snow White stomped into the bathroom and ran her aching hands under the cold water. She bent over the sink and splashed some water on her face before she crumpled to the bathroom floor. Tears sprang to her eyes as she lay on her side with her arms wrapped around her bent knees. After a good, long cry, Snow White took several slow, deep breaths and sat up, her back leaning against the cupboard door.

Snow White slowly got to her feet and dragged herself back into her room. She bent down, scooping the card off the floor. "This is no time to be scared," she said aloud. "I've been wanting answers my whole life. Don't chicken out now." Snow White shook her hands back and forth, trying to force the nerves away. She picked up her phone again and clicked redial. Then she squeezed her eyes shut and waited.

"Noah Wilkins' office, this is Janette. How may I help you?"

"May I speak to Mr. Wilkins, pl-please?" Snow White's voice was barely a squeak.

"I'm sorry, could you repeat that, please?"

Snow White took a deep breath and forced her fears aside. "May I speak to Mr. Wilkins, please?" she asked, louder.

"May I ask what this is in reference to?"

"Elizabeth Princess." Snow White wasn't sure if her mom's name would mean anything to this admin, but she figured it was worth a shot.

"Hold, please."

Snow White was surprised when the next thing she heard was a man's voice. "Hello? Is this Ms. Princess?"

"No, well, sort of. I'm her daughter. Do you remember me?"

The man sighed. "Yes, I do. What can I do for you?"

"I just want answers." Snow White could feel a lump rising in her throat and tried to swallow it back down.

"I don't feel it's my place to divulge any information at this time. I think you need to ask your mom these questions."

"But she won't tell me anything! Please, Mr. Wilkins, why did you come here? Why does my mom need a lawyer? Does it have anything to do with my dad? Do you know who he is?"

There was a long pause and Snow White feared he had hung up on her. "Hello?"

"I'm still here, Ms. Princess. I'm just thinking."

"Just call me Snow White."

"Like the princess?"

"Yes, like the princess."

"All right, Snow White, perhaps we can help each other. But aren't you a minor? You legally can't help me without a guardian's consent."

Snow White knew her mom would never agree to that. She had to think fast. "I'm not a minor. I just turned eighteen last week." The lie flew out her mouth before she had time to think about it.

Noah Wilkins chuckled. "Now, Snow White, I'm pretty sure you're lying to me. And if you really are eighteen, then my timeline doesn't fit and you can't help me anyway."

Snow White gritted her teeth. "Yes, I lied," she whispered.

"I was kind of hoping that was the case," he said. "You see, Snow White, I was hired to put a very bad man in jail, hopefully for a long time. If you were eighteen, then you would be too old to fit in with my theory."

"What's your theory?" Snow White asked, not sure if she wanted to hear his answer.

"If my assumptions are correct, that bad man might be your father."

The hair on the back of her neck stood up and she shivered, despite the August warmth. "How can I help you then?"

"I can't divulge any of the case to you without your mom present, Snow White, but I do have an idea forming. Do you and your mom go out to eat very often?"

"Do we what? What does eating out have to do with anything?" Snow White could feel her temperature rising. This phone call was going nowhere.

"If you could get your mom to take you out to eat one night, and I just happen to be at the restaurant..." His voice trailed off.

She was starting to understand. "Then we could corner her together," Snow White finished. "Yeah, she really likes this place called Boston's. I could probably talk her into it."

"How about next Friday?"

"That should work," Snow White said.

"Look," Noah Wilkins started, "I don't want to deceive your mom, Snow White, but I think if I talk to her, with you there, then we might both get some answers. I truly just want to help her. I don't understand why she won't let me."

"Well, you sure made her angry last time you came here. I've never heard my mom yell like that in my entire life!"

"I understand why she doesn't want to talk to me, but this man might walk if she doesn't. I need her help. I need your help. Do you think you can get her there?"

Snow White nodded, even though he couldn't see her. "Yes, I think I can."

"Great," Noah Wilkins sighed. "I'll see you next Friday then. Does 7:00 work?"

"Six would be better."

"All right, Snow White Princess, I will see you at Boston's next Friday, 6:00 sharp."

"See you then."

# Chapter Two

Belle dropped her large stack of clothes on top of Cinderella's bed, and then fell backwards onto her pillows.

"You can't just drop them there. Hang them up!" Cinderella said, coming into the room with her arms equally full. "I told you we should have packed your clothes into suitcases."

"I thought this would be easier," Belle said, unmoving. "I'm tired. Can't we just finish tomorrow?"

"Yeah, because I'm sure the family moving into your house won't care if you take your sweet time getting all your crap out over the next month."

Belle rolled her eyes and sat up. "Awww, come on Cindy, you're going to love having me as a roomie! Remember when we were little and used to wish we could have sleepovers every night? Well, now we can!"

"You were supposed to be working on moving out all week!" Cinderella said, placing her hands on her hips. She started lining up the hangers and attempting to fit the large stack in her closet. "Why do you have so many clothes anyway?"

"Options, darling," Belle said, smiling.

Cinderella just shook her head and pushed harder to force the clothes to fit. She looked back at Belle, who picked up a magazine and was flipping through it.

"Oh, no, please don't get up. By all means, continue your reading while I do all the work."

Belle closed the magazine and threw a pillow at Cinderella. "Well, look at who's being miss sassy pants today. I thought that was normally my role."

"It is. I just borrowed your crown for a while." Cinderella dropped the remaining clothes on the floor and plopped onto the bed beside Belle.

"Hey, those still need to be hung up."

Cinderella glared at her cousin.

Belle snickered and got to her feet, retrieving the clothes from the floor and resuming where Cinderella left off. "Spill," she said. "Why the mood tonight?"

"Tomorrow is our Lagoon day."

"I know! We look forward to this every year!"

"Scott will be there…and so will Brian."

"I still don't understand why you invited them both," Belle said, shaking her head.

"I was trying to be nice. Besides, Brian and I have become pretty good friends."

"Does he know that?"

"What?"

"That you're just friends? The way that boy looks at you, it's like a dog hungering after a bone."

Cinderella jumped to her feet. "He does not!"

"Oh, please, Cindy, you are completely clueless. Brian has got it for you bad! I still can't believe he hasn't tried to kiss you or anything yet."

"Because we're just friends!"

"Uh-huh."

There was a grunt at the door and both girls turned. "Where do you want this, babe?" Craig asked, clutching a box that covered most of his face.

"Drop it by the dresser." Belle pointed.

Craig did as he was told, and then turned to face Cinderella. "I overheard what you guys were talking about and, yes, Brian totally wants you."

"He does not!" Cinderella said, storming from the room. "I'm going to go grab more clothes," she yelled over her shoulder.

***

Cinderella paced nervously up and down the sidewalk in front of the Lagoon entrance.

"Stop moving!" Aurora yelled. "You're starting to make me nervous."

"Sorry," Cinderella said. "I'm just excited, and scared about today."

"As you should be," Aurora said. "You should take it from me and just have one boy at a time."

"Who is This Week?" Ariel asked.

Without skipping a beat Aurora said, "James."

"This Week?" Snow White asked, eyebrows raised.

Aurora laughed. "That's what Ariel has taken to calling my many boyfriends. I think she started saying it to make me mad, but I actually think it's quite fitting. I enjoy trying out a new guy each week. And I'm not ashamed to admit that."

"Speak of the devil," Ariel said as they watched a tall young man approach. "How do you keep their names straight?" she whispered.

"Hush!" Aurora ran towards James and squealed when he picked her up and tossed her over his shoulder.

"Hey, Princess."

Cinderella smiled at the familiar endearment and turned to find Scott standing behind her.

"Hey!" she said, throwing her arms around his neck. He picked her up in his familiar bear hug and held tight.

"I've missed you!" He spoke softly into her neck.

"I know. I've missed you too!" she said.

"Hey, guys," Dave waved.

The only person who didn't seem happy to see him was Craig. Their group continued to grow until they were only waiting for Brian to arrive.

"Maybe he decided not to come," Ariel said, shrugging.

"It's not like him not to call," Cinderella said, looking around.

Scott raised his eyebrows. "How well do you know him?" he asked.

"We hung out a lot this summer," Cinderella said. She knew Scott had told her to go out with other guys, but she couldn't bring herself to look him in the face. "Here he is," she said, pointing.

"Sorry I'm late," Brian said. He gave Cinderella a nice, long hug while Scott watched on.

Scott's lips thinned into a straight line and he started to walk toward the entrance. "Well, let's go then," he said. The others followed.

Brian reached down as they began walking and wrapped his hand around Cinderella's. "What do you want to ride first, Cinderella?"

She looked at Brian and then down at their hands. "I...uh...I'm not sure," she said, stumbling over her words.

"Let's go to the white roller coaster," Scott said. He paused on the asphalt and allowed everyone to walk past him. When Cinderella and Brian neared he stopped them. "I don't think we've met yet," he said, extending a hand to Brian.

"I'm Brian."

"Scott," he said. Brian had to drop Cinderella's hand briefly in order to shake hands with Scott. Scott returned the handshake, then quickly threw his arm around Cinderella's shoulder, boxing Brian out, and led her toward the ride.

# Chapter Three

"So why didn't you move to California with your mom?" Scott asked Belle as they stood in line.

"I wanted to finish out my senior year here. I'll join my parents in California after graduation."

"That makes sense," Scott said. "Senior year at a new school would be rough. Are your parents...married then? 'Cause I don't remember receiving an invitation," Scott said, feigning hurt.

Belle laughed. "Yes, they got married just a few weeks ago. My dad didn't want the media getting ahold of the story, so he and my mom were married in a tiny, private ceremony. Family only."

Cinderella nodded. "It was small, but it was beautiful."

"And totally romantic," Ariel added.

"So where are you living, then?" Scott asked.

"Thankfully my awesome aunt Dana is letting me move in for the year. And Cindy and I get to be roommates."

Cinderella grumbled. "She has so much crap!" she said. "It's like we need a second bedroom just for all her stuff."

Craig nodded vigorously. "I can second that. I moved most of it last night."

The group laughed.

"It's going to be weird having new neighbors next to us," Ariel spoke up. "We've been between Snow White and Bell's houses practically our whole lives."

"It will be weird to watch someone else living in my house," Belle said.

"Do you know when the new people are moving in yet?"

"This week sometime, I think." Belle shrugged. "I'm not really sure. I just know I had to be out last night."

"How's your mom doing in California?" Dave asked.

"Really well! She's been going to auditions with my dad. She's even going to have a very small cameo on my dad's show! I'll let you guys know when it airs and we can all watch it together."

"Wow, that's awesome!" Dave said.

"How is everything going with being an SBO, Mr. President?" Belle smiled at Dave.

"So great! Senior year is going to be awesome! And I have you to thank." Dave winked at Belle.

Craig instinctively wrapped his arms around Belle's waist and rested his chin on top of her head. Belle snuggled into him, but continued talking with Dave.

"What do you mean, you have me to thank?"

"At the end of sophomore year you said I should go into politics. Remember? 'Cause I'm so good at lying." His blue eyes sparkled when he laughed.

"Oh yeah!" Belle laughed along with him.

Craig tightened his grip around Belle's slender waist. He pulled her toward the ride as the line began to move.

"Okay, apparently we're done talking now," Belle said. She narrowed her eyes at Craig. "What are you doing?"

"I'm sorry, weren't you done?" he asked.

Belle opened her mouth to protest but Craig covered it with his lips instead. Dave saw them kissing and moved away, ending beside Snow White in the back of their group.

"How are you doing, Snow White?" he asked glumly.

Snow White smiled at him. "At least she's friends with you again, right?"

Dave looked up into her eyes. "Yeah, I guess. So anything new going on with you?"

Snow White thought about her conversation with the lawyer, and the snippets of information she'd gotten. She decided against sharing that yet. "No, not really. You?"

"Just getting ready for school. I can't believe we're seniors this year! Do you have plans for after high school?"

Snow White froze in place. The question had caught her off guard. "Umm, I honestly don't know." Snow White had spent so much time stressing about high school itself that she hadn't really spent much time thinking past it. What *was* she going to do after high school? "Do you have plans?" she asked Dave.

"I was thinking about looking into schools in California." He glanced through the crowd in Belle's direction.

Snow White followed his gaze. "You're not going to follow her to California, are you? Dave, that is like stalker creepy!"

"What? No! I'm not moving there to be closer to her. That would just be a bonus." He smiled slyly. "I honestly think it would be nice to go somewhere on my own. You know, act like a grown-up and all."

Snow White shook her head and smiled. "You know that grown-ups don't refer to themselves like that, right? They are adults."

"Fine, whatever. I want to be an adult then."

"All right." Snow White eyed him skeptically. "I just wouldn't be surprised if Craig has a similar mindset. He's probably looking into California schools, too."

Dave grumbled as they stepped into their car and sat down.

Snow White nudged him playfully. "Come on, Romeo, cheer up. There are a million girls at school who would love to date you."

***

As the day wore on, Cinderella grew increasingly frustrated with Scott. Every time Brian got close to her, Scott would step between them. And whenever he spoke, Scott cut him off. Cinderella finally had enough.

"Scott!" She interrupted his story, similar to what Scott had just done to Brian. Scott stopped and looked at her. "Can we talk, please?" Cinderella didn't wait for an answer. She stormed away and sat down hard on a bright red bench.

"Why did you get out of line?" Scott asked as he walked toward her.

Cinderella jumped to her feet again. "Because I'm tired of the way you're treating my friend!" She threw her hands up in the air. "Why are you acting this way?"

Scott kicked a small piece of gravel near his shoe. He stared at the black asphalt as he spoke. "I don't like him. I don't think he has good intentions."

"You don't know anything about him! You won't even let him say two words!" Cinderella was shouting loud enough now that passersby stopped to witness their fight. "And how dare you accuse Brian of bad intentions! He is one of the nicest guys I've ever known! We've gone on several dates during the summer and he's never even tried to kiss me! I seem to remember another guy who kissed a minor the first night they met."

Scott looked up at Cinderella like she'd punched him in the gut. His hurt quickly flashed to anger. "I didn't realize you felt that way about our first kiss. Well, don't worry. It won't ever happen again!"

"What do you want me to do?" Cinderella shouted. "You told me to date other guys. In fact, you forced me to. And now you're mad at me for doing exactly what you asked?"

"Well, since I clearly don't have good intentions, I must be a big, creepy predator. Go ahead and be with your boyfriend. I won't get in your way anymore!" Scott pointed at the ride where Brian and the others still waited in line. Scott shoved his shaking hands into his pockets and walked away.

"Scott, come back! Scott!" Cinderella yelled his name, but Scott never turned around as he left. Hot, angry tears flooded her eyes. Cinderella sat on the bench, her forehead in her hands. Her shoulders trembled as her brain tried to wrap itself around what just happened. Was Scott gone for good?

# Chapter Four

Cinderella heard giggling coming toward her. She wiped her eyes with her fingertips and looked up. Aurora was being chased by This Week. He would catch her and tickle her until she squealed and collapsed to the ground. Then he'd help her up and chase her again. It was sickening to watch. Aurora finally stopped, the smile dropping off her face when she saw Cinderella.

"Cindy, what's the matter? Where's Scott?"

"We got in a fight. He left. I don't think he's coming back. Like ever."

"What? What do you mean you fought? I can't imagine Scott and you fighting."

"Well, it was bound to happen." Cinderella shrugged, fighting back the tears that threatened to return.

This Week grabbed Aurora's middle, but she had no reaction. "Not now." She waved him off. "Would you please get me a Coke?" she asked, batting her eyes.

He smiled and nodded. "Sure."

Aurora sat on the bench beside Cinderella and put an arm around her.

"How do you do that?" Cinderella asked, nodding in the direction he'd gone. "Do you give them love potion or something?"

"No, I think they all like that they have to chase me. I refuse to choose one of them, so they all keep competing to win."

Cinderella watched as the remainder of their group climbed off the ride and walked toward them.

"What's going on?" Ariel asked.

"Scott left," Cinderella and Aurora said in unison. Most of the group frowned, but Cinderella couldn't help but notice Brian was trying to hide his grin.

"Uh, is he gone for good?" Dave asked. "'Cause he was my ride."

Belle shoved him with her shoulder and pointed to Cinderella's red, splotchy skin and swollen eyes. "Not the time," she hissed.

Brian pushed his way through the group and, taking Cinderella by the hand, he lifted her to her feet. Without a word uttered between them, he placed her hand on his offered arm and escorted her to the next ride. The others followed without question.

Cinderella smiled up at Brian. "Thank you," she whispered. "Everyone was staring at me."

"Not a problem," he smiled back. "You looked like you needed rescuing."

"I'm sorry Scott was so mean to you," Cinderella said.

Brian shrugged. "I'm not going to say it was okay, but he really likes you. That was extremely obvious. I do, too, but I don't want to act like a jerk to get your attention."

Cinderella looked at Brian in surprise. His ears turned pink.

"I guess I should have told you sooner," he whispered, staring straight ahead as they spoke. "I didn't realize you were already taken."

Cinderella stopped walking, forcing Brian to stop and look at her. "I'm not taken, though. Scott doesn't want to date me until I graduate."

"Idiot," Brian muttered. He shook his head and began walking again. Suddenly he stopped and pulled Cinderella behind one of the game buildings.

"What's the matter?" she asked.

Brian's hands were visibly shaking as he turned Cinderella to face him. His trembling fingers calmed when they brushed the warmth of Cinderella's cheek. "You're really not taken?" he asked, inches from her face.

"No, but I…"

Brian cut her off. With one hand on either side of her face, Brian tilted her head up gently and bent down for a kiss. His lips were warm and soft against hers. Cinderella was too shocked to respond. He pulled away slowly and smiled into her sunflower eyes. "I've been wanting to do that since prom," he said, releasing a huge breath of air.

Cinderella smiled weakly at him and allowed Brian to continue to guide her. She was glad to be holding his arm. She wasn't sure she would make it on her own at this point. A headache started to form in Cinderella's temples and she wished now, more than ever, that this day could just be over. She liked Brian a lot, but he was just a good friend to her. She didn't even think of him in a romantic way, although she had never really tried to, either. Her heart already belonged to someone else. But maybe he didn't want it anymore?

***

When the Princess sisters and Dave arrived home, well after dark, they saw a light on in Belle's old house.

"So weird," Belle said, staring out her car window. Cinderella pulled into her parking stall and they all climbed out.

"Do you think it's too late to go introduce ourselves?" Ariel asked. "The light is still on."

"It's too late," Cinderella spoke up. The last thing she felt like doing was putting on a neighborly face and meeting new people. She just wanted to crawl into bed and crash.

"I guess we can introduce ourselves another time," Aurora said.

"Are you going to make them brownies, like you did for me?" Dave asked.

"Probably not," Belle said. "You only got a treat because you were hot."

Dave laughed. "Really?"

"Yes, really," Ariel confirmed. "We saw you unloading the moving truck and thought, 'what better way to win over the new, hot guy?'"

"Well, it definitely worked!" Dave said goodbye and crossed the street to his own condo.

The girls pulled out their keys and said goodnight as they each went to their own houses.

"You comin'?" Aurora turned when she realized Ariel wasn't behind her.

"I actually think it feels really nice out here," she said. "I just want to sit outside for a minute."

Aurora shrugged. "Suit yourself. I'll leave the door unlocked."

"Okay." Ariel waited for the door to click shut. She plopped down on the top step and looked up at the bright, full moon. She leaned her head against their white door and closed her eyes. She opened them a moment later and walked about a hundred feet to the mailbox. After unlocking it, she took a deep breath and opened the lid. Ariel pulled out the stack of bills, catalogs, and magazines and began flipping through them. When she came upon a brochure addressed to her, she squealed in delight.

Clutching the paper to her chest, she tossed the rest of the mail back inside and closed the little door. She returned to her place on the steps and flipped through the brochure, her eyes wide and round.

"USC? Is that where you're going to college?"

Ariel jumped at the voice, a small squeak escaping her lips. She looked up to see a tall, dark boy standing in front of her. He smiled, his bright, white teeth almost glowing in the dark. "I didn't mean to scare you," he said, still trying not to laugh.

"I just thought I was alone," Ariel said.

He indicated the brochure in her hands again. "Is that where you're going to school?"

"Probably not." Ariel looked longingly at the brochure again and shook her head. "Tuition is crazy expensive. But it's my dream school, so I'm going to drool over it while I can."

"Do you mind if I sit?" The boy pointed at her steps.

"Oh, sure." Ariel scooted over and patted the cement next to her. He sat right beside Ariel, his warm, black skin rubbing against her own. Ariel's heart raced and her face flushed red. He smiled at her and now that he was closer, she could see his eyes were light brown. They popped against his dark features. He smiled at her again and she realized she had been staring.

"I'm Jordan," he said.

Ariel had to think for a moment. Name? Did she have a name? "Ariel," she finally spoke. "I'm Ariel."

"It's nice to meet you, Ariel."

"You too, Jordan. So did you guys just move in?" *What a stupid question*, she chastised herself. *Of course he did!*

"Yup, today. I was starting to think we were the only ones who lived here. This place was dead all day."

"We all went to Lagoon," Ariel said, pointing down the row of condos to her cousins' homes. "We just got home, actually."

"We?" he asked.

"Yeah, I went with my cousins and a bunch of friends. My cousins all live in these condos, too."

"Oh, cool. One more question. What's Lagoon?"

Ariel smiled. "It's an amusement park. It has lots of fun roller coasters and stuff. It's not too far from here."

Jordan nodded, and then reached for the brochure. "May I?" he asked.

Ariel handed it over. "Sure."

"So what is it you want to study? Why USC?"

"I'm obsessed with movies!" Ariel brightened. "I'm just fascinated by the whole process and I want to be involved in making them. I honestly think directing would be really cool! The University of Southern California is considered one of the top film schools in the United States. Did you know both Ron Howard and George Lucas are alumni?"

When Jordan smiled, his nose crinkled. "No, I didn't, but that is pretty cool." He chuckled softly.

"What's so funny?" Ariel asked.

"You," Jordan looked at her and handed back the brochure. "You seemed really shy just a second ago, but as soon as you started talking about film school and movies, it was like you woke up. Now you don't seem shy at all."

Ariel grinned. "It's my passion! And it tends to drive my cousins all crazy. I can quote just about any movie and also tell you who acted in it, who produced it, and who the director is. No one else seems to get it. That's why I'd love to go to school with a huge group of people who are as passionate as I am." When she looked over, Jordan was still watching her, smiling. "What?" she asked, her face flushing again.

"I've never met a girl like you before. At my high school, all the girls just seemed to care about hair and makeup and clothes. None of them had passions or hobbies, at least not like you do. I think it's cool."

"Well, that's exactly why I have a passion for movies, simply to impress other people." Ariel flipped her long, blonde hair over her shoulder and batted her eyes at him, mocking the type of girl he just spoke about.

Jordan laughed loudly and Ariel joined in. "Actually," she said. "My sister is kind of like those girls you just described. She's smart, though. Really smart. She just doesn't want people to know it."

"Why would anyone hide that?" he asked.

"I don't know, but she gets a lot of guys by being super flirty and playing a little ditzy. So I guess it works for her."

"Hmmm. I'm not sure I'd call that success, but to each his own, I guess."

"How old are you, Jordan?" Ariel asked. She crossed her fingers it wasn't too old.

"I'm eighteen," he said. "I actually just graduated high school in June."

Ariel could feel her heart racing again. Eighteen was doable. "Then why'd you move here with your parents?" Ariel asked.

"My grandma is really sick," he said. "We moved here to be closer to her and to help take care of her."

"Oh, I'm sorry," Ariel said.

Jordan shrugged. "It's not your fault, but thanks."

"Are you going to school then?"

"No, my passion is actually cars, much to my dad's dismay. I think he wanted me to go to college and go into business or something boring like that. But I want to be a mechanic. I love working with my hands! Sitting at a desk all day is definitely not my idea of a fun job!"

Ariel made a face. "Me neither," she said.

"I knew I could get on at a garage here in Utah just as easily as I could have back in Oregon."

"Wow, you're from Oregon?"

"Born and raised."

"I was born in California, but we moved here when I was one and I've never been anywhere else since," Ariel said. "Maybe that's the other reason I'd love to go to USC. Just to get out of here and try something new on my own."

"I know what you mean," Jordan said. "I probably would have done that if it weren't for my grandma. But I want to be close to her before she's gone."

"I get that," Ariel said. "I actually just met my grandma for the first time last year. I didn't know I had one before then."

"You didn't know you had a grandma?" Jordan looked at her, his eyebrows furrowed.

Ariel paused for a minute, trying to decide how much to tell him. She really didn't know this kid at all, but she felt really comfortable with him already. Ariel took a deep breath and ended up spilling everything from how her parents met to meeting Grandma B. last year. As she spoke, Ariel found herself scooting closer to Jordan for warmth. They had been talking for almost two hours and it was getting late. When Ariel began choking up a little, Jordan put an arm around her shoulder, which gave her the strength to continue.

"Wow," Jordan said. "I can't believe you've been through all that."

"I know," Ariel said. "Sometimes I feel like it's really surreal. I don't know how my mom lived through it. She's stronger than I am, that's for sure."

"I dunno," Jordan said. "You seem pretty strong to me."

A loud rustling in the tree right in front of them made Ariel jump. "What was that?"

Jordan laughed again. "You're jumpy, aren't you?"

"Not normally!" Ariel argued. "But I don't normally sit on my porch in the dark until midnight either."

"Wait, do you see that?" Jordan asked.

"What?"

Jordan raised the arm that was strung over Ariel's shoulder and pointed up at the tree before them. "I think that's an owl. Look!"

Ariel's gaze followed where Jordan pointed. She squinted, trying to see through the dark branches. Sure enough, there was a large barn owl, perched on one of the branches.

"Ew! Is he eating something?" Ariel squirmed.

"Yeah, it looks like he's got a mouse or something in his talons. Look!"

Ariel looked up in time to see the owl devouring his prey, head first. She quickly turned away, right as Jordan turned to face her, laughing. Their noses bumped and Jordan's laughter melted away. Ariel could feel his breath against her face as they stared into each other's eyes. He truly had the most beautiful eyes she'd ever seen. She instantly felt lost in his bright, tan orbs. His breath was enticingly sweet, as his thick lips drew nearer to hers. She could feel her heart quicken as heat creeped up her neck.

Jordan's gaze danced back and forth from her eyes to her lips as they neared.

Realizing what was happening, they both pulled back quickly. Jordan whipped his arm off her shoulder and stood. "Well, I better get to bed."

Ariel jumped up and shoved the brochure under the welcome mat by her feet. "Yeah, me too." Jordan gave her a questioning look. "Can we just keep USC between the two of us for now? Please?"

"Uh, sure, but why?"

"Because I want to hold onto my dream a little longer. I know as soon as I approach the subject with my mom, money will come up and the possibility of my going will be dashed away. I'm not ready to deal with reality yet."

Jordan smiled and Ariel felt her heart race. "Your secret is safe with me."

"Thank you. It was nice meeting you, Jordan."

"You too, Ariel," he said. "Goodnight."

# Chapter Five

The next morning Cinderella awoke to a soft knock on her door. Dana poked her head in. "Can I talk to you for a minute?" she whispered. Cinderella stretched and yawned. She carefully crawled out the bottom of her bed, so as not to disturb a sleeping Belle. With the trundle beds pushed up right beside each other, there wasn't any excess space in her room. At least during the day, Belle's bed was safely stored below her own so they had room to move around. Cinderella squeezed past the foot of the beds and froze when Belle rolled over, but she remained asleep and Cinderella continued until she was able to slip through the door. Pulling it behind her quietly, she asked, "What's up?"

"I just go off the phone with your dad."

Cinderella brightened. "Oh yeah? How is he?"

"Well, he actually needs to come into town on business and wants to stop by and visit."

"Really?" Cinderella squealed.

Dana smiled. "Yes, really. So don't make plans with Scott or anyone else. He wants to take us to dinner Monday, to celebrate your first day of senior year."

Cinderella's stomach lurched at the mention of Scott. "Us?" she asked.

"Yes, he wants to take us both out."

"And you're okay with that?" Cinderella's eyes widened.

"Yes." Dana actually smiled, which Cinderella found strange, but didn't say anything. No sense in jinxing it.

"Wait, Monday? You mean tomorrow?"

"Yes, I guess tomorrow is Monday. Wow. Okay, yes, tomorrow then."

Cinderella clapped her hands together. "Is he bringing the girls?"

"Not this time." Dana shook her head. "They have school too, so they're staying with a friend. It will just be a quick trip."

Cinderella felt even more excited for tomorrow to come. But school meant she would have to see Brian and she still wasn't sure about how to handle that situation. She had never really considered another guy after Scott. Maybe she should give Brian a chance. She could feel a headache forming again and decided to crawl back into bed.

\*\*\*

"Ariel, wake up! Look out your window!"

Ariel peeked her eyes open and found Aurora inches from her face. "What?" she moaned, pulling the covers back over her head.

"There is a super hot guy next door, mowing his back lawn."

Ariel sat up straight in bed, and then dashed to the window. Sure enough, Jordan was outside mowing the lawn, and he was shirtless. Ariel's face flushed pink as she looked away. Aurora was oblivious to her reaction and continued to talk.

"I suddenly don't think it's sad that's not Belle's house anymore. Quick, get dressed! Let's go bring him some lemonade or something!"

Ariel wasn't sure what to say. Last night, getting to know Jordan had been amazing, but things ended a bit awkwardly. She wasn't sure how he would react to her today. She slowly pulled on some denim shorts as Aurora continued to babble about how she planned on making him next week's boy of choice. She really wasn't sure she wanted to go downstairs and watch as Aurora attempted to make him her next victim. She plopped back down on the bed without changing from her pajama shirt.

"What are you doing?" Aurora shrieked while teasing her hair into place. "Get up! Let's go!"

Ariel dragged to her feet and went through the motions of pulling her hair into a messy ponytail and putting on a touch of makeup. She didn't know why, but she just didn't want to share her special night with Aurora.

"Aren't you ready yet?" Aurora dashed from the room. "I'll meet you downstairs. I'll start making the lemonade."

Ariel took each step slowly, one at a time. When she reached the kitchen, Aurora had three tall glasses of lemonade lined up on the counter and was carefully adding ice to each one. "Geeze, slow poke, did you stay up too late staring at the moon, or whatever you were doing?"

"Yeah, I was up pretty late," Ariel admitted. Her mind thought back to Jordan and the way it felt with his warm body pressed up against hers. The way his comforting arm enveloped her made Ariel feel safe. She smiled as she envisioned his eyes staring back into hers. A grin split her face and Aurora looked at her sister, her eyes narrowing. She set down the glasses of lemonade she had just picked up.

"Okay, Missy, spill."

Ariel, pulled from her memories, focused in on her sister. "What?" she asked.

"What happened last night?"

"I don't…"

"I'm not stupid, Ari, I can see you are clearly focused on something else. And from that goofy look on your face, my instincts are telling me it's a boy. So spill! Who did you meet up with last night?"

Ariel turned beet red and stumbled through her words as she tried to make excuses.

"No, no, no, sister, give it to me straight. What guy did you see last night?"

Ariel glanced out the kitchen window, where they could still see the mower going strong, pushed by Jordan's slender frame, sweat dripping under the August sun.

Aurora followed her sister's gaze and her jaw dropped. "You little liar!" she teased. "You've already met the new guy! Why didn't you say anything?"

Ariel watched Jordan wipe his forehead with the back of his hand. She looked away quickly when he glanced in their direction.

"Oh, I get it," Aurora said, nodding. "You like him. You really like him! Well, shoot, Ari, why didn't you just stop me from rambling then?" Aurora walked over to the kitchen sink and dumped one of the glasses down the drain. She picked up the other two glasses and handed them to her sister. "Go!" she said, nudging Ariel toward the back door. "And don't be afraid to tell him you like him. It's about time!" Aurora smiled at her sister and, with one final push, moved her out the door. Aurora went back inside and disappeared.

Ariel took a deep breath and stepped over to their shared fence. "Hey, Jordan, you thirsty?" She held up the lemonades as she shouted over the mower. Jordan shut the mower off and walked over to the fence, opening the gate between them.

"Hey, thanks!" he said, taking the cold beverage from her and drinking most of it in one gulp. "Did you sleep well?" he asked. "I don't know about you, but I had images of that owl decapitating the mouse running through my mind all night." He smiled teasingly at her.

Ariel shuddered and laughed. "Gross. Don't bring that up again!"

Jordan walked over to his lawn mower and removed the bag before dumping the clippings into a large, round, blue trash bin.

"Are you finished?" Ariel asked.

"Yeah, I am with our lawn. Your cousin must not have been much of a mower," he said. "This grass hasn't been cut in weeks."

"Yeah," Ariel smiled, "Belle and her mom aren't big on yard work. You'll understand better when you meet her."

"When do I get to meet these elusive cousins?" he asked.

Jordan pushed the mower toward the opposite end of his small yard and tapped on the other connecting gate.

"What are you doing?" Ariel asked. "I thought you were done."

"I am with my yard," he said. "Now I gotta do my grandma's." Jordan pointed to the yard next door to his own.

"Wait, your grandma is Grandma Johnson?" she asked.

Grandma Johnson opened the latch on her side of the gate and swung it open. Jordan pushed the mower through the opening. Ariel crossed through Jordan's yard and approached the two of them. She looked from Jordan to Grandma Johnson, confused.

Jordan chuckled. "You're wondering how we're related, aren't you?"

Ariel nodded.

"My dad is white," he said.

Ariel looked at Grandma Johnson's frail frame and gasped. "Wait, you're not the grandma…you're sick?" She turned to the first grandmother figure she'd ever known.

*Smack.* Grandma Johnson slapped Jordan's bare chest. "You told her? I thought I made it clear I didn't want people knowing and feeling sorry for me."

"Sorry, Grandma, I didn't know you guys knew each other."

"Of course we know each other! This is one of the Princess girls! She's practically your cousin!"

Ariel thought she saw Jordan wince at the mention that they might as well be related.

"I've raised her and the others like my own grandchildren since they were tiny babes."

Jordan's eyes lit up with recognition. "You're one of the girls from the Popsicle picture!" He smiled. On her piano beside her grandchildren's portraits, Grandma Johnson had a picture of Ariel and all her cousins when they were little, with red Popsicle mouths.

Ariel was too concerned to feel embarrassed. "How sick are you?" she asked. Grandma Johnson looked at Jordan. He looked down, his mouth set in a grim line. "Grandma?"

"I have stage four lung cancer, sweetie. They've given me about six months."

Tears pricked at Ariel's eyes. Her hand covered her mouth, and she shook her head.

Grandma Johnson took Ariel's hand and patted it, guiding her over to a lawn chair on her patio. "Now, now," she soothed, pulling Ariel into a chair. "I've lived a good, full life. Don't mourn over me. Just enjoy your life and be happy. That's the greatest gift a child can give to their grandparents. Besides, I'm looking forward to being with my Richard again. Lord knows how much I've missed him!"

Ariel dabbed at her eyes and gave Grandma Johnson's hand a squeeze. "Please tell us if you need anything," she said.

Grandma Johnson smiled. "You're such a sweetheart. My son and his family have taken care of a lot. I told him not to drop his life and move out here, but he wouldn't listen to me. That boy's stubborn like his father was."

Ariel watched Jordan as he walked up and down the lawn, his back glistening with sweat. She noticed how muscular his legs were as he walked, his calves flexing with each step, and wondered if he were a soccer player.

Grandma Johnson giggled and Ariel turned to look at her. She smiled at Ariel and then moved her gaze over to Jordan. "He's cute, isn't he?" she said with a wink.

"Grandma!"

"What? I still have eyes, you know. I can see the way you're looking at him."

Ariel glanced at Jordan to make sure he wasn't looking, and then nodded quickly.

Grandma Johnson clapped her hands together and hooted. "Oh, goodie! I just love the two of you together! You'll make such cute babies!"

"Grandma!" Ariel choked on her lemonade.

"What? I'm a dying woman. I can dream about my great-grandbabies if that's what I want to do."

# Chapter Six

"She's such a tease!" The girl's mousy voice cut through the air.

"Oh my gosh, do you know what she said to James after his week was up?"

Aurora couldn't hear the answer, but the cackling that followed clattered and bounced against the walls, echoing down the hall toward her.

Aurora's stomach plummeted. She had been looking forward to starting cosmetology school, but as she neared the classroom, her pace dropped down to a crawl.

It felt weird to leave the high school during the hours she should be there, but Aurora decided to sign up for cosmetology school. She was excused the last two periods to leave campus and come to the tech school. The best part was she got credit for it, too. College didn't really appeal to her like it did for Ariel. She was hoping to graduate cosmetology and high school at the same time, so she could get a job straight after graduation.

Aurora shook off her fears. So what if the other girls didn't like her? Raising her chin and fixing her brightest smile into place, she stepped into the brightly lit room and looked around. The room went eerily silent. Her classmates watched her with disdain. Some sneered, while others snickered behind closed hands.

Aurora pulled her gaze from the girls and looked around. She could see shelves and shelves lined with mannequin heads, wigs, and more hair products than Aurora ever knew existed.

A short, slender woman bounced into the room and welcomed them. "If you love to do hair, then you're definitely in the right place!" she said. "Go ahead and pick a work station, sweetie." She gestured for Aurora, who stood still in the doorway, to pick a seat. Aurora watched as the other girls seemed to spread themselves out, taking up as much space as possible and covering the empty chairs. Aurora slinked to the back of the room and sat against the wall. The girl on the other end of her table scooted her chair even further from Aurora. It was sophomore year all over again.

*** 

"How do you all know what you want to do?" Snow White asked, falling onto one of the soft couches.

Their last first day of school was officially over. The girls sprawled on the comfy sectional in Aurora and Ariel's basement. The TV was on in the background, but no one watched it.

"What do you mean, Snow?" Cinderella asked.

"I mean Aurora wants to go to cosmetology school, Ariel wants to go to college for film, and Belle is moving to California after high school. Everyone has dreams and plans and I have nothing. What about you, Cindy? Should we become bums on our mom's couches?"

"Actually," Cinderella said, "I got my application for Utah State in the mail today."

"I thought you weren't going to go, since Scott is there and everything."

"It's still my number one school. It's a big enough place that I might never see him. Or maybe things will be okay. I just wish he'd call me." She looked out the window to avoid eye contact with any of her cousins.

"Why don't you call him?" Ariel asked.

"Because he's the one who was acting so stupid and jealous!" Her words came out stronger than she felt. "He needs to call me and apologize."

"Just don't shut him out too long," Belle whispered. The girls looked at her in surprise. "I wasted a lot of time with my dad doing that."

Cinderella wiped away the stray tear that had escaped her eye.

"Well, that's just great," Snow White complained. "So I'm alone again. You all have these fabulous lives planned and I'm just going to be stuck here with my mom forever. Maybe I should get a cat and start going crazy early."

Ariel couldn't listen anymore. "Stop it, Snow!"

Snow White jumped, along with her cousins. They all stared at Ariel.

"I'm so tired of hearing you complain about your poor, little life. If you don't like something, then change it! If you want to be something, then go out and do it! We're not all going to give up on our own dreams just to spend our lives here on these couches, listening to you whine. Pick a dream! College, trade school, sign up for the army, join the circus, just pick something! The only one holding you back is YOU!"

Snow White's lip trembled as she rose from the couch and ran from the room.

"Geeze, that was a bit harsh!" Aurora said. They could hear the front door slam upstairs. Snow White was gone.

"Don't tell me you guys aren't tired of listening to her complain. I wish she would just take ahold of her own life and do something with it, instead of resenting the rest of us for the things we've worked for."

"Maybe you could have worded it just a little nicer," Cinderella said.

Ariel got to her feet. "I gotta go," she said. She ran up the stairs after Snow White and left.

"What do you think that was about?" Belle looked at Aurora.

Aurora shrugged. "I dunno. She's been kinda moody lately."

"I actually have to get going, too." Cinderella rose to her feet. "My dad is in town tonight," she added excitedly. "Can someone go after Snow?"

"I got it," Aurora said.

"I'll come with you," Belle said, getting to her feet. "It's usually you or me offending Snow," she said to Aurora. "This feels strange."

Aurora nodded. "I know."

***

Cinderella and Dana pushed the glass door open and stepped into the restaurant. Her dad was sitting behind a small table, looking over the menu. When he saw them approach, he stood and pulled out each of their chairs. Cinderella was surprised to see her dad give her mom a kiss on the cheek when he greeted her. And she didn't even punch him! Cinderella gave him a big hug before he pushed her chair back in.

"How are you?" he asked, looking straight at Cinderella.

"Pretty good. I got my application for Utah State, so that's been interesting to look over. I'm definitely going to need to look into scholarships and student loans, though."

"Tell you what," Steven said. "I'll do for you what my dad did for me. I'll pay for half of your first year, to help get you established. After that, I'd be happy to loan you any money you need for schooling, but you'll be on your own and expected to pay it back."

Cinderella nodded. "That seems fair. Thanks, Dad!"

Her mom smiled at him. "I was afraid you were going to offer to pay for everything."

"Definitely not. Eighteen year olds are adults and need to behave as such. I definitely don't think leaning on mommy and daddy for financial support is a healthy way to go through college."

Dana's smile split her face. She reached out and placed a hand on top of his. "That is exactly the way I feel," she said.

Cinderella looked between her parents. What on earth was going on here?

*** 

The sun was just starting to fade when Ariel stepped out of her house and looked around. She removed the USC brochure from its hiding place under the mat and sat down. She loved reading over the class options. Each one sounded more interesting than the last.

"Do you only leave your house at night?"

Ariel looked up, the butterflies in her stomach awakened at the sound of his husky voice. Jordan stepped away from his truck, his hands and shirt front stained with oil.

"I could say the same for you," she said. "How do I know you're not a vampire or something?"

Jordan smiled, sending tingles down her spine. "Because I don't sparkle."

Ariel laughed. "Actually, you were kind of glowing in the sun yesterday."

"When I was mowing the lawn? Yeah, that was my glistening sweat."

"Yum."

"Oh, you like that, huh? I can give you lots more," he said, stepping closer and wiping the sweat from his brow.

Ariel put up her hands in defense. "No, no!"

Jordan stopped at the foot of her steps. "Any closer to talking to your mom?" he asked.

"No. My cousin really ticked me off today, though."

"Oh yeah? You wanna tell me about it?"

"She just likes to complain. A lot. But she won't do anything to change her circumstances. It's so frustrating to watch!"

"Kind of like hiding your dream from your mom because you're afraid it won't come true?"

Ariel glanced down at the brochure in her hands. "Yeah, shut up."

Jordan leaned closer to her. "Is it possible you got mad at your cousin, when you were really frustrated with yourself?"

Ariel's cheeks reddened. "How'd you get to be so smart?" she asked.

Jordan shrugged. "My grandma."

Ariel nodded. "So I guess I should probably go find Snow White and apologize then."

"Probably," Jordan said. "I'm not really sure I believe they exist, though."

"What? Why?"

"You talk about your twin sister and these elusive cousins, but I've never actually seen any of them."

"Kind of like sparkling vampires?" Ariel asked.

Jordan's smile spread across his face. "Yes, exactly like sparkling vampires."

Forever After

# Chapter Seven

Belle wandered through the kitchen for the third time. She opened the fridge and stood, staring at the contents inside. Nothing appealed to her, yet her stomach grumbled with hunger. It was well past dinner time and she hadn't eaten since school. She closed the fridge again and began opening cupboards. Still, nothing jumped out at her. Her mom and Dana might have been sisters, but their taste in food could not be further apart. Belle missed her own house, with her own food. Her super comfortable bed was set up and lavishly decorated with pillows in her California bedroom. Here, she slept on a thin mattress with absolutely no support. She was tired of waking up with a stiff, sore back.

That morning when she woke up and stretched, her hand whacked Cinderella in the face. The room was definitely too small for two beds. Belle opened the fridge again, hoping she'd missed something. Nope. Dana had absolutely nothing with sugar, carbonation, or high fructose corn syrup, three of Belle's favorite food groups. Everything was raw and fresh and needed to be cooked. Belle stuck out her tongue and slammed the door shut again. She whipped her cell phone from her back pocket and speed dialed number one.

"Hey, beautiful girl! How was your first day of school?"

Belle had not expected to feel emotional, but at the sound of her mom's voice, she wanted to cry. She took a slow, deep breath so her mom wouldn't hear the emotion in her voice. "Your sister is a freak," she complained.

"Are you looking in the fridge again?"

"Yes! I'm starving and she doesn't keep any real food in here! Where is the Coke? Where's the pudding? Where's the leftover Chinese food or pizza wrapped in foil?"

Mary laughed. "Just order a pizza or something, honey. Although it probably wouldn't hurt to learn a few eating habits from your aunt. I was never an award-winning mom when it came to meal time. For awesomeness and beauty, of course I was! But I failed in the dinner department."

Belle smiled. She missed her mom so much it hurt. And she had only moved a week ago! "Everything just takes too long to cook. She doesn't even have macaroni and cheese in her pantry. I think she may be trying to kill me."

"Oh, I miss you so much, sweetie! Your dad and I are having fun together, but our family won't be complete until you get here."

"Well, actually, that's one of the reasons I called. I didn't think I'd miss you guys this much! I mean, a year is practically nothing, right? But I'm not so sure I made the right decision. Is my room still waiting for me, or did you rent it out to some bum?"

"No bums here, except your father and me. Look, honey, there is nothing I would love more than to live in the same house as my daughter again! But…"

"But? Your only daughter is asking to move home and there's a 'but?'"

"But," Mary continued, ignoring her interruption, "don't make a hasty decision. If you jumped on a plane and came out here, you'd be homesick for your cousins, and you know it."

"Meh. I could just buy new friends." Belle tried to shrug it off, but she knew her mom was right. Dang it.

"What about school? You told me how awful you thought it would be to transfer to a whole new school for senior year."

"I'll just take online classes and become a hermit. Then I won't have to worry about social status."

"And what would Craig think?"

"He's not that great anyway." Even as the words left Belle's mouth, they made her heart hurt.

"Honey?"

"All right, fine, so I have a lot of things I'd miss here, too. Why couldn't dad just move Hollywood to Layton? He's so selfish sometimes."

Mary chuckled. "Just take some time and think about it. Don't rush to a decision. If you decide you want to move, I'll call the party planners and have a limo meet you at the airport. Give yourself another week to adjust before you decide anything."

Belle sighed dramatically into the phone. "Yes, moth-er."

Mary gagged. "Yuck, don't call me that!"

Belle giggled. "You miss me, too. Admit it."

"More than words can express," Mary said. "Now go eat some food. You know you can't think well and tend to be extra emotional when you're hungry. I love you, sweetie!"

"Love you too, Mom."

Belle hung up and immediately called the nearest pizza place. She went down to the basement and turned the TV on while she waited for her food to arrive. A re-run of *Locker Partners* popped onto the screen. Watching her dad in HD did not help her feelings of loneliness. Belle switched the TV off and called Craig.

"I just ordered pizza. Do you want to come over and join me?" she asked.

"Sure, I already ate, but I can eat more."

Belle grinned down at her phone, but then her smile quickly faded. This was one of those things her mom mentioned. If she lived in California, she definitely wouldn't be able to call up Craig on a whim and have him arrive at her house moments later. This decision sucked! If being an adult meant having to make difficult choices like this, then maybe she didn't want to grow up after all.

Belle ran upstairs when she heard a knock on the door. She threw the door open to a gangly delivery boy. His smile widened when he saw Belle standing there. She handed him the money, thanked him, and closed the door on his pimply face. There was a knock on the door again and Belle opened it, much happier with the boy who stood on her porch this time.

"Hey, babe, why didn't you just come in?" Belle asked. She held a slice of Hawaiian in her open hand and took a bite off the tip.

"I just had a super embarrassing moment," Craig said, sitting down. "But you can't make fun of me."

"I can't make any promises," Belle said, taking another bite.

"I just went to your old house."

Belle choked on her pizza. She put a hand up to catch the piece that threatened to spew out her mouth. "You did what?"

"I know, I know!" Craig put up a hand, shaking his head. "I helped you move and everything! My body just got into autopilot and I knocked on your old door. At least I didn't just walk in!"

Belle was clutching her side, she was laughing so hard. The remainder of her slice slid out of her hand and splattered on the floor.

"Your new neighbors are very nice," he finished.

Belle ran to the kitchen to get a rag and clean up her mess. "I haven't even met them yet," she said, scrubbing the floor. When she was finished, she tossed the rag into the sink as they walked through the kitchen on their way back down to the basement. Belle turned on the TV while they ate.

"So where are Dana and Cinderella tonight?" he asked.

"Cindy's dad is in town so he took them out to eat."

"And he didn't invite you? That's kinda rude."

"Not really. If my parents came to town, I'd want to go out with them alone, too. I get it. She doesn't get to see him often."

"So how's the long distance thing going with your mom?" Craig asked. He chomped his pizza slice in half with one single bite.

"Actually, that's why I called you over tonight. I was feeling pretty lonely. I even talked to my mom about moving out there." Belle looked at Craig to gauge his reaction.

Craig froze mid-bite, his eyes piercing into hers. "You're not serious?" he asked.

"Well, I don't know. Kind of. I miss my mom like crazy! I love Dana and Cinderella, but they're not her. And I feel like I'm missing out on this time I could be getting to know my dad better."

Craig's face was void of emotion. Belle had no clue what he was thinking. "If I were to move, we'd still be together, don't you think?"

"I dunno, probably not," Craig said, picking up his pizza again.

Belle's stomach lurched. "What? You wouldn't want to be my boyfriend anymore if I lived in California?"

"It's not that I wouldn't want to, it would just be really hard, ya know? Long distance just never seems to work."

"And how much experience do you have with it?" Belle asked. She was getting flustered by his reaction.

"I don't know. It would just be really hard to never see you and still be able to keep something going."

"So what were you thinking for after graduation? I'll go my way and you go your way? We'll just chalk this up to a silly high school romance?"

"It's just so far away, I wasn't really worried about it yet. I thought we'd figure that out when we get there."

Belle turned away from Craig, sitting back against the couch, her arms folded across her chest. She was speechless. Craig tried to shift her face back toward his, but Belle remained stiff and unwilling to move.

"Belle, come on! We're only seventeen. Were you planning on us graduating, getting married and living happily ever after?"

"I wasn't really making plans, but I want it to at least be an option! I don't want to break up just because we're kids and that's just what kids do."

"I didn't mean it to come across that way," Craig said, his tone softening. "I just think long distance would be really hard to keep our feelings going."

Craig slid off the couch onto his knees and knelt directly in front of Belle. "Belle," he said, tipping her chin toward him with two of his fingers. "I love you. Let's not stress about the future right now, please? Let's just enjoy being with each other while we're here." He leaned in slowly, hesitating just above Belle's lips. When she didn't pull away, he closed the gap between them, cupping her face in his hands.

Cinderella and Dana walked down the stairs, looking for Belle and found her entangled with Craig on the couch.

"Belle!" Dana yelled her name, causing the two to jump apart.

"Geeze, Dana! You almost gave me a heart attack!"

Dana's face was firm, her eyes narrowing in on Craig.

"I better go," he said. He leaned forward to kiss Belle goodbye, but upon seeing Dana's disapproving face he reconsidered. "Bye," he said, racing up the stairs.

"Seriously, Dana?" Belle shouted. "Did you really have to scare him off like that? You know Craig!"

Dana's face softened. "I know, Belle, and I know I'm not your mom but we do have rules here. You can't be home alone with Craig, or any boy for that matter.

Especially when I didn't even know he was going to be here."

Steven came walking down the stairs. "What'd I miss?" he asked. "I just saw a boy fly outta here like he'd seen a ghost."

"Nope, just Dana," Belle said dryly.

Steven chuckled. "I remember when she used to do that to her sister's dates, too."

"It's just not safe to be alone in the house with the opposite sex. Do you understand?" Dana asked.

Belle rolled her eyes. "Yes, Dana. I get it. Do you mind if Cinderella and I go out for ice cream or something? I've had kind of a rough night."

"All right," Dana nodded, "but hurry back, you've got school in the morning."

Belle grabbed her cousin's hand and pulled her up the stairs and out the door. As they drove to the nearest ice cream shop, Belle unloaded all the details from her evening onto Cinderella.

"Would you really move?" Cinderella asked, the hurt undeniable in her voice.

"I don't know. I feel like no matter what I choose, I'm going to miss people like crazy and it's gonna suck."

"Here, let me see if I can help you feel less homesick." Cinderella shook her hands, and then popped her neck side to side. "Hey, you," she said in her best Mary voice. "The best way to forget about something a dumb boy says is to dance it off."

Cinderella cranked up the music and began jamming in her seat.

"My mom can dance way better than that!" Belle laughed. "Let's just go through the drive-thru," she said, turning the volume back down. The girls placed their orders and headed back home.

"Thanks for coming with me," Belle said as they walked toward the front door. "I really needed that."

"No problem," Cinderella smiled. She turned the handle and, finding it unlocked, pushed the door open with her shoulder. She and Belle both froze. Cinderella's mouth dropped open. Dana and Steven were making out in the front room. They were so wrapped up in each other they didn't even hear the front door open.

Belle smirked. "It's not safe to be in the house alone with the opposite sex," she said loudly.

# Chapter Eight

Steven and Dana both looked like deer caught in the headlights. Their eyes stared wide at the two girls standing before them. Cinderella didn't know what to think. She couldn't remember seeing her mom ever go out on a date, let alone kiss a man. She walked over to the couch and sat down, staring into her ice cream cup. She suddenly didn't feel hungry anymore.

Steven sat beside her on the couch. "I'm sorry you had to find out this way," he said.

"This way?" Cinderella asked. She was so confused, her head was starting to ache. "Find out what?"

Dana sat on the other side of Steven, the two of them holding hands. "I think we better talk," she said.

Belle suddenly felt very intrusive. "Well, I'm super tired, so I'll head off to bed. Goodnight." She moved quickly up the stairs and disappeared.

"Do you want to tell her?" Steven asked. "Or should I?"

Dana held her left hand up for Cinderella to see. A large, sparkling diamond glowed from her ring finger. "We got a little carried away tonight. I'm sorry you had to walk in on that, but your dad proposed."

Cinderella set her melting cup of ice cream on the coffee table. Her head fell into her hands as she tried to process what her mom was saying. "You're engaged?" she asked, looking up at them. "But…how? Last time you saw each other at Lucas' movie premiere, you hardly said two words to each other."

"We actually started calling each other quite a bit after that night and reconnected. We didn't want to get your hopes up, in case nothing came from it. I'm really sorry we didn't tell you sooner," Steven explained. "I planned this trip as a trial for your mom and me to see if we could rekindle our old flame. After spending the day together, we just felt like it was right."

Dana rested her head on Steven's shoulder and sighed contentedly. "Are you okay?" she asked.

Cinderella had never seen her mom glow like this. In fact, both her parents seemed to be the happiest she'd ever seen. And what kid doesn't want their parents to be together? "I'm really happy," Cinderella said, still trying to process the information. "I'm just really confused, too."

"Have you ever shown her the letter?" Steven asked.

"The letter! No, I'll get it now." Dana jumped up and bounded up the stairs.

Steven looked at Cinderella, still hunched over on the couch. "Are you okay with this?" he asked.

"Yes, I really am happy!" Cinderella sat up taller and gave her dad a sitting hug. "Congratulations, I guess," she said.

Steven chuckled. "Boy, that was heartfelt!" He nudged her playfully with his broad shoulder.

"I'm sorry, Dad, this is just a lot to take in."

"I know, sweetie. I'm just teasing you. We didn't give you a lot of time to process. I'm really sorry about that."

Dana appeared at the top of the stairs, waving a faded and tattered envelope. It looked familiar to Cinderella. "Wait, did that come out of the box?" she asked.

"Yes," Dana said. Last year when Cinderella was learning about her dad, Dana had snatched this exact envelope out of her box of memories before Cinderella could examine its contents. "I didn't let you see it then because I was embarrassed I still had it. Now I'm glad I do." She smiled warmly at Steven, who grinned in return. Dana carefully lifted the flap on the envelope and pulled out a once-white piece of paper, fading yellow and thin from use.

"Shortly after we filed for divorce, I realized my mistakes and tried to win your mom back," Steven explained. "I stopped by the apartment one night to drop off this letter. That was actually the same night your aunt Rachel, well, that I helped her out. I never did see your mom, but Elizabeth took the letter and promised to give it to her. Little did I know your mom was pregnant and didn't want me to know, since we were divorced before she found out."

"Here." Dana handed the worn page to Cinderella. "I want you to read it."

Cinderella gingerly took the letter from her mom's hands and began to read:

*My dearest Dana,*

*I am a fool. I am not only a fool for being selfish and sabotaging our marriage, but also for not fighting for us. I love you! I wish I had beautiful, eloquent words to express how I feel about you, but I am a simple man, so my words are simple. I. Love. You. No one else has ever captured my heart and held it the way you do. I feel so lost and incomplete without you. You are my other half. You are the reason I wake up in the morning, the reason I breathe, the reason I strive to be a better person each day. Everything is for you. I'm so sorry I lost sight of that and let my hurt dictate my actions instead of my love. I know I've blown more chances than any man deserves. If you could ever find it in your heart to give me just one more, I swear to you, I will never lose sight of that love again. Please forgive me. If you could see me, I am on my knees, begging you to love me even half as much as I love you. My heart is in your hands forever more. Please, be my wife and let me spend the rest of my days trying to make you happy. I want to have a family with you and hold hands in our rocking chairs when we're old and grey. Dana, you are my one and only love.*

*Always and forever, Steven.*


Cinderella closed the letter slowly and placed it back inside the envelope. She sniffled, wiping at the tears that pricked her eyes. "Wow," she whispered. "How did you not run back to him after that?" Cinderella asked.

Dana looked at Steven and shook her head. "I don't know. I read that letter every single night. I picked up the phone to call him more times than I can remember but never dialed. I was too wrapped up in my own anger and my own pride to forgive him and allow myself to be loved."

Steven looked at Dana and pulled her in for a kiss. Cinderella's heart swelled, watching the tender love exchanged between them.

"That letter is what helped bring us back together," Dana said. "In one of our first conversations I asked your dad if he remembered it. He was able to quote almost the entire thing to me over the phone, almost nineteen years later. That's how I knew he was sincere and decided to give him another chance. If the words stuck with him after all this time, they must have been sincere and from his heart."

"So what does all this mean?" Cinderella asked, looking between them. "Do Monica and Sophie know?" Her parents exchanged a worried look and Steven shook his head. "No, we weren't expecting everything to happen so fast. But then we realized we have already wasted over eighteen years apart, so why throw away any more time?"

"This is going to be a lot harder for them," Cinderella said.

Dana nodded. "We know. We've spent hours debating back and forth on what we should do and what would be best for the three of you."

"And..?" Cinderella asked, her eyebrows raised.

Steven smiled. "And it looks like we're moving to Utah!" he said.

"Yay!" Cinderella brightened. "Wait, here?" she asked.

"No," Dana shook her head. "This house is too small for a family of five. Even if it were big enough, we thought a new family should have a new start in a new house. We'll still be in Layton, so you can finish out high school in the same place."

Cinderella breathed a sigh of relief. "So what about the girls? They're going to have to move and leave everything behind?"

Dana pat Steven's leg, giving him control of the conversation. "That was another thing that sparked our...speed in all this. If we move now, it's still the beginning of the school year, so it will be easier to transition."

"What about your job?" Cinderella asked.

"I actually have been talking with a firm here for quite some time and we finalized my transfer this morning."

"Wow," Cinderella said. "You guys have really thought of everything."

"We're not rushing into anything, sweetie. We really have spent so much time thinking over all the details. We know this won't be easy and will come as quite a shock to your sisters, I'm sure. But this is right. We both know it is." Dana smiled and Steven nodded his agreement.

Cinderella yawned.

Dana glanced at her watch and rose quickly. "It's getting late, and we've been keeping you up. I'm sorry — we can talk more tomorrow. You better go get some rest." Cinderella gave her mom a big hug, holding her tight for several seconds. "Congratulations, Mom. I'm so happy for you guys!" She reached down and picked up the letter from the table. "Can I borrow this?" she asked.

Dana looked at her quizzically. "Sure," she said, "just be careful with it, please."

Steven stood and pulled Cinderella in for a tight embrace. "I love you, sweetie."

"I love you too, Dad." Cinderella began walking up the stairs and paused. "Now you two better behave," she said, pointing an accusatory finger at them.

They both laughed and waved her away. "Goodnight!"

Cinderella found a fully dressed Belle already asleep on top of her covers when she entered their room. She was relieved. She knew Belle would have a million questions and want to know all the details, but there was something else Cinderella needed to take care of first. Reading the words from her dad's letter had pushed her toward a decision. Despite the late hour, she grabbed her phone and slipped into the bathroom so she wouldn't bother Belle.

"Princess, is that really you? It's late. Is everything okay?"

Cinderella sat on the floor, pulling at the fuchsia rug. "Hi, Scott," she said. Just hearing his voice again brought a sad smile to her face.

"I'm so glad you called me," Scott said. "I was afraid I was never going to hear from you again."

"You could have called me too, you know," she argued.

"I know, but I wasn't sure if you wanted me to and then when I didn't hear from you, I convinced myself that you didn't. I'm sorry for being such a stupid, jealous jerk! I know it was really unfair of me."

Cinderella cut him off. "Can I read something to you?" she asked, pulling the letter out.

"Of course. What is it?"

Cinderella briefly told him about her parents getting back together and their engagement. She explained the letter before reading it aloud to him.

"Wow," Scott said. "So many of those words are what I wanted to say to you, but didn't know how."

Cinderella nodded. "I know. In reading the letter, I didn't hear my dad's voice, I heard yours. And it made me realize I was being angry and prideful, just like my mom. She wasted so many years of her life being bitter because of it. I don't want to waste my life away holding onto resentment, but I don't want to have regrets either.

"So what are you saying?" Scott asked.

"I'm saying I forgive you, and I understand why you did what you did, at least to some extent. But I also realized I don't want to be with someone who doesn't trust me, and gets jealous of every guy I talk to."

"But I..."

"Please let me finish," she broke in. "I'm going to give Brian a chance. I want to give Brian a chance. I'm finally going to listen to the advice you gave me almost two years ago. I need to experience high school and dating a little more, and I can't do that with you looking over my shoulder."

Scott was silent and Cinderella feared she had lost him. "Scott?"

"I'm still here." His voice was barely above a whisper.

"I care about you very much, Scott. That's why I wanted you to know first that I forgive you and I'm not doing this out of anger. I'm just..." Cinderella struggled with getting her words out. "I feel like I need to."

"I understand." Scott's voice sounded deflated.

"Goodbye, Scott."

"Goodbye, princess."

# Chapter Nine

Ariel stepped from her house and twirled the single key around her finger. She took slow, deliberate steps toward the mailbox, glancing around as she moved. She stopped twice to tie her shoe, glancing at Jordan's front door and hoping it would open. When it suddenly did, Ariel fell back with a start, her stomach leaping into her throat. Instead of Jordan, a tall, slender, gorgeous woman appeared. Her dark, flawless skin was framed by perfect ebony curls. She grinned at Ariel as she approached, her red heels clicking against the pavement.

"You must be one of the Princesses," she said as she forced her key into the hole and removed a stack of mail. Ariel stood and nodded. The woman's beauty was intimidating. "Wait, let me guess," she said, holding up a hand. "Are you Ariel?"

"Yes, how did you know?"

"Jordan has told me all about you."

"He has?" Ariel squeaked.

Her smile widened. "Yes, of course. Well, I need to be getting off to work but it was good to finally meet you."

"You, too." Ariel felt hot and tingly. He had told his mom about her? Then, before she could lose her nerve, Ariel called out, "Is he home right now?"

"No, sorry," she said, pausing and shaking her head. "He's at work. But I'm sure he'll be home soon."

With a wave of her hand, his mother climbed into her car and drove away.

Ariel stood frozen beside the mailboxes. Jordan was talking to his mom at home about her. Was this a good sign? It had to be, right?

A smile spread across her face as his beat-up, blue truck pulled into the parking lot. Ariel pretended not to notice, turning her back to him as she finally retrieved the mail.

"Hey, Ariel," Jordan called, coming up behind her.

Her face flushed at the sound of his voice. Why did he have this effect on her? Ariel had never been nervous around boys before! She took a deep breath, steadying her racing heart and turned to meet his gaze.

"How are you?" he asked.

"Pretty great," she answered with a smile. "How was work?"

"Is it that obvious?" he asked.

Ariel looked from his torn, grease-stained jeans to the tattered, blue, button-up shirt he wore over a soiled white beater. She laughed. "Not at all, just a lucky guess."

"Right…so what are you up to?" he asked, sticking his hands in his pockets.

"Just getting the mail," she said, holding up the small stack of white envelopes. "Then I think we're going to watch a movie and hang out in a little bit. Wanna come?"

"Really?" he asked, his eyes brightening. "Can I really meet your cousins?"

Ariel nodded. "I think Dave is coming, too. Think you can handle the whole gang?"

"Dave? Who's Dave? Is he my competition?"

"Your competition for what?" Ariel asked, quirking her eyebrow.

Jordan smiled as he took a step closer. "Well, there's this really cute blonde I met a few days ago and I'm hoping this Dave guy doesn't already have a claim on her."

This time Ariel couldn't hide her face as her cheeks reddened. She tried to look away but Jordan's broad smile indicated he'd already seen her reaction.

"No, he's got his eye set on Belle. But Belle has a boyfriend already, so he hangs out with us and pretends he doesn't care about her when we all know he really does. It's all very complicated." Ariel stumbled over her words, trying to cool the heat in her face and avoid Jordan's eyes.

"I'm sorry," he said, shifting his feet. "I didn't mean to make you uncomfortable."

"No," Ariel said, searching her foggy brain for what to say next. She returned his gaze and noticed the warmth in his eyes. "I'm just not sure how cute you'll still find a certain blonde once you meet her gorgeous cousins."

"They're gorgeous? Well, why didn't you say so? Let's go!" Jordan pushed past Ariel and began walking towards her front door.

Ariel laughed. "Oh, I see how it is! As soon as someone better comes along, I'm left in the dust!" She reached out and grabbed Jordan's arm, pulling him backwards. With the mail in her other hand, she began swatting him playfully on his back. Jordan turned and grabbed Ariel's wrist in an attempt to snatch the weaponized envelopes away. She spun the other direction, shielding the envelopes with her body.

Ariel always thought 5'9" was tall, but she suddenly felt very small when Jordan grabbed her from behind, his 6'2" frame towering above her. He wrapped his long arms around her, pinning her own arms against her stomach.

Ariel squirmed and squealed, but Jordan's grip held her firmly in place.

"Hey, you let go of her right now!"

Jordan released Ariel quickly as Grandma B. came racing toward them. Their laughter died instantly. Grandma B. yanked Ariel away, waving a terrifying finger in Jordan's face. "If you ever so much as come near my granddaughter again, I'll call the police! Do you understand?"

Jordan put his hands up in defense. He looked to Ariel with wide eyes. "This is your grandma?"

"Yeah, my dad's mom. She's the one I told you about." Ariel turned toward the old woman. "We were just goofing around, Grandma! What's the big deal?"

Grandma B. held her ground. "It didn't look like you were goofing around to me. It looked like he was attacking you."

"Only because I attacked him first," Ariel joked, trying to lighten the mood.

"Well, from what I've seen, I don't think this boy is the kind of company you want to keep. You better get home, Ariel. I'll be speaking with your mother about this."

"My mother..?" Ariel looked to Jordan, confused by her grandmother's words.

Everything about Jordan had changed. He stood stiffly, his face grim, his eyes cold. "You better listen to your grandma, Ariel." The playful tone was completely gone from his voice. "I don't want to cause any trouble."

Grandma B. nodded.

"This is stupid, Grandma! Jordan and I were just goofing off. I know you worry about me because of your husband and your son, but seriously, Jordan would never hurt me! He is absolutely nothing like them!"

Both Grandma B. and Jordan broke their standoff and slowly softened.

"I'm sorry." Grandma B. finally tore her eyes away from Jordan and looked at her granddaughter for the first time. "I don't do wrestling well. Seeing things like that just sends me back to those dark days." She shivered.

Jordan suddenly broke into laughter. Given the topic of conversation, both Ariel and her grandma stared at him in surprise. "I'm sorry," he chuckled, stepping forward and taking Grandma's hand between his own. "Ariel has told me about her past, I should have known what this was about and why you were so upset."

"What did you think the problem was?" Ariel asked.

Jordan blushed. "I thought your grandma was racist."

***

"Is he really coming?" Aurora practically bounced in her seat.

"Unless you scare him away," Ariel said.

Cinderella clapped her hands. "I can't believe we finally get to meet your mystery man."

"Okay, well he's not exactly mine...yet." Ariel smiled.

The Princes sisters all laughed.

"He's so hot, you guys!" Aurora gushed. "When did you say he was coming over?"

"I'm already here!" Dave grinned as he came down the last step and entered the twins' basement.

Belle threw a pillow at him, which he dodged. "Oh I'm sorry, you weren't talking about me?" He winked and tossed the pillow back.

"No, we're talking about Jordan. He's our new neighbor who also happens to be Ariel's new 'friend,'" Belle explained.

"Come on, you guys, please don't embarrass me when he gets here." Ariel covered her face with her hands.

"There's an attractive new guy in the condos?" Dave asked. "Well, that sucks! I don't want to share my Princesses!" He plopped on the couch between Ariel and Aurora, putting an arm around each of them.

"Is Craig coming?" Snow White asked, earning a glare from Dave, which she didn't notice.

"No, he's at work," Belle pouted.

"What about This Week?" she teased, looking at Aurora.

"Yeah 'Rora," Cinderella said. "I don't think I've seen who your flavor of the week is yet."

Aurora thought back to her brief encounter with the other girls at beauty school. She didn't normally have a problem with her cousins teasing her about boys, but those wounds were still fresh. She didn't really want to talk about it, but saying nothing would make them suspicious. Aurora buried the incident in the back of her mind and plastered a smile on her face. "I just haven't chosen the lucky winner yet," she said.

The doorbell rang, causing Ariel's heart to jump into her throat.

The other girls squealed. "He's here!"

"Okay, I'm seriously not going to bring him down here if you all can't chill."

Her cousins each pulled the most serious faces they could muster. Ariel rolled her eyes as she walked up the stairs to answer the door.

Jordan, freshly showered, smelled incredible. The scent of his cologne made her heart flutter and she longed to have his arms envelope her again.

"Am I late?" he asked.

"No, just in time." Ariel smiled and stepped aside so he could enter their small family room. She began leading him toward the stairs when Jordan stopped her.

"Are we okay?" he asked.

"Well, except for the fact that my grandma is apparently racist," she joked.

Jordan smiled. "I feel so dumb!" he said. "But really, after I left you guys, your grandma didn't warn you to stay away from me anymore?"

"No! In fact, she apologized over and over again for misreading the situation. I'm kind of glad I told you my history, or you really would have been weirded out by her outburst."

"Only kinda?" Jordan's eyes twinkled.

"Yeah, it probably would have been more entertaining for me if you'd been completely in the dark!" Ariel laughed.

"You're mean."

"Not as mean as you getting grease all over me," Ariel teased.

"Oh no, did I?" Jordan looked horrified.

"No!" Ariel assured him. Even though the back of her clothes did have a new stain that probably wouldn't wash out, she wasn't about to tell him the truth and hurt his feelings. *Besides*, she thought, *I wouldn't trade that moment of being wrapped in his arms for anything.*

"You guys coming or what?" Aurora yelled up the stairs.

Ariel looked at Jordan and smiled. "You ready?"

He rubbed his hands together eagerly. "Let's do this!"

# Chapter Ten

Snow White reached out a clammy palm and pushed the glass door open, allowing her mom to step through the doorway first. The bustle of the busy restaurant buzzed in front of them. A waiter, weighed down with his heavy tray, squeezed past the hostess as she welcomed them.

"Is it just the two of you?"

Elizabeth nodded.

"No, three," Snow White corrected.

Elizabeth looked at her quizzically. "Who are we meeting?" she asked.

"It's a surprise," Snow White muttered.

"It'll be about ten minutes."

Elizabeth nodded. "This is nice," she said, smiling. "The two of us don't go out by ourselves very much. We're usually with the whole family."

Snow White couldn't look her mom in the eye as they waited for a table. She couldn't believe she was doing this. Her heart raced against her chest. She feared her mom would figure something out and make them leave before Mr. Wilkins ever got there. She was surprised her mom wasn't hounding her with a million questions already. She was usually so psychic when something was up, but she continued to stare happily at the TV mounted behind the reception desk. Sweaty baseball players ran around the bases, trying to beat the ball. With each whack of the bat, Snow White feared her heart would pound right out of her chest.

The hostess reappeared moments later with three menus in her hand. Snow White glanced back through the glass doors, out into the parking lot. If she turned around now, she could make a run for the car, claiming she didn't feel well. It was now or never.

Balling her hands into tight fists, Snow White straightened up and marched after her mom. *I guess it's now!*

Once seated, Snow White held the menu high, trying to hide the sweat pouring down the sides of her face. The words blurred together in a big jumble of letters.

"Can I get you anything to drink?"

"No, thanks." Snow White spoke without even thinking. She lowered the menu slowly. Both her mom and the waitress were looking at her like she'd lost her mind.

"Not even water?" The waitress asked, her pencil poised above the black pad.

"Ummm, sure, water. Yeah, water."

Elizabeth's eyes widened as she cocked her head. "You okay, sweetie?"

"Yeah, sorry. I've just got a lot on my mind."

"Like this mystery guest?" her mom asked. Elizabeth reached out and lowered Snow White's menu to the table. "I promise I'll be nice to him," she said.

Snow White's face blanched. Did her mom know? No, she wouldn't have come if she knew. And given their history, she definitely wouldn't be nice. "Who?" she finally stuttered.

"Oh, come on honey, the sudden desire to go out to eat with just me, all the secrecy. You want me to meet a boy, don't you? It's okay," she said, holding up a hand to stop Snow White's protests. "You're a senior in high school. I knew this day would come eventually. I'll be super pleasant to whoever this mystery guy is."

Snow White shook her head, about to tell her mom she had it all wrong, when she had a better idea. "You promise?"

"What, dear?"

"That you'll be super pleasant to him?"

"Of course! I want you to feel comfortable bringing the guys you're dating to meet me."

Snow White smiled. When the waitress returned with their beverages she said, "Could I actually get a Coke instead, please?"

"Sure thing, hon. You feelin' better?"

"Much, thank you." She smiled at the waitress.

"Mind if I join you?" Mr. Wilkins sat beside Elizabeth in the booth, blocking her exit.

Elizabeth stared at him. Her face quickly went from white to red. "What are you doing here?" she demanded.

"I invited him, Mom," Snow White said, biting her lower lip.

"WHAT?" Elizabeth's face shifted from red to purple with rage. Several people from nearby tables turned and stared, forcing her to calm down.

"Good call on the public place," Snow White mumbled to the attractive young lawyer sitting across from her.

"It's good to see you again, Snow White, and it's very good to see you again, Ms. Princess," he said, turning toward her and offering a smile. "Before you get up and throw me out, please hear what I have to say."

"I think I've heard plenty from you. And given the fact that you've now conspired against me behind my back, with my daughter, no less, I really don't care what you have to say. We should go." Elizabeth rose to her feet. "Come on, Snow White."

Snow White folded her arms against her chest and stared hard into her mother's eyes. "I need answers, Mom. And if you're not willing to give them to me, I'll just ask Mr. Wilkins for them. He told me he thinks he knows who my dad is, and I'm not leaving this booth until I find out."

The lawyer didn't move from his seat, causing Elizabeth to sit back down. She slumped over the table, defeated. "You told my daughter that?" she asked, her sad eyes pleading. "You had no right! I should have you arrested for talking to a minor about a case anyway!"

"I did not divulge any information to your daughter, Ms. Princess. In fact, when she called me, I told her that because she was a minor I couldn't. But I'm losing this case. I need your help." He was the one pleading now. If they weren't already sitting, Snow White was certain he would have dropped to his knees. "Bart Denum is going to walk if you don't help me. I can't live with myself knowing a man like that is free to roam the streets when I had an opportunity to put him away for life. Why won't you help me?"

Elizabeth's face fell into her hands. She leaned against the table, sniffling. Her shoulders began to shake.

The waitress returned, but upon seeing Elizabeth, she backed away quickly. "I'll give you some more time," she whispered.

*I'll bet she wishes she didn't get our table tonight,* Snow White thought. She reached a hand across the table and placed it on her mom's arm. "It's okay, Mom. Please tell me," she soothed. "I'm old enough to know now, don't you think? I'll be eighteen next year. Besides, if this guy is really as bad as Mr. Wilkins makes him sound, why wouldn't you want to help?"

Elizabeth finally looked up. Her eyes were red and swollen. Black mascara pooled on her cheeks and ran down her blotchy face. "Because of you," she whispered. "I've spent almost eighteen years trying to protect you from him. I didn't know what he would do if he ever found out."

Mr. Wilkins cautiously lowered a hand on Elizabeth's trembling shoulders. "It's okay, Ms. Princess. He's in custody right now. He can't hurt you or Snow White. And if you help me, he'll never leave that prison again."

Elizabeth nodded. She unraveled her silverware and wiped her dripping nose with the paper napkin. "You say the words, and I understand them, but I just…can't. I can't go back and relive that night. I'm not strong enough…" Her voice trailed off.

"Why don't we eat while you mull things over?" Mr. Wilkins asked. He opened his menu with his left hand, keeping his right firmly secured around Elizabeth's shrinking frame. "I would never have pegged you ladies as sport's bar fans. So what's good here? It's my treat."

"We don't ever watch the sports, the food is what keeps us coming back," Snow White said. "The pizza here is delicious. So are the burgers and the pasta. You can't really go wrong." Snow White looked at her mom, who seemed to be lost in another world. Maybe this wasn't a good idea after all. She snapped her attention back to the menu when the waitress cautiously approached for the third time.

"I will take a medium all meat pizza," Mr. Wilkins ordered. "And do you serve homemade root beer here? This looks like the type of place that might carry it."

"Sorry, sir, just Mug root beer."

"That sounds great! Bring me a glass of that, please." Mr. Wilkins tipped his blond head toward Snow White, his caramel eyes stared into her emerald green ones. "What would you like, Snow White?"

Snow White and her mom placed their orders next, each naming the first dish their eyes fell upon. After the waitress walked away, Snow White couldn't even recall what she said. *Oh well*, she thought. *I guess it will be a surprise then.*

The three of them sat awkwardly in silence until their food arrived. Then they had forks and chewing to keep themselves occupied. About halfway through the meal, Elizabeth finally broke through the quiet. "What would you need me to do?" she mumbled.

Mr. Wilkins jumped at the sound of her voice. He tried not to appear too eager. "Well, I'd need you to get up on the stand. I need you to testify what happened to you that night and explain why you dropped the charges against Burt Denum so soon afterwards."

Elizabeth's gaze flicked across the table at Snow White, but she couldn't really look at her. Snow White froze, her fork poised above her plate. "What charges?" she asked.

Elizabeth inhaled deeply, looking around the noisy, crowded restaurant. "All right, you win," she said, staring down into her plate of half-eaten pasta. "But not here. I don't want to talk about this anymore where someone might overhear us."

When the waitress returned for refills Mr. Wilkins asked for the check and some to-go boxes. He left a generous tip and hurried the two women out of the restaurant. "Why don't we go for a drive?" he suggested. "That way you can speak freely without the chance of someone overhearing you. I'll drive so you can just relax. Then I can bring you back here to retrieve your car when we're done."

Elizabeth didn't indicate whether she heard what the lawyer was suggesting, but she walked silently behind Mr. Wilkins. Snow White trailed a few steps behind her mom. Her stomach twisted around in knots with each step, every stride bringing her closer to some answers.

Mr. Wilkins held the door open for each of the ladies in turn. Once behind the wheel, he turned to Elizabeth. "Would it be possible for me to record this?" he asked, holding up a small digital voice recorder. "For reference during the trial," he clarified at the look of horror on her face.

"I suppose," she finally conceded. "But I haven't agreed to take the stand yet. I don't think I could face him again." Elizabeth shuddered.

"We'll just take it one step at a time," Mr. Wilkins said. His smile was genuine, his face kind. Snow White was glad her mom seemed to be warming up to him. Mr. Wilkins pulled out of the parking place and drove towards the mountains. "Nothing like a drive through the canyons in the fall," he said.

"I thought you were from California?" Snow White piped up from the backseat.

"Ah, well, I am, but my grandparents used to live in Utah. I spent a lot of time here as a boy. It's kinda nice to be back." He glanced over at Elizabeth's crumpled body, which was pressed against the passenger door. "I do, however, wish it were under different circumstances." Mr. Wilkins then held his digital recorder just below his lips and pressed a red button. "Interview with Elizabeth Princess, on the record. Witness and first victim to Burt Denum, accused serial rapist."

Snow White, who had remained mostly quiet in the backseat, wringing her hands in her lap, jolted when she heard those words. *First victim? Rape? Could this mean…* Snow White's hand flew to her mouth to cover the gasp which threatened to escape past her lips. She knew if she had any sort of reaction to Elizabeth's testimonial, her mom would stop speaking and probably never open up about it again. She had to keep her emotions in check.

"I had just graduated high school," Elizabeth's shaky voice whispered, "and I was taking some classes at the community college. B-B-Burt," Elizabeth stumbled over his name, "had an art class with me."

Her mom took art? Snow White couldn't recall a time when her mom held so much as a crayon.

"He asked me out a couple times, but I wasn't interested. He came across as debonair with me and the other girls, but I had also overheard him with other guys where he acted very vulgar and chauvinistic. I knew he wasn't genuine. Something about him always gave me the creeps. Anyway, it was one night after I stayed on campus late to study for midterms. It seemed like someone was following me, but I couldn't see anyone. When I was…crossing through a parking lot…someone hit me…hit me over the head from behind." Elizabeth began hyperventilating, gasping for breath between each word.

Mr. Wilkins stopped the recording and placed a comforting hand over hers. "Elizabeth," he spoke very softly, "you are safe here. Burt cannot get anywhere near you. Take some deep breaths for me and we'll continue whenever you're ready."

Elizabeth's gaze flicked up at Mr. Wilkins and she nodded briefly. She sucked in a deep breath through her nose and dispelled it. With eyes squeezed shut, she blew out a second breath and continued. "When I woke up, I was behind a dumpster alongside one of the buildings. He was…he was…on top of me." Elizabeth's shoulders began to tremble again as she buried her face in her hands.

Snow White stared down at the grey upholstery of the rental car. It took every ounce of self-control she possessed not to cry out for her mom. Her mind refused to wrap around the reality of her mother's stinging words. A silent tear slipped past her frozen gaze, and she angrily wiped it away. Why did she want to know the truth? Why did she push so hard? Knowing him as the sperm donor hurt a lot less.

"And you recognized the man attacking you as Burt Denum?" Mr. Wilkins whispered.

"Yes," Elizabeth said. "I don't think he expected me to wake up, but I was groggy and disoriented. I couldn't fight him off. When I tried to move, I realized my hands were tied. That's when he hit me again and yanked a bag over my head. Then he just left me in the alleyway to die."

"And how did you get out of that alleyway and make it home?" the lawyer asked.

"Campus police found me. I don't know how long I lay there for. It felt like an eternity. I was afraid to try and get up on my own. I didn't know if he was still there, watching me." Elizabeth shuddered.

"And that's when you filed your police report, naming Mr. Denum as the perpetrator?"

"Yes," Elizabeth choked.

"And why did you go back and drop the charges only six weeks later?"

Elizabeth was silent for several minutes before finally responding. "Because I found out I was pregnant." Her voice was barely above a whisper, yet the words felt hot and loud to Snow White. Elizabeth might as well have been yelling them. "I didn't want him to know about the baby. I was afraid he would hurt her, too. Right after she was born, my sisters and I moved to Layton."

Snow White thought her mom looked like the crumpled shell of a person, broken and hollow.

"I'm so sorry!" Elizabeth turned in her seat to try and look at Snow White, but she couldn't look her mom in the eyes. "I'm so sorry," she said again. "I just wanted to keep my daughter safe from that evil man."

Mr. Wilkins stopped the recording again. "I think that's enough. Everything you said matches the police reports exactly. Thank you, Elizabeth, for being so brave tonight." He gave her hand one final squeeze before parking the car and coming around to open their doors. Snow White never even noticed they had left the canyon. As she peeked out her window, she found they were back in the restaurant parking lot.

The rest of the evening became a blur. Snow White couldn't recall getting out of the car and driving home, but soon she found herself lying on top of her comforter in her own bedroom, the tears flowing freely. Now she understood. She knew why her mom never wanted her to know where she came from. Because Elizabeth couldn't admit to Snow White that she was never wanted in the first place.

# Chapter Eleven

The doorbell rang, causing butterflies to appear in Cinderella's stomach. Not the same excited anticipation butterflies that Scott always caused, but fearful and nervous ones. She threw the door open and welcomed Brian inside.

"You ready to go?" he asked, smiling widely.

"Hey, you got your braces off!" Cinderella exclaimed.

"Yeah," Brian said, rubbing his tongue over his smooth teeth. "I'm so excited!"

"You look great," she said, returning her own goofy grin. "Let me just grab my purse." As Cinderella turned, she blew out a large breath of worry and then plastered a smile back on her face before following Brian down the front steps.

He opened her door, always a gentleman, before climbing in beside her. "I thought we'd go miniature golfing and then to dinner. Does that sound good?"

"Sure," Cinderella smiled. Back when she thought Brian was just her friend, another pal, she felt completely relaxed and comfortable around him. Since she found out he liked her, and ever since that kiss at Lagoon, things had become awkward between them. Cinderella had been avoiding him at school a little bit. Not really on purpose, but it seemed like she always needed to hurry somewhere else when he came walking down a hall toward her. This was their first official date since Lagoon. Cinderella hoped the awkwardness would dissipate and they could return to normal again. She realized they had been sitting in the car in silence for several minutes while these thoughts ran through her mind. *Great. Not off to a good start,* she thought.

"What are your plans after high school?" Cinderella asked. "Have you applied to any colleges yet?"

"Yeah, I think I'll go to the University of Utah and study business. My dad and all my brothers have gone there. It's kind of family tradition."

"So is that what you want to do? Or are you doing it just out of tradition?"

"A little of both, I guess." Brian shrugged.

Cinderella waited for him to go on, or to ask about her future plans, but he grew silent instead.

"Are you excited for graduation?"

"Yeah."

Cinderella stared at him, waiting for something, anything she could grab onto to resuscitate their conversation. But no, it dried up and died. Cinderella took to looking out her window instead. When they pulled into the Boondocks parking lot, Cinderella was so excited to see more people that she leapt from the car without waiting for him to get her door. Brian stood there, looking shocked and a little hurt.

"Oh, sorry," she said, realizing too late. "Let's just go in."

Brian led the way past several loud, flashing arcade games and a laser tag arena to the mini golf counter at the back of the complex. "For two," he said, holding up his fingers. They handed him two clubs and directed him to pick out a couple balls for play. Brian reached into the box and grabbed a bright green one. He then pulled out a baby pink ball and handed it to Cinderella. Cinderella pinched the ball between two fingers and placed it back in the box, trading it for a bright blue one.

"You're not a pink fan?" he asked.

"Not at all," Cinderella said, scrunching her nose. "Blue is my favorite color, actually. Aurora and Belle both like pink things. Especially Aurora. I think her dream car would be a hot pink convertible."

"Cool," Brian said. He led the way to the miniature golf course. Cinderella rolled her eyes and followed him. So far the score was Cinderella-0 and awkwardness-3.

"Ladies first," Brian said, motioning for Cinderella to play.

"Okay, but you can't laugh at me," Cinderella joked. "I haven't played mini golf in a long, long time." She approached the green turf and squatted near the small black dot which served as the tee. Setting her blue ball in place, Cinderella stood, surveying the first hole. It was fairly simple—no huge obstacles stood in her way, just a small curve around the first hole. She stood and, after taking aim, whacked the ball with all her might. The ball flew into the air, whizzed over several players who had to duck, and landed somewhere on the opposite side of the arena. "Oops," she whispered. Her shoulders scrunched, her face bright red in the fading sunlight.

Brian stared, open-mouthed before he burst out laughing. The awkwardness between them seemed to melt away with Brian's laughter. "I'm sorry," he said, "but you weren't kidding!"

Cinderella smiled and gently poked him with her club. "Hey, I said no laughing!"

"I'm sorry," Brian said again, bending over as he clutched his side. "I've never actually seen anyone do that before! You could have taken someone's head off!" He continued to laugh until his face turned purple.

Cinderella couldn't help but join him. "All right, you big dope," she said, offering him a hand, "now what?"

"We get you another ball, and maybe some insurance." Brian began laughing again. Cinderella dropped his hand, causing him to fall onto his backside. "Okay, okay," he said, trying to control his laughter. "Let's go get you another ball." Brian rolled over and got to his feet, pushing his glasses back into place. He casually threw an arm around Cinderella's shoulders and walked her back to the entrance counter.

"I'm sorry," Brian said, approaching the desk, "but I seem to have lost my ball. Could I get a new one, please?" He flashed the young girl a winning smile. She rolled her eyes and shoved the box of balls toward them. Cinderella quietly reached up, closed her hand around a ball without even glancing at it, and turned back toward the green.

"I thought you didn't like pink?" Brian nudged her shoulder playfully.

Cinderella glanced down and noticed the bright pink ball resting in her fist. "Oh, great," Cinderella said, sticking out her tongue.

Brian chuckled and reached for her ball. "Here," he said. Cinderella placed it in his palm and then watched as he lined the ball up on the black dot once again. He waved Cinderella closer and told her to get ready, but not to swing. She shuffled forward and placed her hands on the club, hunching over the ball. Cinderella's face began to burn when Brian came right up behind her and pressed his body against hers. Goosebumps burst out across her skin as he wrapped his arms around her and placed his hands along the club. "Try holding it like this, with your thumbs down," he explained. Cinderella had a hard time focusing while Brian spouted off instructions. When Scott wrapped his arms around her, she melted. Right now, she didn't feel like melting. She felt suddenly stiff and uncomfortable as he moved the club back in slow motion. "We're not on a real golf course. You can just tap the ball gently."

Cinderella took the opportunity to escape, jabbing her elbow back into Brian's stomach. He bent over, laughing, and released her. "Just hit the ball quick and smooth," Brian instructed.

Cinderella shifted her feet a little and pulled the club back, tapping it swiftly this time. The ball shot forward, bounced off the wall in the curve and came back to her. Cinderella growled.

"That was better!" Brian encouraged.

"How was that better?" Cinderella asked, feeling silly that she was being beaten by such a simple game.

"Well, you didn't almost kill anyone this time." Brian grinned, revealing his most charming smile.

Cinderella shook her head and hit the ball again. The ball rolled around the corner and landed right beside the hole.

"You're getting it!" Brian cheered.

Cinderella walked forward and tapped the ball in with a clunk. Brian then took position and hit his own green ball. It turned the corner with ease and fell perfectly into the hole for a hole-in-one. Brian looked at Cinderella and grinned sheepishly. "Beginner's luck?"

"Yeah, right," she answered, smiling.

After twelve holes, Cinderella felt like she was really getting the hang of things. She stepped up to swing when Brian came up right beside her.

"You're really getting pretty good," he said. "What do ya say loser buys dessert?"

"Well, seeing as my first ten holes were a joke, that doesn't seem like a very fair bet."

"I mean starting now, with this hole."

Cinderella looked at his face. "You're on!" She hit the ball, which swerved perfectly for her first hole-in-one. Cinderella jumped up. "I did it!" She held her hand up for a high five. Brian slapped it in return, but held onto her fingers as their hands dropped. Cinderella wasn't sure how to proceed. She could feel the hairs pricking the back of her neck as their clammy hands squished together. She bent down to retrieve her ball, hoping he'd let go, but Brian bent with her. As they stood, she slipped her hand out of his. "You're up," she said, trying not to blush. "Beat that!"

For the remainder of the game, Cinderella gripped her golf club tightly between both hands. Why was she feeling so weird about Brian touching her? She liked him, didn't she?

After the game ended, Cinderella wished she could just go home, but they still had dinner…and dessert, which she had to buy. Cinderella sighed as they walked out to his car.

"Everything okay?" Brian asked.

"Yeah," Cinderella smiled. "I'm just hungry, I think."

"I can fix that. How does Italian sound?"

"Sounds great," Cinderella said, forcing a smile.

When they arrived at the restaurant, Cinderella was surprised to see it wasn't terribly crowded for a Friday night. The hostess showed them to a booth almost immediately. Cinderella sat on the squishy leather and picked up her menu, unnerved when Brian chose to sit next to her instead of across the table. Cinderella scooted over so they would both have enough space, but Brian closed the gap between them again. Cinderella opened her menu and stared at the words, which seemed to blur together. Brian placed an arm around Cinderella's shoulders and she immediately tensed.

"I...uh...need to use the restroom," she said, standing.

Brian slid out of the booth, letting her pass. "Do you want me to get you something to drink?" he asked.

"Just water," Cinderella answered without turning. She hurried toward the ladies room and pushed the door open, sighing heavily when she arrived inside. She stepped cautiously toward the mirror and glanced at her reflection. Grabbing a towel from the wall dispenser, Cinderella dampened it and placed the cold rag against her cheeks. "This was a mistake," she whispered. "I just want to go home." Cinderella lingered in the bathroom for as long as she could get away with before returning to their table.

"You okay?" Brian asked. "You seem to have gotten quieter."

"Yeah, Scott, I'm fine," she said, waving her hand.

"My name's not Scott," he whispered.

"What?" Cinderella looked up at him. Her eyes widened. Her face burned scarlet. "Oh my gosh, Brian, I'm so, so sorry!" she exclaimed. "I don't even know why I said that."

"I do," Brian mumbled. "You're in love with him."

"But I..."

Brian put up a hand to stop her. "It's okay," he said. "I knew that before I ever asked you out. I kind of hoped he had screwed things up at Lagoon, but I can see now you're really not available. Let's just go," he said getting to his feet.

Cinderella slowly stood and followed Brian from the restaurant, staring at her feet as she walked. He opened her door for her. They drove home in silence. When Brian pulled up to the condos and opened his door, Cinderella reached out a hand to stop him.

"Wait," she said. "Brian, I really loved having you as a friend. Can't we just go back to being friends and forget about all of this?"

Brian looked at Cinderella, his face drooping. He removed his glasses and wiped his eyes. "I don't think I can do that, Cinderella. I'm sorry. I just can't be around you and pretend I don't care." Brian got out of the car and opened Cinderella's door.

Her body felt heavy as she slowly climbed out and got to her feet. Cinderella moved to hug Brian goodbye, but he stepped around her, closing her door, and returned to the driver's side.

Cinderella spoke through the open passenger window. "Thank you, Brian. I really did have fun when we were just laughing and hanging out at the miniature golf course. Are you sure we can't go back to that?"

Brian stared down at his dashboard, unable to return her gaze. "Goodbye, Cinderella."

# Chapter Twelve

Belle bounced down the stairs, her arms weighed down with a tray of goodies. She couldn't keep the smile off her face as she spread the various treats and snacks around the top of the card table. She walked along the two couches, fluffing pillows and straightening the cushions. A step creaked behind her, and she spun around to find Cinderella moseying down the stairs. She looked lost and forlorn as her glassy eyes scanned over Belle's decorations.

"You okay, Cindy?"

Cinderella shuffled over to the nearest couch and plopped down in the center, causing the perfectly puffed pillows to tumble over.

Belle clicked her tongue. "Cindy? You in there?" she asked again.

"Huh?" Cinderella looked up. Belle could see dark purple shadows beginning to appear below her eyes.

"When was the last time you slept?" Belle asked.

"I dunno," Cinderella mumbled. "I've got too much on my mind right now. I wish I could sleep, I really do, but I just end up tossing and turning all night."

"You seriously need to take a sleeping pill or something to help you get past this slump. You'll never make it to graduation at this rate."

Cinderella nodded her head, mumbling something incoherent before slumping over and resting her head on a pillow.

"Yeah, okay, don't worry about helping me get ready for the party. I'll just do this myself."

Cinderella stretched an arm in the air and waved Belle off, who rolled her eyes in return. Belle ran back up the stairs for another load of food from the fridge. Grateful her mother had given her an allowance, Belle loaded another tray of artificially flavored snacks and treats loaded with high fructose corn syrup she had purchased and carried them down the stairs. She was filling a pitcher of water when the front door opened.

"In the kitchen," Belle called.

"Do you need a hand with anything?" Dana asked.

"Nope, we're just about ready."

"Did you see the hummus I bought for tonight?"

Belle stared at the water pouring from the sink. "Uh-huh."

"I also bought a bunch of fresh vegetables to dip in it. Have you had a chance to cut those up yet?"

"Not yet…" Belle's voice trailed off.

"Okay, I'll work on those." She set her keys on the counter and stepped over to the fridge, removing a variety of vegetables to be sliced.

"So how was the goodbye?" Belle asked, shutting the water off.

Dana sighed dramatically. "So hard! I tried my best to get him to stay another night for your mom's premiere, but Sophie has a dance recital and he really can't miss it."

"Is that gonna be weird, having three kids now?"

"It's definitely going to be an adjustment," Dana said. "Especially going from one teenager to two teens and a little girl. I thought I was past the Barbie dolls and hair bows stage. It will be interesting to relive those years again." Dana paused, a small grin coming over her face. "It will be nice, though. I was a little nervous, with all you girls going off to college next year. I definitely won't be lonely now! Have you met Sophie?"

Belle nodded, laughing. "Oh, yeah."

"She's a fireball, that one!" Dana chuckled, and then returned to chopping vegetables.

Belle glanced over at her aunt, who had grown very quiet. Dana was chewing her bottom lip as her eyebrows furrowed together. "Something wrong, Dana?" Belle asked.

Dana glanced up at Belle. "Oh...it's just...I don't know, really."

"Are you worried about Steven's girls?"

Dana stared back down at the cucumber in her hand, but the knife remained motionless. "Yes," she whispered. "I'm just not sure what they're going to think of me. What they're going to think of all of this. Everything with their dad has happened so fast—well, fast for them, not for me—and they only lost their mom a few years ago..." Dana paused, lost in thought.

"I'm sure they'll love you, Dana!" Belle set down her water and placed a hand on top of her aunt's. "I don't think it will be easy, but I'm sure it will be nice having a mother figure in their lives again. I for one didn't realize I would miss mine so much until she moved. Now I miss her like crazy. The difference is I at least can reach my mom by phone."

Dana patted Belle's hand and smiled appreciatively. "Thank you, sweetie."

"Just a word of advice," Belle said, picking up the large plastic pitcher once again. "Don't be completely health nutso all the time. Especially with the little one! Let her have sugar once in a while if you ever want her to like you." Belle left Dana with a mischievous grin before carrying the water downstairs to add to the table.

Belle had her foot on the first step, about to run back upstairs, when she heard a muffled cry. Stepping back down, she peered around the side of the couch. Cinderella remained in the same hunched position where she had been when Belle left her. Only now Cinderella's shoulders quivered as she sniffled into the pillow.

"Cindy?" she whispered. "You okay?"

Cinderella sat up, wiping at her red, swollen eyes. "I'm such an idiot," she said.

"Well, only sometimes," Belle joked, trying to coax a smile from her cousin.

Cinderella smiled weakly.

"Is this about Brian?" she asked. "Or Scott?"

"Both, in a way. I thought going out with Brian would be fun and I already knew we got along really well, but it didn't take very long to realize we're just friends. We'll never be anything more than friends. Everything he said, everything he did, I couldn't help but compare to Scott. Scott is not perfect, but he's my kind of perfect. Does that make any sense?"

Belle smiled warmly. "Yeah, it sounds really goopy," she teased, and then added more softly, "and I think it's a clear sign that you are completely and totally head-over-heels in love."

"But I pushed him away," Cinderella whispered sadly. "He asked for my forgiveness and I shoved it back in his face."

"I don't think you shoved it."

"That's what it feels like I did!"

"So just call him," Belle said, shrugging. "Tell him you made a terrible mistake and you're sorry."

"I wish it were that easy…" Cinderella trailed off as she stared at nothing in particular.

"It is that easy!" Belle exclaimed. "Pick up phone, push speed dial." She held her hand up to her ear as if speaking. "Hi, Scott, I'm stupid and made a mistake. I love you. What? You love me too? Great, let's get married and have a million babies. Bye." Belle dropped her hand and glared at Cinderella with wide eyes. "Super simple!"

Cinderella shook her head. "It's so much more complicated than that. I told him I was going to do what he requested and date other guys. So I should just give up after one date?"

"Yes!" Belle exclaimed. She was becoming increasingly exasperated with her cousin. "Is it fair to date another guy you don't even care about, just to experiment?"

"Maybe I should just take a break from guys altogether," Cinderella murmured.

Belle threw her arms up in the air. "Cinderella," she said, looking her straight in the eyes, "what is going to make you the most happy? If you want to take a break from guys, then take a break from guys. But there is no doubt in my mind Scott still loves you like he always has. He's not going to let you go that easily, unless you want him to." Belle got to her feet and patted Cinderella on the leg. "Just think about it before you give up too easily."

The doorbell rang, encouraging Belle to hurry up the stairs. "Are you okay?" she asked Cinderella.

Cinderella wiped the remaining moisture from her eyes with the back of her hand and nodded. "Yes. Thanks, Belle." She smiled. Waving her cousin to continue up the stairs, she added, "I'll be fine. Go on."

Belle approached the front door right as Dana was opening it.

"Hi, Dave," Dana said, stepping aside so he could enter.

Dave's bright blue eyes lit up with his smile. "Hi Dana, hi Belle. So this is pretty exciting stuff! I can't believe your mom was on *Locker Partners*.

"Well, she will be in," Belle glanced at her watch, "twenty minutes or so." She returned Dave's smile. "Come on downstairs. It's just me and Cinderella so far."

Belle waited until Dana returned to the kitchen before she grabbed Dave's arm and pushed him against the wall.

"Okay!" Dave said, wrapping his arms around Belle's waist.

"What? No!" Belle pushed him back and then whispered, "Maybe you can help me out with Cinderella. She's being completely stupid about your brother."

Dave straightened up and shook his head. "Nope, I'm staying out of it. I've already talked to Scott and I think they're both just being stupid and stubborn."

"I do, too! That's why we need to fix it."

"No way," Dave said, putting his hands up. "I've tried and I'm done. They need to figure this out on their own."

"Traitor," Belle mumbled.

"Sorry, Belle, but you can't force them."

"I could if I had a really sharp stick. Then I could just poke some sense into them." She pretended to jab at the air.

Dave chuckled. "Nice try. Now tell me what I can do to help get this party started."

The front door opened again and Aurora, Ariel, and Jordan all entered the house together.

"Our mom had to work late, but she should be on her way soon," Ariel said.

"Okay, great! Head downstairs, guys. I'll be down in a minute. Have you seen Snow yet?"

"Do you want me to text her?" Aurora asked.

"No, she still has a few minutes before the show starts. She's just seems kinda off lately. You guys noticed?"

"Yeah, but we all know she doesn't deal well with change. And high school ending and all of us leaving for school is a huge change. I think it's just got her feeling a lot of pressure lately," Ariel said.

Aurora and Belle agreed. Belle glanced at her watch again and squealed. "Okay, hurry downstairs. We need to be all set before the show starts. Hurry!" She shooed them all away. Jordan reached for Ariel's hand and they walked down together. Belle and Aurora exchanged a look of excitement behind their backs. Aurora followed them as Belle turned to help Dana carry her large tray of veggies down to the basement.

When Dana saw the huge spread of sugar-loaded snacks and processed foods, she gasped. "Where'd all this come from?" she asked.

Belle played coy. "Oh, my mom just sent me some money for a few refreshments." She grinned innocently, batting her long lashes in Dana's direction.

Dana huffed but said no more.

Elizabeth showed up a few minutes later.

"Where's Snow White?" Belle asked.

Elizabeth folded her arms over her chest and sighed. "She didn't feel like coming."

"What? Why?" Belle put a hand on her hip.

"I wish I knew, hon," Elizabeth said.

Elizabeth joined the group downstairs, followed by Craig and a new This Week from the basketball team who snuggled up beside Aurora on the floor. Belle turned on the

TV and hushed everyone, even though they were only commercials. When the theme music for *Locker Partners* began playing, everyone cheered. The first scene aired a shot of her dad sitting behind a large desk. Belle couldn't help but smile. It was strange how much she loved this show just last year. Now she watched it to feel closer to her dad more than anything.

Rachel came dashing down the stairs. "Did I miss anything?"

"Not yet," Belle whispered. "Come sit down."

Rachel glanced from the crowded couches to the bodies filling up most of the floor. "Where?" she asked.

Jordan jumped up from his spot on the couch beside Ariel and Cinderella. "Here, take my seat," he offered.

Ariel was disappointed until he stood behind her and began rubbing her shoulders from behind the couch. She flushed a little when her mom glanced from Jordan's hands to her, eyebrows raised. Ariel just smiled and pointed to the TV. "Shhhh, let's watch your sister," she whispered.

Mary had two quick scenes towards the beginning of the episode, but they all cheered loudly when each one ended.

"Do you have any more popcorn?" This Week asked Aurora.

Aurora remained glued to the episode. "Ummm, no," she responded without looking at him.

"I'll go make some," Ariel said, sliding off the couch.

Jordan reached for the empty bowl This Week held out. "I'll come with you," he offered.

Ariel smiled and the two walked upstairs together.

"I thought you were a TV buff. Why'd you choose to leave the show?" Jordan asked.

Ariel grabbed a bag out of the open box Belle had left on the table. "I don't know. Having Lucas for an uncle kind of ruined the magic for me, I guess. But if you noticed, the rest of my cousins remain entranced."

Jordan chuckled. "You definitely stand out from them," he said.

Ariel placed the popcorn in the microwave and began pushing buttons. "You mean because I'm gangly and strange?" she teased.

"Gangly? Definitely not. Strange? Maybe a little." He smiled playfully. "But I like strange. You're not like any other girl I've ever known." Jordan took a step closer to her. Ariel turned toward the microwave and watched the numbers counting down. Her face felt hot and her heart began to race. "I'd really like to kiss you," he said. "Is that okay?"

Ariel felt like her heart might beat straight out of her chest. Her hands began to tremble. Her breath quickened. She turned and looked at Jordan, whose caramel eyes held hers in their gaze. Ariel didn't even know how to respond. "Why me?" she asked quietly.

"Because you're beautiful, and intelligent, and sassy, and I've never been able to talk to another person as easily as I can with you. I like you, Ariel, but if you don't feel the same I can..."

Ariel stepped closer and grabbed the back of Jordan's head, pulling him forward. She kissed him gently on the lips before pulling back. The microwave beeped and Ariel reached up to open it, but Jordan stopped her. He placed both of his large hands on either side of her face and pulled her in for another kiss. Her lips tingled as they melted into each other. Jordan's hands moved up into her hair. Ariel responded by wrapping her arms around his waist and pulling him closer.

Belle came up the stairs, looking for the popcorn. She froze when she saw the two of them kissing, and her smile widened. She turned and walked back down the stairs.

"What's taking them so long?" Rachel asked.

"Looks like they burned the first bag, so they're just starting another one," Belle answered. She snuggled back into Craig, unable to hide the smile from her face.

***

Snow White sat in her dark basement, alone, watching Mary's appearance on *Locker Partners*. She sniffled over her bowl of popcorn. Everyone was next door at Cinderella's house, probably laughing and having a great time. She sniffled again. She didn't belong there anymore. Not since she learned the truth.

# Chapter Thirteen

Ariel peeked her eyes open the next morning and almost jumped out of her skin. "What are you doing?" she screamed.

Aurora lay on her side beside Ariel, staring at her, their faces only inches apart. "Were you and Jordan sucking face last night?!"

Ariel grinned at the memory as she stretched.

"That's a yes! Woo-hoo!" Aurora shot up and bounced off the bed. "Oh man, I am so proud of you, sister! So...how was it?"

Ariel climbed out of bed slowly. "A lady never kisses and tells."

"Oh bull! Come on, tell me, tell me, tell me!"

"You're like a two-year-old," Ariel laughed.

"You're going to want to tell me," Aurora pressed.

"Oh yeah?"

"Yeah, because if you don't, I can guarantee what I make up in my mind will be far worse. Wouldn't you prefer to set the record straight?"

Ariel rolled her eyes. "Fine." She sat back down on the edge of her bed, Aurora plopping beside her, looking eager. "We went up to make popcorn and were just talking. Then he asked if he could kiss me."

Aurora jerked back. "He asked you? Wow, I don't think I've ever had a guy ask me."

"That's because Jordan is a gentleman and most of your This Week choices are not."

"So…" Aurora ignored her comment. "Was it good?"

Ariel closed her eyes, replaying the memory of his soft, warm lips in her mind. She felt a chill go up her spine, her body tingling all over. Ariel grinned and opened her eyes to see Aurora watching her closely again. Her twin smiled back. Aurora clapped her hands and squealed. "I knew you had it in you!"

Ariel's entire face lit up as she smiled back. "Well, we better get ready for school."

Reluctantly, Aurora shuffled to the closet and began pulling out clothes. Ariel sighed and stood again. She couldn't keep the smile from her face.

*\*\**

Ariel scanned the parking lot for Jordan's truck as they pulled into their own parking stall after school. She slumped back down against her seat when she realized he wasn't home. Snow White climbed out of the car the moment it stopped and hurried inside her house without muttering a word to anyone.

"Have you talked to her lately, Cindy?" Belle asked. "She usually tells you things more than the rest of us."

Cinderella peered out the window at Snow White's closed door. "I have no idea! I've tried asking, but it's like she's shutting us out."

Ariel remained sitting while her cousins all piled out of the car.

"I've gotta lock the doors now, Ari," Belle said, holding up her car keys.

"Huh?" Ariel looked around and realized she was in the car alone. She unclicked her seatbelt and climbed out. "Sorry," she grinned sheepishly.

"Last night really took a toll on you, huh?" Belle asked with a hint of laughter. "Going without air for that long will really affect your brain the next day."

"Shut up," Ariel said, smiling.

"Wait, what?" Cinderella asked. "Did I miss something last night?"

The other three girls all laughed. "You were pretty out of it last night, Cindy," Ariel said. "I would've thought you were the one with a kissing hangover."

As they filled Cinderella in on the story, a large blue truck turned the corner and parked. "He's here!" Ariel hissed. "Go inside, go inside!"

Aurora, Cinderella, and Belle dashed into Cinderella's house, wishing Ariel luck in whispered voices as they ran. Ariel could still see them peeking through the curtains of the large, front window. "Smooth," she mumbled. Ariel tried to ignore them, turning toward Jordan as he approached. His smile split his face as he neared. Without warning, Jordan walked straight up to Ariel. With one hand behind her head and the other around her slender waist, he pulled her in and kissed her passionately. Ariel stumbled back a step when he released her.

"Sorry," he said, running his hand down her arm and holding her fingers. "I couldn't resist. I've been thinking about you all day."

Ariel squeezed his hand and stood on her tiptoes to kiss him again lightly on the lips. "I've been thinking about you all day, too," she admitted.

"Well, then, Ms. Ariel Princess, I need to take you out on a proper date. Would you have dinner with me tonight?"

Ariel's eyes crinkled as her smile widened. "I'd love to!"

"Great! I'll pick you up at 6:00. Let me go shower and cleanup from work, before I get any more grease or grime on you," he said, trying to rub the black smudge from her hand.

As soon as Jordan left, Ariel's cousins came back outside, whooping and cheering.

"You guys are so cute!" Aurora exclaimed, hugging her sister.

"I'm still in shock he likes me," Ariel said quietly.

"Oh, stop!" Cinderella nudged her arm. "Why wouldn't he like you? You're incredible!"

Ariel shrugged. "I've never been here before. You guys are the ones who usually get dates and boyfriends."

"Please," Belle said. "Might I remind you that minus the hair color, you and Aurora look exactly the same?"

"Yeah, but I don't flirt like Aurora does."

Cinderella and Belle both laughed. "No one flirts like Aurora does!"

"She could make it a career!"

Aurora bent over and took a bow.

"Well, Craig's coming over to study. I better get home."

"Have fun!" Ariel watched as they all trickled away. "I'll be right in," she said to Aurora. "I'm just going to grab the mail real quick." Ariel unzipped her backpack and pulled out her small keychain. She opened the mailbox and gasped. There, on the very top, was a large white envelope addressed to her. The return address was labeled University of Southern California. Ariel reached in and grasped the envelope with a shaking hand. She held it up, staring at the university logo and her name. She slammed the mailbox shut and ran down the sidewalk. Ariel hurried up the three small steps and knocked.

"Geeze, I thought I was picking you up at 6:00. Are you that anxious to go?" Jordan stood in his open doorway, running a towel over his wet hair. His eyes shone bright as he watched Ariel trembling on his front stoop.

Ariel couldn't find the words. She just held the envelope up for Jordan to see.

His face lit up. "No way! Did you get in?"

Ariel shook her head, trying to get the right words to come. Her throat felt suddenly very dry. "I don't...I don't know," she answered, breathlessly. "I'm too scared to open it."

Jordan reached out and took Ariel by the hand. He led her into his house and sat her down on the soft leather couch. Sitting beside her, he reached for the envelope. "May I?" he asked.

Ariel nodded, covering her face with her hands. "Do it quick-like a Band-Aid."

Jordan chuckled. "Dear Ms. Princess," he read, "Congratulations! I am pleased to inform you of your admission to the Cinematic Arts department at the University of Southern California for the fall semester."

Ariel ripped the paper out of Jordan's hand before he could finish reading. "Are you serious?!"

"Ow!" Jordan said, holding up his hand. Ariel glanced at him. "Paper cut." He held up his injured finger.

"Sorry."

Jordan got to his feet and pulled Ariel up into an embrace. "I'm so proud of you!" he said, holding her tight. "Does this mean you told your mom?"

Ariel slowly backed out of his arms. "Not exactly."

"But you got in!"

"I know! I sorta thought if I applied and didn't get in, then that would be that. I wouldn't have to stress about telling her, and I wouldn't have to be disappointed. But this changes everything! I got in. I wasn't supposed to get in. Now I have to tell my mom and be disappointed when she reminds me we can't afford it."

Jordan lifted her chin and looked her square in the eyes. "Then don't tell her today. Tonight, we will celebrate this amazing accomplishment. Forget McDonalds. I'm taking you somewhere super nice."

Ariel pulled a face. "You were going to take me to McDonalds for our first date?"

Jordan laughed loudly. "You should see your face! No! Of course not. I think I know exactly where to go. You're gonna love it."

Ariel smiled. "Tonight we celebrate. Disappointment can wait one more day."

"That's right."

"In that case, I will go home and change. See you in a bit."

"Bye."

"Bye."

***

Aurora had insisted on doing Ariel's makeup for her first real date with Jordan. Ariel thought it was too heavy, but Aurora didn't listen. When Jordan came to the door, his jaw dropped when he saw her. "Wow," he said.

Aurora smiled. Her work was done. "Have fun, you two," she said, waving.

"You look incredible," Jordan said as he led her towards his truck.

"You clean up pretty nice yourself," she smiled back. "You don't think it's a bit…too much?" she asked, tugging at the frilly top Aurora had shoved over her head.

"Well, frankly, I'm a jeans and T-shirt kind of guy. And you can seriously rock a pair of jeans."

Ariel blushed.

"But I think it's nice to get dressed up every now and then. You look stunning tonight, and it makes me feel really good that you went to all that work for me. I appreciate it." He squeezed her hand. "Now if you did this all the time, I would probably think you were too high maintenance," he teased.

Ariel smiled appreciatively. "So where exactly are we going?" she asked as Jordan helped her up into the seat.

"You'll see."

When they pulled up to the restaurant, Ariel's eyes sparkled in amazement. "What is this place?" she asked. Jordan got out of the truck and came around the front, opening Ariel's door for her. He placed his hands around her waist and lowered her easily to the ground. "This is where my dad proposed to my mom," he said. "And where my grandparents celebrated every anniversary up until my grandpa died. And where my mom took my dad to announce I was coming. It's where my family has always gone to celebrate special occasions."

Ariel put a hand to her throat. "And you brought *me* here?"

"We're celebrating, aren't we?" Jordan tugged Ariel forward.

The entrance to the restaurant was shaded by a small grove of trees, small, twinkling lights adorning each branch. As Jordan led her through the trees, Ariel stared upwards. "Wow," she mouthed. Jordan reached out and pulled open the heavy wooden door. Ariel's thoughts immediately went to *The Secret Garden*. She couldn't wait to see what they would find on the other side. Ariel looked around, wide-eyed, as she took in the enormous restaurant. Vines hung and twisted around the walls. Beautiful fresh flowers embellished each table. The thing which stood out the most to Ariel was a beautiful waterfall in the center of the room, running down the main wall, between rows of vines. The combination of the trickling water, sparkling lights, and sheer beauty of the room held Ariel captive until the hostess appeared. She snapped from her trance when the young woman asked, "Do you have a reservation?"

"Yes, it's under Jordan," he responded. Once the hostess seated them, he said, "Geeze, maybe I should have picked another place."

"What? Why?" Ariel asked.

"Because I don't think you've even looked at me since we walked in the front doors."

Ariel reached across the table and held Jordan's hand. "I'm sorry!"

Jordan smiled. "I'm only teasing you. This place is pretty mesmerizing, isn't it?"

"It's incredible! I can't believe I've never even heard of it." Ariel opened her menu and then gasped, slamming it shut again.

Jordan looked at her, his eyebrows crinkled in concern. "What's the matter?" he asked.

"The prices!" Ariel whispered.

"Oh, that." Jordan looked around for a moment before unraveling his silverware and holding up his dark blue cloth napkin. He opened Ariel's menu once again and placed the napkin, spread out, over the prices along the right column. "There," he said. "Just look at the food and pick something that sounds good. Don't worry about the cost. I've got it covered."

"I don't suppose you'd believe me if I said all I wanted was a side salad and a glass of water?" Ariel flashed him her most endearing smile.

"Not for a second. Now pick something, or I will choose. And I'll pick the most expensive thing on the menu."

Ariel tried to slide the napkin over just a smidge, but Jordan grabbed both of her hands in his and pulled them across the table. "I'm not going to let go of these until you can behave."

Ariel glared at him in mock anger. "But this is too much."

"Hey, we are celebrating something huge tonight. You got accepted to your dream school! Ariel, that's so amazing! Now, come on, I've seen you eat so I know you can."

When their dinners arrived, Ariel couldn't believe how beautiful the dishes looked. "It's like art!" she exclaimed.

The pair talked easily through dinner, which was the best food Ariel had ever tasted. When the waiter came over to ask if they would like any dessert, Ariel and Jordan both groaned. "I wish!" Jordan said. "Your cheesecake is amazing, but perhaps another time." He turned back to Ariel once the waiter had taken their check. "So, are you up for a movie?"

"Always!" Ariel said. "Did you have one in mind?"

"I was going to let you choose, since I picked the restaurant." He smiled.

Twenty minutes later, Jordan and Ariel sat in their seats and looked up at the giant white screen. Jordan reached over and held Ariel's hand, causing her stomach to flutter. Almost instantly the lights went out and previews played across the screen. Jordan's phone began singing loudly, causing several heads to turn.

Ariel giggled. "Oh, you're *that* guy in the movie theater," she said as she watched him try and silence the obnoxious beast.

Jordan glanced at his screen before returning his phone to his pocket and froze. He stared at the bright monitor, which attracted more attention.

Ariel squirmed in her seat, glancing over at him. "Jordan, you've gotta put that away," she whispered. "People are really starting to stare."

Jordan jumped up in his seat and bolted down the theater stairs. "We gotta go," he said loudly. Confused, Ariel jumped up and quickly followed him. She found him in the lobby, pacing back and forth as he continued to stare down at his phone. "I'm sorry, but it sounds really urgent. We need to leave now."

Ariel reached out and grasped his arm, just above the elbow, causing him to pause. "What's going on?" she asked.

"It's my grandma."

# Chapter Fourteen

When they arrived home, Ariel and Jordan saw several cars parked along the road outside of the condominiums. Jordan gasped. "Oh, no," he muttered.

"What's the matter?" Ariel asked, straining her neck to see.

"Those are my aunts' cars, which means everyone is here…"

Ariel studied Jordan's face, observing his tightly clenched jaw. He sniffled once when he put the truck in park and sat back, watching his front door. Ariel moved in slow motion as she unclicked her seatbelt and tried to slide out her door.

"Wait," Jordan said, putting a hand across her lap to stop her. "Please come with me." His soft brown eyes looked like they might melt with sadness.

"I don't want to intrude on your family," Ariel said quietly.

"You are family."

Ariel squeezed Jordan's hand as they approached Grandma Johnson's door. They each took a deep breath and pushed it open together. The air in her small condo felt warm and thick. With so many bodies in the room, Ariel wasn't sure how they would get through the door.

Grandma Johnson's couches had been removed from her living room. In their place, a long hospital bed sat against the far wall. The hospice nurse hovered over Grandma's small, frail body, checking vitals and answering questions. Both Jordan's parents sat in kitchen chairs beside her bed. Grandma's other two daughters and their families were sitting or standing in groups around the room, talking in hushed whispers. Ariel was surprised to see Aurora and her own mom speaking to one of them. Ariel rushed over, and she and Aurora embraced. They held each other for several minutes, neither having to say a word. Ariel finally released the tears she had been holding in and looked up to find Aurora was doing the same. Ariel glanced around and found Jordan, with his head on his mother's lap. In that moment, he reminded Ariel of the old school picture that used to be displayed on Grandma Johnson's piano of Jordan with his big goofy grin, minus his two front teeth.

The front door opened again and Dana entered with Cinderella, Belle, and Snow White. A few minutes later, Elizabeth joined them. Jordan's family welcomed them warmly, embracing Ariel's family and thanking them for taking care of Grandma Johnson for all these years.

Ariel stepped away from her sister and knelt on the ground beside Jordan. He placed his hand on her back and slowly traced his fingers around in circles. Ariel really looked at Grandma Johnson for the first time. Her face appeared sunken, her skin grey. She looked like she had lost weight and her thinning hair lay matted against her head. All signs of the lively, happy old woman from a few weeks ago disappeared. The cancer had worked quickly.

"I don't think we've been introduced yet." Ariel looked up to discover the deep voice had come from Jordan's father. He reached out a hand and Ariel shook it.

"I'm Ariel," she tried to smile.

"This is one of the famous Princess sisters," Jordan explained.

"From the Popsicle picture?" he asked.

Ariel's smile widened. "The very same one."

"It's a pleasure," he said, nodding his head, "although I do wish we were meeting under different circumstances. My mother referred to you girls with nothing but fondness."

"Would you like to meet the rest of them?" Jordan asked.

"Yes, please," his dad responded, looking around.

Ariel called to her cousins and waved them over.

"Dad, this is Snow White, Belle, Cinderella, and Aurora. Aurora is Ariel's twin sister."

"I never would have guessed," his dad said, smirking.

"It's so nice to finally meet you all."

"I'm impressed you kept us all straight," Cinderella said.

Ariel smiled. She was impressed, too!

"So tell me, ladies, what is the story behind the picture my mother has displayed so very proudly on her piano?"

"I don't really remember," Belle admitted.

"Just a summer day, I think," added Cinderella.

"I can answer that," Dana said, joining their conversation. "It was when the girls were about eight years old. It was close to dinner time. In fact, I believe we were having a barbecue with several of the grandmas in this complex that night. We were trying to grill the food and the girls kept pestering us for some popsicles. I think the exact words they used were 'we might die if we don't get one, it's so hot.'"

The cousins all smiled, the memory suddenly coming back to them. "Oh, yeah!" Belle said. "And you told us not yet because the Popsicles were for after dinner."

"So what did you girls do?" Dana asked.

"We walked down to Grandma Johnson's house and asked her if she had any popsicles," Cinderella said. "Which she, of course, gave to us."

"Then we sat on her porch and ate them so we wouldn't get caught, and that's when she took the picture," Ariel added.

"We thought we were so sneaky," Aurora laughed.

"But then when you all came back to the barbecue, your mouths were so stained, it was obvious what you had done. When I confronted Grandma Johnson about it, she just smiled and said, 'it's a grandmother's prerogative to dote on her grandchildren,' and a month later, the picture appeared on her piano next to all her other grandkids."

Everyone laughed. "That sounds exactly like Mom," Jordan's dad said. "Did you ever hear about the time my mom chased a bear?"

"What?"

"No!"

"You've gotta tell it, Dad," Jordan said.

"When we were all younger, our parents took us camping for the first time. All the kids were in one tent and my parents were in another. My mom woke up before anyone else the next morning to start breakfast, and there was this huge black bear sniffing around our tent."

"Because you left food out!" Jordan's aunt said, pointing from across the room.

"Yeah, you promised mom and dad you'd take care of it and then you didn't!" his other aunt added.

Jordan's dad smiled. "All right, so it may or may not have been my fault that we had a bear. Anyway," he said, glaring at his sisters, "my mom saw the bear and she was afraid it was going to eat us. So she picked up her frying pan and charged towards the bear, screaming and waving the pan around like a crazy person. We all woke up to find our mom chasing the bear out of the campgrounds."

The room burst into laughter. They began swapping stories about Grandma Johnson, going around the room and sharing their favorite memories.

"I like this," Jordan whispered to Ariel.

She looked back at him and nodded.

"I like hearing all these awesome stories about my grandma and celebrating her life."

Grandma Johnson's oldest daughter stopped mid-story and gasped. "Mom?"

Everyone in the room stopped talking and turned toward the hospital bed. Grandma Johnson was peering at them through tiny slits. She couldn't speak, but she began to lift a shaky hand above her bed. Her three children moved forward. Her daughter grasped her hand and held it tight. "We love you, Mom!" she said, kissing her spotted, wrinkly hand. She stepped aside and let her sister say goodbye.

"You say hi to Daddy for us, okay?" She bent over the bed and kissed her mother's forehead.

Jordan's dad stepped forward and said, "Don't worry about us, Mom, we'll be fine. I promise I'll look after everyone. It's okay to go. You fought hard." His voice cracked as he whispered goodbye. He placed a kiss on his mother's cheek, and then turned his head so she wouldn't see his tears.

Grandma Johnson gasped and closed her eyes again.

"It will be any time now," the hospice nurse whispered. "If you all would like to have a turn to say goodbye, she can still hear you, even if she can't respond."

The grandkids surrounded her bed, all with red eyes and stained cheeks.

"Goodbye, Grandma."

"We love you, Grandma."

Jordan pulled Ariel forward. She planted her feet and tried to push back. "No, you go first," she said.

"We go together," he responded. Ariel allowed herself to be pulled right beside Grandma Johnson's bed. The frail woman lying there didn't look like Grandma Johnson anymore. If her chest weren't rising and falling with each ragged, shallow breath, Ariel would have thought she was already gone. They both reached out and placed their hands on hers. Grandma moved, causing Ariel to jump. Grandma tried to grab Jordan's hand, but her strength was gone.

"What is it, Grandma?" he asked, setting his hand back in hers. She tried to grab Ariel's hand, too, but her eyes never left Jordan. He seemed to understand. Jordan grabbed Ariel's hands in his own and looked at grandma. "Is this what you wanted?" he asked.

They watched as Grandma Johnson seemed to smile and close her eyes again. Jordan wrapped an arm around Ariel's shoulders and whispered, "Don't worry, Grandma, I'll take good care of her."

Cinderella, Aurora, Snow White, and Belle each said goodbye next. They kissed the first grandmother any of them had ever known and whispered their own farewells. Grandma Johnson gasped again, and then she was gone.

\*\*\*

Four days later, when they arrived home from the funeral, Ariel ran to her room and retrieved both the brochure and her acceptance letter.

"Mom, I need to talk to you," she said before Rachel even had time to change.

"Okay," Rachel said, giving her a quizzical glance. "Let's sit down." Rachel started to sit on the couch when Ariel stopped her.

"I mean in private."

Rachel cocked her head, "Ok-ay," she said. She stood and followed Ariel up the stairs and into her bedroom.

Ariel sat on her mom's bed and took a deep breath. She clutched the papers close to her chest. Once Rachel was seated beside her, Ariel lowered her treasures and presented the brochure to her mom. Rachel looked at the cover, surprised, and began flipping through it. "My biggest dream in the whole world is to go to the University of Southern California and study in their film department. I want to be a director someday. And I knew it was a long shot, and I know we don't have a lot of money, but I decided to apply anyway, just to see what would happen. Well, I got accepted." Ariel placed the letter on top of the brochure, in front of her mother. "I never thought in a million years that I would get accepted, so I didn't bother telling you about it. I know, especially with the out-of-state tuition, that it's way out of our price range, but I just wanted it so badly. I didn't even care whether or not it was realistic." Ariel looked at her mom with large, round, hopeful eyes. Her lip quivered as she waited for a response.

"Ariel, this is incredible!" Rachel said, reaching over and hugging her daughter. "Why didn't you tell me as soon as you were accepted?"

"I got the letter the same day Grandma Johnson died," Ariel explained. "I wanted to tell you, but then with how hectic these last few days were, there just wasn't ever a good time."

"But I don't understand why you wouldn't tell me about this." Ariel could see the hurt etched on her mother's face. "If this is your greatest dream, why wouldn't you want to share it with me?"

"I guess I was afraid you would think it was dumb, or tell me directing wasn't a viable career. Mostly I didn't want to face the reality that we can't afford it. If I kept the dream to myself, I could keep it alive..." Ariel trailed off. "It seems silly now," she added.

Rachel stared hard into her daughter's eyes, her lips tight and straight. "Dreams are never silly or stupid. If this is what you want to do, what you truly believe your path is, we can figure out a way to make it work. We can take out student loans if we need to, or you can see if you qualify for any scholarships. You'll probably have to find work while you go to school, so you can pay for an apartment and food. If you stayed here and did community college, those things would be free, of course."

Ariel's face fell, but Rachel quickly continued. "I don't want you taking classes on subjects you don't even care about just because it's easier. If this is your dream, you have to go for it!"

Ariel jumped off the bed, barely able to control her excitement. "Really?" she asked.

"Yes, really," Rachel smiled. "Now go accept the offer and register for classes before they try and give your spot to someone else!"

Ariel tore from her mom's room, screaming excitedly as she dashed down the hall. Aurora had to squish herself against a wall as Ariel flew past to avoid getting trampled. Aurora wandered into her mom's room.

"What was that all about?" she asked.

Rachel turned from her small desk, her hands filled with a stack of papers. She placed the papers on the bed and began flipping through them. "Your sister wants to go to

USC in the fall to become a director." Rachel said the words casually, but her creased forehead and drooping shoulders told another story.

"Wow," Aurora said. "I mean, it's not a huge shock because she's always been obsessed with the film industry, but I'm just surprised she hasn't said anything until now."

"She was scared, because of the money," Rachel said, opening a manila envelope and searching the papers inside.

"That will be weird having her so far away." Aurora plopped down on Rachel's bed, causing the pile of papers to bounce. "So what's all that?" she asked, indicating the papers on the bed with her chin.

"Just going through some of my finances," Rachel said. "I wonder if I could take out a second mortgage on the house."

## *Chapter Fifteen*

Aurora pulled open the glass door, but hesitated before going inside. She loved learning how to cut and style hair, but was all this really worth it? It was getting exhausting having to sit alone in class and always having to partner with the instructor because the other girls wouldn't go near her. No, Aurora stood her ground. She wasn't about to give up. She pushed the loose strands of hair behind her ears and charged forward.

It was unusually quiet when she entered her classroom. The other girls were huddled around a table across the room. Aurora chose a seat and pulled one of the dummy heads closer. She began braiding the long, stringy hair while she hummed to herself and waited for class to begin.

Aurora jumped when another girl plopped into the seat beside her, slamming her binder on the metal table. Aurora stared at her, her mouth slightly open.

"Is this saved?" the girl asked, seeing Aurora's face and pointing to her chair.

"Ummm, no," Aurora said. She eyed the girl skeptically. She recognized her from school and knew she was friends with Sara, the queen bee herself. They may not be BFF's, but she knew the girl at least hung around Sara and her other cronies.

"All right, ladies, today's the da-ay!" the instructor sang cheerily, clapping her hands together. "Everyone partner up with the person next to you. We're going to practice some coloring techniques."

Aurora's eyes narrowed in on the girl sitting beside her. *So that's why the sudden interest in changing seats.* "What's your name?" Aurora asked.

"I'm Ruby," the girl smiled sweetly. Too sweetly. "I guess we're partners today," she said excitedly.

"Listen up, Ruby," Aurora said, rising to her feet. "I may be blonde, but that doesn't mean I'm stupid. I'm on to your little plan. You're going to give me a terrible coloring job so you guys can make fun of me and mess up my rep with the boys."

Ruby's mouth dropped open. She looked over at Sara and then back to Aurora again. "I don't—I don't know what you're talking about," she stuttered.

"Uh-huh, sure." Aurora flipped her hair with the toss of a hand and strutted into the salon.

Ruby entered the room, her shoulders slumped over as she walked. She slid into the chair Aurora was standing beside, her eyes darting nervously around the room. "You're not…going to do something terrible to my hair now, are you? My mom would absolutely kill me if I came home with a crazy color or something." Ruby bit her thumbnail and stared, pleadingly at Aurora.

Aurora rolled her eyes in return. "No, because unlike you and your friends, I'm not actually a mean person."

Ruby seemed to cower in her chair while Aurora administered a nice weave of blonde highlights to the girl's mousy brown hair. She sat in silence, with frequent glances at the mirror to see what Aurora was doing. When she was finished, Aurora smiled at her handiwork. Not bad for her first time on an actual human being. Ruby admired her hair as Aurora climbed into the seat.

"Very nice work, Ms. Princess," the teacher said as she walked past.

Aurora beamed at the compliment. She felt as though she were born to do hair. Ruby gulped behind her, stumbling as she gathered some different colors for mixing. Aurora looked in the mirror and thought Ruby looked as though she might cry. Aurora sighed. "Go ahead," she whispered, watching Ruby's reflection.

Ruby stared at her. "What?"

"Go ahead and do whatever evil plan Sara has concocted. Make my hair purple or whatever."

Ruby's eyes widened. She shifted from one foot to the other. Finally she spoke. "Why?"

"Because I've been bullied before. I know what it's like. And from your hesitancy and constant glances over in Sara's direction, I get the feeling she coerced you into this. I don't care what other people think of me. It took me a long time to get there, but I honestly don't. Besides, it's just hair! Other than shaving my head, which I ask you please don't do, you can do whatever. Maybe you'll finally be included in her group by being nasty to me, or whatever it was she promised you. If you need to do this to feel accepted, be my guest."

Sara came over at that moment, pretending to look for a color she needed. She pulled out a small bottle from the reds section and set it near Ruby's hand. She then glared at Ruby expectantly, clearing her throat loudly in her direction, and then left. *Wow, subtle*, Aurora thought. Ruby stood frozen in place, looking from Sara to Aurora and down at the small bowl in her hand.

"Oh, for heaven's sakes," Aurora said, getting to her feet again. She glanced over to be sure Sara was busy before grabbing the bottle and squirting a good amount into

Ruby's mixture. Aurora then plopped back down and waited for the prank to commence.

"I...I can't do this," Ruby said, shaking her head.

Just then the teacher came up beside Ruby. "Oh, sure you can, hon!" she said. "No need to be nervous." She then took Ruby's hand and plopped a decent glob of the mixture onto Aurora's hair. "Now smooth it out, just like we've been practicing," she coaxed.

The teacher walked away, leaving Ruby stunned. Aurora began to giggle and soon they were both laughing. "No going back now," Aurora said. "Come on, make it truly terrible and give everyone a good laugh."

Ruby smiled at Aurora and got to work.

An hour later, Ruby spun Aurora around and pretended to look horrified. "Oh no," she said, as loudly as she could. "What have I done?"

Right on cue, Sara and the other girls gathered around, pointing and laughing at Aurora. Ruby had dyed the top of her hair a horrid pale pink, in a perfect circle. It looked as though Aurora had been wearing a pink hat with wet paint around the brim.

"Oh dear," their teacher said as she approached. "Well, we're out of time, dear," she said, placing a hand on Aurora's shoulder. "Come in tomorrow and I'll fix things for you," she said, gritting her teeth. "Or run to the store tonight and buy a box of color. Any color."

"I thought you told us never to use the grocery store boxed stuff," Aurora said. "You said it was cheap."

"It is cheap, dear, but sometimes, well, you really should run out and buy a box."

As soon as their instructor had walked away, Sara pulled out her phone and snapped a picture. "Let's see what all the boys think of you now," she sneered.

Aurora gathered her things quietly and prepared to head home.

"I had an idea," Ruby whispered. She pretended to clean their work station while she explained her plan to Aurora.

Aurora's smile deepened. "Ruby," she said, "You are absolutely brilliant!"

Ruby beamed in return. "See you tomorrow," she whispered.

***

When the Princess sisters arrived at school the next morning, Aurora could already see a small crowd gathered around the front doors. Sara stood eagerly in the center of them all, passing her phone around and laughing heartily.

Aurora stepped from the car and Sara's face fell. Her laughter quickly turned to anger. Her face turned beet red. Aurora smiled warmly, half expecting steam to pour from Sara's ears. Eyes widened and jaws dropped as Aurora approached the group with her cousins.

Aurora's head still had the pale pink circle along the top of her hair, but after a trip to the beauty shop last night, the pink now darkened as it extended down her hair, so by the time it reached the tips, it was hot pink. Aurora looked stunning in her black leggings, silver top and hot pink heels to match. Her makeup was bold, adding to the new look.

"Good morning, Sara," Aurora smiled brightly. "You look lovely today."

Sara glowered back at her.

"Could someone be a doll and help me with my bag please?" Aurora asked, pouting her lips. Two boys jumped forward, grabbing Aurora's things from her and following at her heels as she entered the building. "Oh and Sara," she said, pausing in the doorway, which one of the cute boys held open for her. "Thanks for the prank. I never would have been bold enough to try this without you." Aurora kissed her admirer on the cheek and walked away.

***

"Oh, this is so exciting!" Grandma B said, climbing up into the black chair. "To have my own granddaughter do my hair! What an honor."

"You're too sweet, Grandma," Aurora smiled. "Wait until I'm done before you go praising my handiwork.

"Do whatever you like." Grandma B. smiled. "Except," she added, eyeing Aurora in the mirror, "not quite as drastic as your own."

Aurora laughed. "No offense, Grandma, but I don't think you could pull this off. It's not really your style." Grabbing a lock of pink hair, she said, "Actually, I didn't think it was my style either, but I'm glad I did it. It's been really fun!"

"If anyone can pull off pink hair, dear, it's you."

"Thanks."

"So," Grandma B. said, shifting in her seat, "what's new at the Princess house?"

"Let's see." Aurora tapped the comb against her chin. "I'm in beauty school and absolutely loving it. I can't wait until I can graduate and work in a salon full time."

"And what about your sister? She's so busy with that boy these days, I feel like I hardly see her anymore."

"You and me both."

"And he's…a decent guy?" Grandma B. asked.

"Oh yeah, Grandma, you have nothing to worry about with Jordan. He's super nice and treats her like, well, a princess."

"What about you? Any special boyfriends?"

Sara walked by at that moment and snorted as she overheard their conversation.

"What was that about?" Grandma B. asked.

"Oh, she's just got some jealousy issues. I like to go out with a lot of the boys in our class, to find out who I really like and what I really want. But Sara, on the other hand, can't get a single guy to even look her way."

"Now, Aurora, I love you dearly, but talk like that won't get you anywhere."

Aurora paused, her scissors held just above Grandma B.'s hair. "She started it," Aurora mumbled.

"Oh, honey, they had mean girls back when I was your age, too. But I've seen too much anger and fighting in my lifetime. Don't waste a second hating on another person. In the end, you're only making yourself more miserable."

Aurora sighed heavily. "I'll try, Grandma."

"That's a good girl. Now, on to happier topics. Do you plan on staying here in Layton with your mom after graduation?"

"Yeah, I'm going to stay here while I start working and hopefully save up some money. I'm not in a huge rush to move out."

"Oh, wonderful. Can I plan on you as my new hairdresser then?"

"Absolutely!"

"What about your sister? What are her plans after graduation?"

"She's going to USC to study and become a famous movie director," Aurora said.

"Well, that sounds exciting! All the way to California, huh?"

"Yeah," Aurora murmured.

"What's the matter, dear? Are you going to miss your sister?"

"I am, but that's not what's bothering me," Aurora said.

"What's the matter then?"

"It's just that this college is going to cost a lot of money. Money that my mom doesn't really have to spend. She's talking about taking out another mortgage just to pay for it! I don't want to tell Ariel, because I know she'll just freak out and decide to stay here if she knows how much of a stress it is on our mom. She deserves to live her dream. I'm just not sure what to do."

"Why don't you just let me handle it?" Grandma B. said.

"What do you mean?" Aurora asked.

"Oh, you'll see."

# Chapter Sixteen

"Snow White, we need to talk."

Snow White groaned before plunking onto the couch. "What?" she asked her mom.

Elizabeth ignored Snow White's annoyed attitude and sat gently beside her daughter. "You've been storming around here for weeks now. You rarely say anything, you don't hang out with your cousins as much anymore, and even your grades are slipping. What is going on?" she asked, patting Snow White's leg.

Snow White shifted away from her mom and shrugged. "I dunno."

"I think you do know, honey. Come on, please talk to me."

Snow White laid her head back on the couch and stared up at the ceiling.

"All right, if you won't talk, I will. You've been off ever since we had dinner with that lawyer from California."

"He has a name."

"Fine. Ever since you and Mr. Wilkins cornered me at the restaurant and you finally heard my story, you've been acting distant and withdrawn. I'm really worried about you. I knew I never should have told you what happened. This is exactly what I was trying to protect you from." Elizabeth grew more upset as she spoke. "I think," she said, pausing to calm her voice. "I think it's time for you to see someone who can help you process this difficult situation."

"Like a shrink?!"

"Yes, sweetie. It's a lot to take in and the trauma of this information is obviously upsetting you."

"You're the one who's upsetting me! I can't believe you never told me the truth! I feel like my entire life has been a lie. And now you want me to go and blab my sorrows to some idiot stranger who will pat my hand and tell me everything will be fine? No! You can't make me go!"

Elizabeth sat stoically while Snow White continued to scream out her frustrations. "Fine," her mom said, when Snow White paused for a breath. "I can't and won't make you go. But I do think it would be a really good idea. Talking to someone really helped me overcome a lot of the emotions and trauma from my past."

"You've seen a therapist?" Snow White was caught off guard by this new information.

"Yes, I have. I had a lot of PTSD symptoms after the attack and she really helped me work through them."

Snow White still didn't like the idea of talking to a complete stranger about such a sensitive subject. Her mind raced to change the focus of their conversation. "So when are we going to California?" She blurted the question she'd been wanting to ask for weeks.

"Excuse me?" It was Elizabeth's turn to get caught off guard.

"For the trial," Snow White said. "When do we need to be there so you can testify against...?" Snow White hesitated, not sure what to call the man. "Against him."

Elizabeth shifted uncomfortably. "I'm not," she murmured.

"What?" Snow White jumped to her feet. "Why wouldn't you testify? You already told your whole story to

Mr. Wilkins and now that I know everything, why wouldn't you help to put him in prison?"

"Mr. Wilkins and I had a very long talk on the phone last night. I told him he can use my testimony and he even has my permission to play the recording in court. But I've already watched the effect all this has had on you. I'm not going to put us in the spotlight of a major trial, too. And there is absolutely no way I could be in the same room with that man ever again."

"Mom! This is my history too, you know. I want to be there to help in any way that we can."

"You are not to have any more contact with Mr. Wilkins, do you understand me? I made that very clear to him last night. If he so much as talks to you again, I will press charges." Elizabeth's mouth was set in a firm line, her face strong and void of emotion. "I just want all of this to be over. I want my daughter back."

"That's not possible, Mom." Snow White spit out the words as she stormed from the room. "You don't have a daughter. All you have is a mistake," she mumbled.

***

"What do you mean you have a present for me?" Ariel asked. She and Jordan walked hand in hand, enjoying their frozen yogurt as they walked home from the store. "It's not my birthday." She grinned up at him.

"I know, but when I saw it, I couldn't resist." He smiled mischievously at her.

Ariel's pace quickened as they moved down the sidewalk.

"Geeze, where ya goin', turbo?"

Ariel tugged on Jordan's fingers to make him speed up. "To get my present!"

Jordan laughed heartily and allowed himself to be pulled forward. "All right, I'll go get it," he said when they came up to their complex.

"You mean I can't go with you?"

"Fine, but you have to wait downstairs. And no peeking!" he added, with a pointed finger in her direction.

"Who, me?" Ariel asked innocently. She wandered around Jordan's living room, following the timeline of photos from when he was a baby, to a small boy, and up until now. It was fun to watch that same crooked grin age with time. Ariel's eyes settled on a picture of Jordan with his arm around Grandma Johnson's shoulder. It was taken at his high school graduation. Ariel smiled at the familiar crinkles by the old woman's eyes. Ariel began to get misty and had to turn away.

"Well, don't cry, you haven't even seen it yet!" Jordan stood at the foot of the stairs, watching her.

Ariel smiled, wiping the tears away. "I just miss her."

"I know," Jordan said, wrapping his arms around her slender frame. "I do, too." He rubbed his hands up and down her back until Ariel stepped back.

"Okay," she said, blowing out a breath. "Let's see what you got."

Jordan held a gift bag in front of himself and waited eagerly for Ariel to open it. She quickly removed the tissue and pulled out a cardinal and gold sweatshirt with the USC logo on the front. Ariel feared she might start tearing up again.

"Oh, Jordan, thank you!" She returned to his embrace. She stood on her toes and wrapped her arms around his broad shoulders, kissing him on the lips. "This was so sweet of you!" She beamed up at him.

"I thought you should have something you can wear to get excited about school. Then when you leave, it can double as a reminder of me."

Ariel sat on the sofa and held the sweatshirt in front of herself. "It's the most perfect gift." She rested her head on his shoulder, not wanting to think about needing a reminder of him. "So what was the good news you wanted to tell me?" she asked, hugging her gift.

"Oh, so we had a meeting with my grandma's lawyers yesterday," he said, sitting up straighter. "Apparently my grandma left me some money. And it's enough money that I'm going to start up my own garage with a buddy of mine."

"Jordan, that's amazing!" Ariel said, grabbing his face and kissing him again. "I'm so proud of you!"

"Thanks, I'm pretty proud of me, too," he said, tickling her side. Ariel squealed and jumped away. She looked into Jordan's chocolate eyes and noticed his teasing fingers as they threatened to attack again. Her face fell and she grew somber.

"What's the matter?" he asked gently.

"What's going to happen to us?" she asked, looking down at her hands. "I know we just started dating, but I really like you. And come August, I'll be moving to California."

Jordan slid across the couch, placing his hand on Ariel's leg. With his other hand, he pushed a lock of hair behind her ear, forcing her to look up. "I like you, too," he said, kissing her gently. "I honestly can't say right now what's going to happen, but I'd like to keep dating you and see where this goes. Then we can make those difficult decisions when the time comes."

Ariel nodded. It wasn't ideal, but at least it wasn't breaking up. Yet.

***

Cinderella's face glowed as she walked down the aisle, stepping over the pastel flower petals laid neatly before her by a skipping Sophie. Never in a million years did she think she would ever witness her mom getting married, let alone to her father. Her yellow sundress swished against her knees as she walked. It was unusually warm for February. Monica, in a matching dress, walked down the aisle beside her with a scowl on her face. Stephen stood at the front of the tiny church, watching his girls walk toward him. He stepped forward and kissed them each on the cheek before stepping back to his proper place once again.

The wedding march began to play and the small gathering all rose to their feet. Dana looked radiant in her simple white gown, escorted down the aisle by her sister, Rachel. When they reached Stephen, standing handsomely beside his best friend Lucas, Rachel hugged her older sister tightly before handing her off. The ceremony was simple and sweet, with only family and very close friends in attendance.

Cinderella watched her father take her mother's hands in his and kiss her tenderly as his beautiful new bride. Sophie screeched, "Ew, gross!" and everyone in attendance laughed. Cinderella reached out and gave Monica's hand a friendly squeeze, but she immediately snatched her hand away and stormed out a side door. Cinderella sighed. This was going to take some getting used to.

An hour later, Cinderella was dancing with Dave and admiring her new family. Dana and Stephen sat huddled close together at a corner table, staring into each other's eyes and acting disgusting, according to Sophie.

"How's your brother?" Cinderella asked.

"Nope, not going there," Dave said, shaking his head. "You should call him and ask him yourself."

Cinderella shook her head. "I can't do that."

"Suit yourself."

"You really aren't going to tell me how he is? I'm not asking for private details about his dating life. I just want to know if he's still alive."

"Yes, my brother is still breathing, last time I checked."

Cinderella nodded. "That's good." After dancing in silence for a moment she said, "So do you have plans for next year? Do you know where you're going yet?"

"Yeah, I actually just got my acceptance letter. I'm headed to UCLA in the fall."

"Wow, congratulations!"

"Thanks. What about you?"

Cinderella looked just over Dave's shoulder, avoiding eye contact. "Well, I actually got into Utah State. It's the only place I applied, but now I'm wondering if that was a mistake."

"I thought you loved Utah State?" Dave asked.

"I did—I do! It's just..." Cinderella was saved from having to answer a question she'd been asking herself for weeks when Sophie came tearing up to them and grabbed Cinderella's knees.

"Where's Scott?" Sophie asked. "Why isn't he here?"

Cinderella paused her dancing with Dave and knelt down to Sophie's level. "Scott goes to school far away from here. He was too busy with classes to come."

Dave raised an eyebrow and Cinderella waved him away. "Go dance with Belle," she hissed. Turning back to Sophie, she asked, "Have you seen Monica?"

Sophie stuck out her tongue and pulled a face. "You mean old grouch puss? She's over there somewhere." Sophie pointed behind her. "Monica said step moms are bad. Is that true?" she asked with a pouting lip.

"No, that's not true at all," Cinderella said. "Don't you think my mom is nice?"

Sophie nodded enthusiastically. "Uh-huh," she said, spinning around. "See? She even did my hair for me!" She pointed at the braided crown, wrapping around the top of Sophie's head. "I think my new mommy is nice, but Monica always yells at me when I say that. You know what I think?"

"What?" Cinderella whispered.

Sophie looked around to confirm her sister wasn't near. "I think Monica is the ugly stepsister!" She covered her mouth and then ran away giggling.

Cinderella rose to her feet and looked around the gathering. Belle positively glowed as she sat near her parents and Craig. Ariel was so wrapped up in Jordan, Cinderella wasn't certain she even knew where she was. Aurora, with her spunky new hairdo, danced happily with This Week. Rachel and Elizabeth joined Cinderella's parents at their table and the four seemed to be lost in conversation. Sophie ran around the group wildly, shrieking with glee each time she passed by Uncle Lucas, who reached out a hand and threatened to grab her.

Cinderella noticed Monica sitting alone at a table, slouched back in her chair, arms folded tightly across her chest. As she looked around, she realized Snow White appeared to be missing. Cinderella walked around the small room, but couldn't see her cousin anywhere. She proceeded down the hall and into the ladies' room. Snow White sat on the counter between sinks, leaning against the mirror.

"Hey, stranger!" she said with a smile. "Where ya been?"

Snow White indicated the empty bathroom with her open palm.

"Why aren't you joining the party?" Cinderella asked. "The food is actually really good."

"I don't feel hungry," Snow White muttered.

"What's the matter, Snow? Come on, you've always been able to talk to me."

"Things are changing," Snow White said. "I don't even know what the point is anymore."

Cinderella hopped onto the counter and looked at Snow White. "The point of what?" she asked.

"You're all leaving in the fall for these awesome new adventures. You've got colleges and boyfriends waiting for you, and I'm just stuck. I'm stuck here forever. No one wants me." She sniffled.

"Snow," Cinderella said softly. "What do you mean no one wants you? Of course we want you!"

"No." Snow White shook her head, her soft red curls bouncing against her wet cheeks. "You don't understand," she whispered. "And just when I thought I had the chance to do something brave and strong, to participate in something that actually matters, it was ripped away from me. Just like everything else in my life."

"Snow, please tell me what's going on," Cinderella pleaded. "I'm trying to understand, but I know there's something you're not telling me. What's been bothering you so much lately? Is it the college thing? Because you are so brilliant! I know you could get into any college you wanted!"

Snow White jumped off the counter. "You don't understand. No one understands," she said, avoiding her cousin's gaze. "Just go live your perfect life with your two parents who both love you and leave me alone!" Snow White ran from the bathroom, leaving Cinderella even more bewildered than before.

# Chapter Seventeen

Cinderella stared out the large bedroom window and watched as the realtor hammered a for sale sign into her lawn. She couldn't believe she had to say goodbye to the only house she'd ever known. She crawled over Belle's sleeping form and wandered down the stairs. Her parents stood on the front porch, arms wrapped around each other as they spoke to the realtor. The conversation was about open house dates and how soon they'd be moved out. Today. The answer was today. Everything had happened so quickly, Cinderella still felt like her brain was trying to play catchup. She couldn't quite wrap her mind around the reality of the marriage, the new house, the boxes, and the moving. She glanced at her phone and realized the truck would be at the house in less than an hour. She didn't have time to be sentimental.

Cinderella traipsed down to the basement to find her little sister's messy blonde head sticking up from the hideaway bed. Sophie rubbed her eyes in confusion as she looked around.

"Where's Daddy?" she asked loudly.

Cinderella put a finger to her lips and pointed at Monica's still sleeping form beneath the covers. "Shhhhhh."

Cinderella stepped up to the couch and grabbed Sophie under the armpits, lifting her from the temporary bed. Sophie jumped as she was lifted, wrapping her skinny little legs around Cinderella and resting her head on her sister's shoulder. Cinderella carried her up the stairs and approached her parents.

"New Mommy!" Sophie said, extending her arms out to Dana. Dana smiled and took her from Cinderella.

"You better go get dressed. The movers will be here soon," she said.

Cinderella nodded and returned to her bedroom. Belle still appeared to be sleeping. Cinderella grabbed her cell phone, set the timer for sixty seconds, and then turned the volume up as loud as it could go. Carefully placing the phone on Belle's pillow beside her face, she grabbed her clothes and slipped from the room. Cinderella stood in the bathroom brushing her teeth when the alarm went off.

"Ahhhhhhh! Cinderella!"

Cinderella smiled to herself and continued to brush. A moment later, Belle shoved the door open.

"What'dya do that for?" she shrieked.

Cinderella spat into the sink. "Good morning, sleepy-head," she said with a smile.

Belle growled in return and stumbled out of the room.

"The movers will be here soon," Cinderella said. "I didn't figure you wanted them to see you in your pajamas with messy hair. So really, I was just doing you a favor." She smiled sweetly.

Belle grumbled in return as she pulled on her pair of jeans and slowly began to get ready. "It still feels weird to be moving into a new house with your new family," Belle admitted. "I feel out of place."

"It's only for the next few months while we finish school, just like my mom said, remember? Besides, she promised your mom she'd take care of you, and we both know how seriously my mom takes promises."

"True," Belle said, nodding. She got to her feet and the two of them yanked the bedding off their beds and shoved the sheets and blankets into a large, black garbage bag for transport to the new house. A loud honk outside informed the girls that the movers had arrived. Belle dashed into the bathroom, throwing on a pair of jeans and a sparkly pink T-shirt. She grabbed her cell phone and the pile of loose makeup off the bathroom counter, dumping them into her backpack. She tossed the bag over one shoulder and ran down the stairs. Two men carried a sofa out the front door while Dana chased Sophie around the room.

Sophie jumped from one piece of furniture to the next singing, "Moving day! It's moving day!" at the top of her lungs.

Monica made an appearance in the doorway, still clad in pajama bottoms and an old yellow T-shirt with a faded concert picture on the front. Her bed-hair stood up in all directions as she yawned and rubbed her eyes.

"You'd better hurry and get dressed, Monica," Dana said, catching Sophie mid-jump and swinging her into the air.

As the movers came back in to grab another piece of furniture, Monica gasped. "You couldn't have given me a little more warning?" she asked, scowling at Dana. She turned and stomped out of the room.

Dana sighed. "This step mom thing is not easy, and it's only been two days."

"You're not a step mom!" giggled Sophie. "Those are the bad guys!"

"Oh, I'm not?" Dana said, her eyebrows raised.

"No! You're New Mommy!" Sophie grabbed Dana's cheeks between her two hands and squeezed them together, giving Dana a kiss on the lips.

"Well, I'm glad you see it that way," Dana said. She smiled and hugged Sophie tightly.

Belle walked past them onto the front porch. Steven was outside, giving instructions to the movers. Cinderella came outside right behind Belle. Her cheeks were pale and she looked as though she might cry.

"What's the matter, Cindy?"

"This is just weird," Cinderella said, stepping off the stairs and sitting on the lawn. "There's someone in my room taking my bed apart. I feel like I can't even watch! This is the only house I have memories in, and they exist in every single room," Cinderella frowned.

Belle squatted on the grass beside her. "I know what you mean," she said. "I felt the same way when I had to pack up our condo. I still feel weird whenever I see Jordan and his family coming and going. But isn't the new house a ton bigger? Your sisters don't even have a room right now. They're just sleeping on a foldout couch."

"I know," Cinderella said. "And it will be nice to have a new start as a new family in the new house. It's just a lot of new all at once, you know?"

Belle nodded. "I know, but as cheesy as it sounds, we're all growing up. You would have been moving out in the fall anyway."

"You're right," Cinderella said. Looking at the movers, she added, "Should we offer a hand?"

Belle held up her manicured nails. "Are you kidding?"

Cinderella laughed.

The front door opened two doors down and the twins emerged. They made their way to the grass and sat down. "Everything is changing," Ariel whispered.

"I know. It's weird," Cinderella said.

Ariel lay her head on Cinderella's shoulder. "I'm going to miss you," she said.

"I'll miss you, too. At least my parents found a house somewhat close, so I can still see you guys at school." Cinderella forced a smile.

"It won't be the same," Aurora grumbled.

"I agree," Ariel said. "Things will never be the same."

The cousins sat together in a small huddle, arms wrapped around each other as they bid farewell to the ending of an era.

***

Snow White watched her cousins from her bedroom window. They held each other and laughed over something Ariel said.

"Aren't you going down to say goodbye?" Elizabeth asked from behind her.

Snow White wiped at her eyes and shook her head. "Haven't you ever heard of knocking?"

"Sweetie, go downstairs and say goodbye. I know your cousins would love to see you."

*No one wants to see a mistake.* Snow White shook her head more forcefully. "Please just leave me alone!" she yelled.

Elizabeth backed out of her room and closed the door.

***

Craig's car pulled up behind the moving truck and Belle rose to her feet. "There's my ride," she said. "I'll have him drop me off at the new house tonight."

Belle's cousins also rose, pulling Belle in for a group hug.

"Wait, aren't you going to help unload the truck and unpack?" Cinderella asked.

Belle looked around. "It seems to me like you have everything under control." She smiled, climbed into the front seat of Craig's sedan, and waved goodbye as they drove away.

"So how are the newlyweds?" Craig asked. "Is it weird being in the same house?"

"No, not too weird. Just a little crowded." Belle began to laugh.

"What's so funny?" Craig asked.

"I was just thinking it isn't too weird, but it's sure a lot noisier with Cinderella's little sister there. She's a riot!"

Craig shook his head. "I can't even imagine that."

"What? Having a little sister?"

"No, having kids! When I get married, I want it to just be me and my wife. No crying babies, no messes. We can have a nice house and nice cars and travel all over the world. Doesn't that sound awesome?"

Belle stared hard at Craig's profile. He didn't seem to be joking. "No," she finally said. "That doesn't sound awesome to me at all! I mean, I don't want a million kids or anything, but I do want to have my own family someday."

Craig shrugged. "Really? Why?"

"Because I loved growing up with my cousins, but I never got the experience of having my own brother or sister. I think what you're describing would be fun for a little while. Like a year or two maybe, but then I'd want to settle down and have a family. What's the point of living life without family? That just seems…sad to me."

Craig grunted. "I have plenty of nieces and nephews and whenever they all come over, the house is just crazy! And none of my sisters and their husbands can afford to go anywhere or do anything fun. Everything is about their kids all the time. That's just not a life I want."

"Why haven't you ever told me this before?" Belle asked.

Craig shrugged again. "Because we're just in high school. Who thinks about marriage and babies in high school?"

"I do!" Belle said. "I like dreaming about my future! The only problem is I always saw you in it. You're telling me you'd never, ever want kids?"

Craig shook his head. "I don't see the point. I mean, I guess maybe, like a long ways down the road, but only after I did everything I wanted to first."

Belle couldn't believe her ears. Craig was changing right before her eyes and she wasn't so sure she liked this new guy.

***

Cinderella liked the view out her window in the new room. In her old room, she could see directly across the street, watching the parking lot, which was super exciting, or stare at Dave and Scott's house. She didn't love the constant reminder of the guy she let get away. Now, sitting on her cushioned window seat and looking out her window, she saw an apple orchard. Tall, beautiful trees smiled at her as they waved in the gentle breeze. Cinderella sighed contentedly and returned to the open box beside her dresser to put her folded clothes neatly away. The doorbell rang downstairs.

It rang again.

Cinderella got to her feet and walked down the elegant front staircase. It was the kind of staircase a girl could lose a shoe on!

Cinderella opened the front door to find a very small Belle, hunched over and huddled in the corner of the porch.

"Belle, what's wrong?" Cinderella rushed toward her and with an arm around her shaking shoulders, half-carried Belle into the house. To avoid suspicion from her prying younger sisters, Cinderella hurried Belle upstairs as best as she could. Once she had Belle comfortably seated on her bed, Cinderella knelt beside her, looking up into Belle's mascara-streaked face. "All right, spill. Tell me what happened?" Cinderella spoke in a soothing voice.

"Craig and I broke up." Belle said the words matter-of-factly, but even as they passed through her lips, she still couldn't believe they were true.

"What?" Cinderella shrieked. Calming her voice, she tried again. "What happened?"

"I…I don't really know. I feel like it's been coming for a little while now, but it still feels completely surreal."

"Well, did he give you a reason?"

Belle's head snapped toward Cinderella. "What makes you think he broke up with me?"

"Well, I just…you seem so upset."

"I am upset! I just did the hardest thing I've ever had to do!" she yelled.

Cinderella lowered her bottom to the carpet.

"Sorry, I'm not mad at you. I just, I thought Craig was it for me. I thought we'd be together forever. I finally realized tonight that we want completely different lives. We could go on pretending through graduation, but that just seemed like a waste of both our time. I can't believe he's really gone." Belle caught her head in her hands and moaned.

"What can I do? Do you want me to call the girls and we'll go out for some chocolate lava cake?"

"No, I need to pack." Belle got to her feet slowly and walked around the room, looking lost. "Where's all my stuff?" she asked.

"Pack? We're already here, Belle." Cinderella looked at her cousin, puzzled.

"No, I'm going to California. Where's all my stuff?" she asked again, tearing open a box.

Cinderella jumped to her feet. "Wait. What? I think you're confused. We just moved today. All your boxes are on that side of the room, see?" Cinderella said, pointing.

Belle walked over and popped the tape off of the first box. She checked the contents inside and after making sure they belonged to her, she nodded and closed the box again.

Cinderella approached her cousin cautiously and grabbed her hand. "Belle, stop moving around and talk to me. What's going on?"

Belle sighed. "Right after I broke up with Craig, I called my mom. She and my dad made arrangements. I need to pack a suitcase to get me through the next few days, and then your mom will ship the rest of my stuff. They tried to get a flight out tomorrow, so I'd have time to say a proper goodbye, but the only flight they could get me on was a redeye tonight."

"You're really going to California? Just like that?" Cinderella began to feel light-headed. She needed to sit down.

"I don't belong here," Belle said, gesturing around Cinderella's large room. "You need to get to know your new family and spend time with them without an intruder always hovering around."

"You never hovered!" Cinderella tried to make a joke, but it fell flat. "Don't leave because of some stupid guy!" Cinderella pleaded.

"The truth is, I haven't been really happy since my mom moved to California. I've been thinking about going there for months. You know that."

"I know, but…"

"I never thought I'd miss my mom so much, but I really do! And I want to experience what you're experiencing. I want to know what it's like to have a mom and a dad for once. This is the perfect opportunity for me to leave, so I'm taking it. Besides, all my boxes are already conveniently packed," Belle joked, patting the top of her pile.

"But what about the others? You're just going to sneak away in the middle of the night?"

"That's the part that really sucks! But it's not like you guys will never see me again. We are related, after all. You girls can't shake me that easily." Belle surged forward and wrapped her arms around Cinderella. She hugged her cousin tightly for several minutes. "Pass that on to the girls for me, will you?" Belle wiped a stray tear that trickled down her cheek. "Besides," she said, stepping back, "we all basically got to say goodbye earlier today. It's like fate."

Cinderella sighed deeply. "Are you sure you don't want to think about it a little longer? A week, maybe. Give it a week before you decide."

Belle laughed. "You sound like my mom. She's been telling me that for months. It really is time."

"But there's only a few months left in school." Cinderella scrambled to find an excuse good enough to change Belle's mind.

Belle smiled. "I know, Cindy, but this is what I need to do. I need a new beginning, a fresh start."

Dana knocked on the door and entered without waiting for an invitation. "I just got off the phone with your mom, Belle. Are you certain this is what you want?"

Belle swung her backpack over her shoulder and nodded. "I'm ready."

Dana pulled Belle in for a tight hug. "I'm not," she whispered.

Belle noticed the tears pooling in Dana's eyes. "Come on, you guys, you're not making this easy on me!"

"Make her stay, Mom," Cinderella pleaded.

"If only I could, sweetie." Dana hugged Belle again. "Steven is going to drive you to the airport," she said, stepping back. "Do you have everything?"

Belle grabbed a couple more outfits and added them to her backpack. "I think I'm good," she said.

Cinderella wrapped her arms around Belle. "Thanks for getting me ready for sisters," she whispered.

Belle smiled. "Anytime."

Dana came up from behind and wrapped her arms around Belle, sandwiching her between mother and daughter. They held each other tight until Steven came to the door.

"Knock, knock," he said. "Belle, I'm sorry, but if you're going to make that flight, we need to leave now."

Belle sniffled and waved a final goodbye as she walked from Cinderella's bedroom. She didn't know when she would see her cousins again.

# Chapter Eighteen

Snow White trudged down her front steps. She glanced over at the empty house next door and sighed deeply. Aurora honked the horn, encouraging Snow White to hurry, but she continued to saunter to the car at a leisurely pace. She sat down and didn't quite have the door closed before Aurora raced from the parking lot. On their way out, they saw a snappy-looking realtor putting up Open House signs.

"What took you so long?" Aurora asked. "We're gonna be late!"

Snow White folded her arms crossly, but didn't respond. She glanced at the twins and sighed again. *And then there were three.*

"You okay, Snow?" Ariel asked.

Snow White continued to stare out her window and pretended not to hear her. Ariel glanced back at her cousin but didn't push her to talk. Soon she and Aurora were lost in conversation about Jordan and beauty school.

When Aurora pulled into the parking lot, Snow White got out and walked toward the school without saying goodbye.

"Goodbye, Ariel. Goodbye, Aurora. Thanks for the ride. You guys are the best!" Aurora mimicked as she and her sister walked toward the building.

Ariel nudged Aurora in the side. "Oh, stop! Something is really going on with her."

"I know. That's what's driving me so crazy!" Aurora said, throwing her hands up in the air. "If she'd actually talk to us, we could help her. But she hasn't spoken to anyone, not really, for months!"

"She'll talk when she's ready. Snow takes longer to process things than the rest of us," Ariel whispered.

Cinderella stood in front of the school, hugging her books close to her chest. A smile brightened her face when she saw her cousins coming. "Hi!" she practically shouted at them. "Did you miss me?" Cinderella side-hugged them each in turn.

"Ummm…no," Aurora said, giving her a funny look. "You moved yesterday."

"Don't mind her!" Ariel said, shoving her twin out of the way. "Of course we missed you! She's just irritated with Snow White this morning."

"What was going on with her?" Cinderella asked. "She didn't even say hi to me as she walked past. It's like she couldn't even see me standing here."

"You and Belle left. I think she feels abandoned," Aurora said, holding open the glass door as the trio entered the school.

"I probably shouldn't tell her about Belle then," Cinderella said, biting her lip. "She might not speak for a month."

The twins both turned around. "Oh, yeah, where is Belle?"

"Shouldn't tell her what about Belle?"

"Ummm, she moved," Cinderella said.

"We already know that. We were there," Aurora said.

"No, I mean she really moved. Belle and Craig broke up yesterday."

"What?" they both shrieked.

"That's not even the worst part!" Cinderella said, trying to keep her emotions in check. "After they broke up, Belle called her mom and before I knew what was happening, she was on a plane for California!"

"Belle's...gone?" Snow White's voice came out in a tiny squeak.

The girls hadn't noticed as they rounded a corner on their way to the lockers that Snow White was now standing right in front of them.

"So much for not telling her," Aurora murmured out of the corner of her mouth.

Snow White stared at the three of them, eyes wide with horror.

"I'm sorry, Snow, she was really getting homesick for her parents and when she and Craig broke up, I think it was just the last straw."

Snow White's lip began to quiver. Her eyes narrowed and her face tensed. "Everything is changing!" she shouted. Breaking through the three girls, she ran down the hall, back the way they came.

"Snow White, wait!" Cinderella yelled. She began going after her when Ariel grabbed her arm.

"Hang on," Ariel said, holding her back. "She needs to process for a little while. We'll talk to her at lunch and hopefully we can find out what's going on once and for all."

The bell rang, causing Cinderella to jump.

"Besides, we're gonna be late," Aurora said.

*\*\*

Cinderella sat beside the twins at their usual lunch table and waited for Snow White.

"What are we going to say?" Ariel asked.

"I think we need to start with how much we love her, and how worried we've all been about her," Cinderella said. "For some reason, she feels like she's all alone right now. We need to let her see that we're all still here."

"Except Belle," Aurora piped in.

Cinderella threw her a dirty look. "All right, miss sassy pants, I mean we're all here in spirit. Even when we go our separate ways next year, we'll always be here for each other."

A cute boy with curly brown hair approached their table and invited Cinderella to a movie on Friday. She politely turned him down.

Aurora stared at her, mouth agape. "What was that?" she asked as the cute boy walked away.

"I'm taking a break from guys for a little while," Cinderella explained unapologetically. "After Scott and then Brian, I just really don't feel like dating right now."

"I think you're nuts! Dating is great!" Aurora said, leaning back. She waved and blew a kiss to some guy who walked behind Cinderella as they spoke.

"You date your way, and I'll date mine," Cinderella said. Looking around, she added, "Where's Snow?"

"Bathroom maybe?" Ariel suggested. "She'll turn up."

The cousins continued to talk and eat lunch while they waited some more. When Snow White didn't make an appearance, they split up and searched all the girls' bathrooms in the school. When they still turned up empty, and it was time to go to their next class, Cinderella began to panic. "We have fourth period together," she said. "We always walk from lunch to fourth period together."

Ariel scoured the lunchroom again. "Something doesn't feel right," she said. Ariel found Dave and rushed across the room toward him. "Dave!" she called.

"What's up, Ariel?"

"You have English first thing with Snow White, don't you?"

"Yeah, but she wasn't here today."

When the girls' faces all turned white, he dropped the smile from his own face. "What's wrong?" he asked.

"She was upset this morning and ran off. We can't find her," Aurora explained.

"I'll help you look," Dave said, leading the way out of the cafeteria. "Did you check bathrooms already?"

"Yes," Cinderella said, glancing frantically at each face as they walked through the crowded halls. "We're supposed to have next period together," she added.

"Let's head there then, and see if she shows up."

Cinderella turned down the crowded hallway and guided them to her choir classroom. She pushed past several students finding their seats and immediately marched up to the teacher.

"Have you seen Snow White yet?" she asked.

"I haven't," he answered, looking puzzled. Sensing their tension, he asked, "Is something wrong?"

"She seems to be missing," Cinderella explained.

Most of the students, aware something was going on, watched intently as the conversation unfolded.

Mr. Bentley got to his feet and pushed the door closed as the final bell rang. Snow White was nowhere to be seen. He turned toward Cinderella, "You better go to the main office and explain the situation. Maybe she got picked up early by her mom or something and forgot to tell you. I'm sure everything is fine," he said, stiffly patting her on the shoulder. He turned toward the twins and Dave. "Mr. Prince, I don't see why these ladies need an escort. You may return to class. And I trust that as soon as this is resolved, you ladies will also return to your classes?"

"Yes, Mr. Bentley," Ariel muttered.

They hurried from the classroom towards the main office.

"I don't care what he says. I'm coming with you guys," Dave said. His brow creased in concern.

After an explanation at the office and a panicked phone call to Elizabeth, Rachel picked up the girls from school. Elizabeth had not checked Snow White out of school. Rachel used her spare key, and after searching their house, discovered several of Snow White's things were gone. The police were on their way to Elizabeth's house for questioning and to file a report.

Snow White was definitely missing.

***

Cinderella sat huddled beside Ariel and Aurora, squished onto a sofa meant for two. The officer continued to ask the same questions over and over again. Where was the last place they had seen her? What was she wearing? How had the conversation gone? Why was she upset? Did she have any other friends? The words continued to buzz around her ears, but Cinderella couldn't wrap her mind around any of them. No, this wasn't really happening. Snow White wasn't gone. This was a scene from a scary movie or the late night news. This was not something that happened to real people. Not to her.

Dana decided to stay at home with Cinderella's sisters until her dad got off work, but Cinderella's phone kept buzzing for updates. Sadly, she had none to give. Ariel and Aurora remained stone-faced as they answered the policeman's questions. Elizabeth, who only resembled a shell of a person, stood shivering in the corner of the room. Rachel got off work early and kept offering her sister some soothing herbal tea, or a seat, but Elizabeth remained frozen in place.

Hours passed. Elizabeth finally broke her composure and began screaming at the cops to get off her couch and find her daughter. She fell into Rachel's arms, sobbing uncontrollably. Unfortunately, since the cops viewed this as a runaway and had no reason to suspect a kidnapping, there wasn't much they could do other than file a missing persons report and encourage them to get her picture out on social media.

"Is there anything that has recently changed in Snow White's life? A major trauma or event can sometimes spur this sort of reaction in teens."

Elizabeth looked up. She wiped her eyes and stared at the officer as if seeing him for the first time. "I know where she is," she whispered.

The officer turned and looked at her. "Excuse me?"

"I know where my daughter went!" Elizabeth said, standing with confidence this time. "I don't know how she would have gotten there, but I'm almost positive she went to California. Los Angeles."

The officer began giving instructions to the other policemen. Handing them a picture he said, "Take this to all the nearest train and bus stations. See if anyone saw her board something for LA. Go!" The police officers scattered.

"Give me your phone," Elizabeth demanded, reaching toward Rachel with shaking hands. Rachel handed her phone over, still confused but willing to play along until she received more information.

"Hello, Belle? This is Aunt Elizabeth."

"Belle?" Cinderella mouthed at her cousins. They shook their heads in return. The group all listened intently for what Elizabeth would say next.

"Are your mom and dad home? No? Hmmmm. Belle, I need you to listen very carefully. Snow White has run away. Yes, I know. Well, I have a good idea where she might have gone." Elizabeth typed something into Rachel's phone and soon came up with an address. "Do you have access to a car? Belle, I need you to do me the biggest favor of your life! Go to this address. It's an attorney's office. His name is Mr. Noah Wilkins. If Snow White is there, see if you can get her back to your parents' house and let me know immediately. If she's there, like I think she'll be, I will be on the next flight out to get her. Belle, I love you! Thank you! Bye."

Everyone stared at Elizabeth, wide-eyed, even the police officer. "Is there some more information I should know about, ma'am?" he asked.

"An attorney?" Aurora asked.

"In California?" Cinderella added.

Rachel looked at her sister, her face lighting up with sudden revelation. "It's not about..."

Elizabeth nodded.

Rachel gasped, covering her mouth. "But how did she find out?"

"It's a long story," Elizabeth said, sitting back down and slumping against Rachel's side.

"Do you want me to have the girls leave?" Rachel asked, pointing at Cinderella and the twins.

"No," Elizabeth said, acknowledging their complaints. "It's about time they knew the truth."

***

Snow White handed the cab driver a stack of bills before climbing from his car. She looked at the remaining five dollars in her hand. That wasn't even enough for dinner! *This better work.* Snow White shoved her precious final bill in her pocket and pushed open the large glass door. She stepped into the grand entryway, her feet echoing with each step. She timidly walked up to a large, glass directory which hung high on the wall beside the elevators. Her eyes scanned over the list of names until they landed on the only familiar one: Noah Wilkins. Taking a deep breath, Snow White pressed the up button on the elevator and waited, her skin twitching with each ding. She nervously stepped through the open doors and pressed the floor to Mr. Wilkins' office. *Would he be happy to see her? Or would he be angry she came unannounced, especially without her mother present?*

Snow White followed the lighted numbers with her eyes as she traveled up each floor. It felt like slow motion and for a moment, she felt dizzy. When the heavy doors gradually opened, Snow White timidly stepped through them and turned down the hallway of a bustling office.

"You lost?" an older woman boomed, wearing lipstick three shades too red.

"Ummm...I'm looking for Mr. Noah Wilkins' office?"

"Down that way, second door on the right," she answered in a loud, gravelly voice. The woman moved on without waiting for a thank you.

Snow White continued to walk, trying to avoid collisions with all the active people as they hurried past her in the narrow hallway. She found the door with Mr. Wilkins name etched in glass and pushed it open. A young lady with pretty blonde curls and a pointed nose sat behind a desk. Another door lay beyond her. *Geeze, was this place a maze of doors, or what?*

The young lady looked up from her computer. "May I help you?" she asked. She sounded much sweeter than the lipstick-lady from the hall.

"I need to speak to Mr. Wilkins, please."

"He's extremely busy with a high-profile case at the moment. Do you have an appointment?" she asked, looking doubtful.

"No, but it's actually about the case. I'm Burt Denum's daughter."

The young lady's ears pricked. Her eyes widened in surprise, as she stood quickly. "I'll be right back," she said, disappearing through the closed door.

Snow White sat in a chair against the wall. She blew out a painful breath. That was the first time she said those words out loud. *Daughter.* She was the daughter of a monster. Did that make her a monster, too? She shook her head to clear those thoughts. That didn't even matter right now. She couldn't lose focus. She'd come here on a mission and this time, she wasn't leaving without a fight.

Mr. Wilkins emerged from behind the forbidden door following closely behind his admin. He gave Snow White an exasperated look and waved her inside.

"Does your mom know you're here?" He didn't wait for an answer. "Because after the last conversation I had with her, my guess would be no." Mr. Wilkins motioned for Snow White to sit. She obliged. He looked hard at her, rubbing his forehead. "You know, Snow White," he said chuckling, "I wish everyone on my team was as feisty and determined as you are. I'd probably never lose a case." Mr. Wilkins finally took a seat behind his impressively large desk and paused for Snow White to speak.

"I know my mom said she wouldn't help you, Mr. Wilkins, but I can testify in her place. I heard her entire testimony. Plus, I'm the creation of what happened that night. What more proof do you need?"

Mr. Wilkins shook his head. "It's sweet the way you are looking out for your mom, but I can't put a minor on the witness stand without parental consent. I just can't!"

Snow White wrung her hands. This couldn't be the end of it. Not yet. "What if I threaten never to come home unless my mom helps? Then she won't have a choice. She'll have to testify for you!" Snow White wondered if he could see through her lie. Would her mom really help? No, it was more likely that her mom was relieved she was finally gone. But Mr. Wilkins didn't have to know that.

He sighed. "I'm on your side, Snow White. As much as I hate to admit it, I'm afraid the evidence won't hold up without your mom's concrete witness to back everything up. But…" he said, wiping the hopeful grin off Snow White's face. "In my experience, threats don't usually work with parents. Trust me, I tried my fair share as a teen. You and your mom need to work things out between the two of you. I can't come between you on this. I'm sorry, Snow White, but my hands are tied."

Snow White stared at her shoes as she left Mr. Wilkins office. Nothing was fair! She couldn't change a thing! As she walked around the door, her head whipped up when she heard a familiar voice talking to his admin. *It couldn't be.*

"Snow!" Belle exclaimed, relief washing over her face.

Snow White stopped in her tracks. Her eyes widened at the sight of her cousin. "What are you doing here?"

# Chapter Nineteen

Belle ran to Snow White, wrapping her arms around her cousin and holding her tightly. "What do you mean, what am I doing here? Your mom is going crazy! She's got cops both in Utah and California looking for you! Once she finally realized where you ran to, she called me and begged me to come make sure you were okay. She's actually at the airport, getting on a flight now. My mom is picking her up after an audition."

So her mom did care after all? Or she at least cared enough to put on a good show for everyone. Snow White reluctantly patted Belle's back in return. Belle pulled away from Snow White and slapped her cousin's arm.

"How could you do that to us? You scared me to death! What were you even thinking, getting on a plane by yourself?"

"You wouldn't understand," Snow White mumbled, looking down.

"Actually, I do," Belle pulled Snow White's gaze back up so their eyes met. "Your mom told me everything."

Snow White's face fell. "Everything?" she whispered, her eyes darting around the office.

Belle nodded. "Yes, but let's not get into it here. Come on, I'm taking you home with me. We'll talk there."

"I'll leave you girls to it," Mr. Wilkins said, returning to his office. "Snow White, thank you for everything. I'm sorry we couldn't help each other more."

"Bye." Snow White feebly waved goodbye and followed Belle out the door.

Belle linked elbows with Snow White as they stepped from the lawyer's office. Together they walked down the hallway back to the elevators, connected all during the ride down, and even outside to her waiting car.

"Aren't you going to let go?" Snow White asked.

"Not until we are safely in the car, with the doors locked. Now that I know you're a flight risk, I'm holding on for dear life until I deliver you safely to your mom."

Snow White rolled her eyes. "Come on, Belle, where am I going to go?"

"Funny, they asked themselves that same question back in Utah and here you are in LA. I'd say you're sneakier than you look." Belle smiled playfully at Snow White, but Snow White continued to soberly look forward. "Hey, mammoth, remember my cousin, Snow White?" Belle tapped on the driver's shoulder as she climbed into the car behind Snow White. "Snow, this is Thor. I don't know if you remember our escorted driver from last year."

The man shook his head, but said nothing as he pulled the car back out onto the road.

"Oh, come on, you know you missed me," Belle teased. "I bet you just cried and cried tears of joy when my parents told you I was coming to live with them." Belle grinned eagerly at Snow White, who continued to sit somberly against the corner of the back door.

"What did my mom actually tell you?" Snow White finally asked. Maybe Belle thought she knew more than she actually did.

"She told me about the rape and about your…dad? If that's even what you can call him. Snow, why didn't you tell us you finally found out? I mean, you were going through something major! Why did you go through all that alone? You know we're here for you. We've always been here for you! Why didn't you let us help you?"

Snow White shrugged as she looked out her window at the darkening sky and the bright city lights. "Everything has changed."

"No, it hasn't."

"Maybe not for you," Snow White said quietly, "but it sure has for me. Your parents loved each other, Belle. At least you had that much of a start in life. I was not wanted by either of my parents. I'm just the messy aftermath of a horrific crime that someone committed. No one ever wanted me." A tear slipped down Snow White's rounded cheek, which she angrily wiped away. The last thing she needed was Belle to feel sorry for her.

"You're wanted by us! Come on, Snow, we're not the Princess sisters without you! You complete the group."

Snow White pressed her forehead against the cool glass and closed her tired eyes, which stung from holding back her tears.

She jerked awake in what felt like a moment later when the car stopped.

"We're here," Belle said gently. "Home sweet home."

Snow White's jaw dropped at the sight of the mansion which stood before her. Tall, white pillars rose like guards on either side of the front door. Belle escorted Snow White inside and past a huge marble staircase. "Are you hungry?" Belle asked over her shoulder.

"Starving!" Snow White answered. "All they gave me on the plane was a lousy bag of peanuts. I skipped lunch...and dinner."

"Speaking of planes, how on earth did you get to the airport and how did you get here without your mom? Did you hijack a plane?"

Belle pulled two bottled waters out of the fridge, sliding one across the granite to Snow White, who sat on a stool. She reheated an assortment of leftover Chinese food. After removing the cartons from the microwave, she handed Snow White a fork and said, "Spill, but not the food, please. This stuff is amazing."

Snow White reached for a white carton and took a large bite out of an eggroll before finally answering. "I just kinda lost it at school. After everything with my mom and her not letting me help with the trial, and then Cinderella moving. When I found out you were gone too, it was just too much to take. I hate change! I hate it!" Snow White's eyes burned with anger, which softened as the tears began to spill. "I don't even know what I was thinking, Belle. Like coming to California would change anything. I guess I thought I could just charge into Wilkins' office and suddenly be a hero and all my problems would be gone. It was just stupid."

"You can't run away from your problems, Snow. They always have a nasty way of finding you. You've gotta face them head on. If you had just opened up to us…"

"I know, Belle. I know I didn't do everything right. Or anything right. But I really don't need a lecture right now. I'm going to get enough of that from my mom when she gets here."

"You're right," Belle said. "I'll back off. But I still want to know how you went from Layton High to that big attorney's office in L.A."

"I hitchhiked to the airport," Snow White mumbled.

"You what?" Belle jumped up from her stool so fast, she knocked it over backwards. It crashed to the ground. "Snow White Princess, that is so dangerous!"

"I know," Snow White said, shrinking away from her cousin. "I had plenty of money in savings but most of it is gone now. Anyway, after I packed a bag from home, I walked up to the freeway entrance and stuck out my thumb." Snow White covered her face with her hands. "I'm so stupid," she whispered.

"No," Belle said, "you aren't stupid, but what you did was very stupid!" She shook her head, and then reached out and gently removed Snow White's hands from her face. "Finish your story."

"Well, I found this nice lady heading to the airport and she gave me a lift. I was lucky to find a flight leaving for California shortly after I arrived there. Then I took a taxi from the airport to Mr. Wilkins' office. It wasn't hard to find. I just had to google his name and tons of hits came up. Apparently this case has been all over the news."

"Well, I think you were really stupid to hitchhike and run away without telling anyone. You could have ended up hurt or kidnapped or any number of terrible things!" Belle's face was stern as she glared down at her cousin.

"I know," Snow White mumbled, staring down at her food.

"But I don't think I've ever seen you do something so...bold before in my life," Belle finished.

Snow White looked up, and she and Belle shared a small smile.

"Now, take this new courage you've found and be smart with it. Tell your mom how you feel. Don't shout or be angry, but be bold. Just give it to her straight. And use your courage to make a decision about your future. You've been so timid, Snow, and so afraid of being left behind, that you've never considered allowing yourself to have a great future."

Snow White wiped her eyes and set her fork down on the counter. She yawned. "I'm really tired," she admitted. "It's been a very long day."

"You're telling me!" Belle said. "My crazy cousin went and ran away from home! No one accomplished anything today except worry!"

Snow White smiled sheepishly when she saw the glint in Belle's eye and realized she was being teased. The front door burst open and Mary's voice echoed through the house.

"Belle? Snow White?"

"In here, Mom!" Belle called back.

Mary came running into the room. "Oh, thank goodness you're all right!" she said, falling onto Snow White and hugging her until her neck ached. She took a step away from her niece and then whacked her across the arm with her purse.

"Ouch!" Snow White grabbed her raw skin.

"Don't you ever do anything like that to us again! Do you understand me, young lady? I about had a heart attack and died when I got out of my audition and listened to a message informing me that my dear, beautiful niece was missing. Darn it, girl! I love you too much for you to run away and scare us all like that. You got it?"

Snow White nodded. "Yes, Mary."

"Good!" Mary stepped forward and hugged her again. This time she grabbed Belle and pulled her into the embrace as well. "If anything ever happened to any of you girls, why, I just don't know what I'd ever do."

The front door opened again and Lucas entered the room, his face as white as a sheet. "Oh, thank goodness!" he said, releasing a huge breath of air when he saw Mary hugging the two girls.

"Dad!" Belle said, breaking from her mother's hug and running towards him. "I thought you had rehearsal until really late."

"I did," Lucas said. "As soon as I heard about Snow White's disappearance, I told the director I had a family emergency and had to get home right away. Are you okay, Snow White? Is everything okay?"

Snow White couldn't respond. Her words were all tied up in her throat. She sniffled and stared back at her new uncle Lucas, a movie star, who had dropped everything today to make sure she, little old Snow White, was okay. She couldn't even believe it. "I'm all right," she finally managed to say.

"Oh, I'm so glad!" Lucas put an arm around Snow White and squeezed her shoulder. "You gave us all a huge scare today."

"I really didn't mean to," Snow White whispered meekly.

Mary snapped her phone shut and looked up. "Well, it looks like your mom wasn't able to get a flight tonight after all. She'll be here in the morning first thing. So, what do you all say we have some ice cream and call it a night?"

"Sounds great, Mom," Belle said.

"Do I need to have Gunther stand guard outside the front door tonight?"

"Gunther?" Snow White whispered the unfamiliar name.

"That's Megatron's real name," Belle explained.

Snow White snickered. She somehow didn't picture the driver's name would be Gunther.

"No, Dad, I definitely don't think you have to worry about Snow White running again. Let Gunther sleep."

Snow White blushed. "I promise I won't," she said.

***

Snow White woke up to the soft touch of someone stroking her hair.

"Mom?"

"Good morning," Elizabeth whispered, smiling down at her daughter.

"But how did you…"

"I caught an early flight this morning and Mary picked me up from the airport. You slept in."

"I was tired," Snow White yawned.

"I would imagine. You had a very long day yesterday."

Yesterday. Snow White groaned and pulled the covers back over her head. How she wished she could go back in time and erase that horrible day!

Elizabeth slowly peeled the blanket away from Snow White's face. "You ready to talk about it?"

Snow White shook her head.

Elizabeth continued to stare down at her daughter.

Snow White slowly nodded and sat up. She squinted her eyes, preparing herself for the assault of words and screaming that was sure to ensue. Instead, Snow White felt her mother's warm embrace as she wrapped her arms around her daughter and held her tightly.

"I love you so much," Elizabeth whispered. "Please, please don't ever leave me again."

Snow White's eyes widened in surprise. She returned her mom's hug. "I love you too…but I…"

"But what?" Elizabeth asked. She pulled Snow White back gently, wrapping her finger around one of Snow White's flaming red curls.

Snow White remembered her conversation with Belle last night. *Be bold.* She took a deep breath and raced forward, finally allowing the question that had been eating her alive for months to tumble out of her mouth. "How can you love a mistake?"

"A mistake?" Elizabeth asked. "How on earth can you think you were a mistake?"

"Mom, please. I know how I was born. You didn't exactly ask for this. You certainly didn't want me."

"Now just a second," Elizabeth said. "What happened to me was truly awful. No woman should ever have to deal with being raped. I certainly did not want or ask for that." Elizabeth raised Snow White's chin, forcing her to look her mother in the eyes. "But you, my beautiful girl, have been the only good thing to come from all this. You truly are my bright spot in all the darkness. From the moment I found out you were on the way, I knew my life had meaning. And I knew I would do everything in my power to keep you safe. I love you, Snow White Matilda Princess. I've loved you from the very moment the strip turned pink."

"Don't I ever make you think of," Snow White gulped, "my father? Don't you look at me and hate me because you remember that awful night?"

Elizabeth shook her head firmly. "Never! He's never been a father to you. Donating sperm does not make a man a father. I don't see him. I see you. I see a beautiful, shy, kind, inquisitive girl. I left California to keep you safe from him, and I've never looked back. Well, until Mr. Wilkins came into our lives." Elizabeth smiled.

"Without getting angry or defensive, can you please explain to me then why you won't help Mr. Wilkins put that horrible man behind bars? I don't want to fight. I just really want to know. I don't understand it."

"I don't want him to find out you exist," Elizabeth stated simply. "He stole everything from me that night. I don't want him trying to hurt you, too. Now I want you to answer a question for me. Why did you run away to Mr. Wilkins' office? Why are you so determined to help him?"

"I was trying to do it for you," Snow White said quietly.

Elizabeth sat back, surprised. "How do you mean?"

"I wanted you to know I'm on your side. And I thought if I helped put that man away, you might not regret your decision to keep me."

"Oh, Snow White!" Elizabeth wrapped her arms around her daughter once again, her shoulders trembling as they cried together.

# Chapter Twenty

Snow White held her mom's hand firmly as they both stepped from the elevator. The busy hallways didn't scare Snow White this time. She squeezed past the bustling people and walked straight up to the heavy office door.

"You ready?" she asked, giving her mom's hand a squeeze.

"No."

"Come on, Mom, you can do this. I'll be with you the whole time." Snow White pushed open the heavy wooden door and smiled when the admin looked up. "Would you please tell Mr. Wilkins that Snow White Princess is here? And I brought my mom with me this time."

The admin jumped from her seat and disappeared behind the door. It didn't even have time to click shut before the door was swung open again and the handsome lawyer was striding the length of the room toward them.

"Ms. Princess! You're here!" The joy and relief shone brightly on Mr. Wilkins face. "Please, come into my office and we'll talk."

Mother and daughter sat across from the large desk in squishy leather chairs.

"Please tell me you have good news. The trial starts in two days." Mr. Wilkins sat behind his desk with his hands clasped.

"I will testify for you."

Mr. Wilkins pumped the air with his fist, his face split into an ear to ear smile. "I'm sorry," he said, clearing his throat. "But I can't even hide how happy this makes me. What made you change your mind?"

Elizabeth looked at Snow White, who smiled in return. "My daughter reminded me that we need to do the right thing, even if it's hard. She also helped me learn to be brave."

Mr. Wilkins smiled so hard at Snow White, it made her cheeks flush pink.

"I do have one condition, though," Elizabeth said. "I want Snow White to be left out of it."

"Unless it becomes necessary," Snow White interjected.

Elizabeth looked hard at her.

"Mom, you promised."

Elizabeth sighed. "You're right. I did." She turned her gaze back to the lawyer. "Unless it becomes absolutely necessary."

"Absolutely!" Mr. Wilkins agreed. "I don't see why we would need to bring her into it. I believe your testimony alone is enough to put him behind bars."

"Very well. Tell us what we need to do."

Mr. Wilkins rubbed his hands together eagerly. "Let's get started."

After their meeting with Mr. Wilkins, Snow White and her mom returned to Belle's house. Elizabeth immediately got on the phone with Snow White's high school to explain their situation. It appeared they would be staying in California until the trial ended. After a very long conversation, Elizabeth turned off her phone and plopped onto the couch with a heavy sigh.

"The principal understands this is a unique situation. She's gathering work from each of your teachers and she'll be sending it tomorrow or the next day so you can still graduate on time. Now I expect you to keep up with your studies. This is not a vacation." Elizabeth's words had a tone of finality to them.

*Yeah,* thought Snow White, *because my idea of a dream vacation is trying to get my father twenty to life.*

\*\*\*

The skirt was snug as Snow White pulled it into place around her hips. She would be grateful to return home to her own clothes when this was all over. Borrowing Belle's clothes also meant becoming Belle's Barbie doll. She turned and faced the full-length mirror, which hung on the other side of the closet door.

"Oh, that blouse looks stunning!" Belle said, walking in without knocking. "I knew that would be the perfect shade of green to match your eyes. Come in the bathroom and I'll help you do your makeup."

"I can do my own makeup," Snow White said quietly.

"No, you can't. Not for a high profile case like this. Come on, Snow, there will be reporters everywhere. Besides, look at your hands. They're shaking like crazy. Your makeup would look like you put it on during an earthquake!"

Snow White glanced down at her trembling fingers and nodded. "Okay, you're right."

Belle chattered on happily about her first day at her new school. Apparently there was a plethora of hot boys in California. Snow White tried to smile and nod at appropriate times, but she really didn't catch most of what Belle was saying. Snow White sucked in a sharp breath and Belle dropped her hands quickly.

"What's wrong, did I poke you in the eye?"

"No," Snow White said, stumbling to her feet, "I just…I'm going to meet *him* for the first time today. I'm actually going to see what he looks like face to face. I don't know what to think. Part of me doesn't want to go at all, but I need to support my mom. I'm afraid without me there, she might chicken out again." Snow White's breathing quickened as she tried to suck in another breath, but felt as though she couldn't get enough air. She couldn't sit still. She began pacing around the small bathroom, wheezing and feeling light headed. Her chest tightened and she had the sudden urge to rip Belle's tight clothes off so she could breathe.

"Snow, you're starting to scare me. I'm going to get your mom."

"No!" Snow White seized Belle's arm. Her wheezing grew even louder as she frantically shook her head. "Please…don't," she said between heaving breaths. "If…she…sees…me…panic…ing…"

Belle cut her off. "Okay," she soothed, stroking Snow White's arm. "I think you're having a panic attack. Just focus on me and take nice deep breaths." Belle guided her cousin back down onto the stool and stared into her emerald eyes, bringing her attention back to the present.

After a moment, Snow White's breathing became steady and normal once again. She closed her eyes and shook her head. "I'm sorry. I've never had that happen before."

"Are you sure you want to go?" Belle asked as she cautiously resumed putting on Snow White's mascara.

"Yes," Snow White answered. "I'm okay now."

Elizabeth appeared in the bathroom doorway a moment later. "Are you almost ready, hon? Gunther is driving us to the courthouse. He's waiting downstairs."

Snow White's jaw dropped at the sight of her mom. It was obvious Mary had gotten ahold of her before leaving for work. The red dress showed off her figure nicely, without being too revealing. And Elizabeth, who normally wore little to no makeup, looked incredibly stunning with darkened eyes and lipstick to match her dress. "Wow, Mom!"

"I know," Elizabeth said, rolling her eyes. "My sister got carried away."

"Actually, I was just going to say how amazing you look."

Elizabeth flushed pink. "Oh, well, thank you."

"She'll be right down," Belle said. "I'm just about done here."

Snow White and her mom drove in silence on the way to the courthouse. They sat close to each other, holding shaky hands, their trembling shoulders bouncing off each other while they watched the busy streets of LA pass by. They were grateful to have Gunther with them when they pulled up and discovered half a dozen camera crews hovering around the court steps. As soon as Elizabeth stepped from the vehicle, the press flew around her like a swarm of angry bees.

"Mrs. Princess! Mrs. Princess!"

"Is it true you are here to testify today?"

"Were you the first victim of Burt Denum?"

"Why haven't you come forward until now?"

Thankfully Mr. Wilkins appeared by their side and, waving the reporters away, guided Snow White and her mom inside.

"Are they always like that?" Elizabeth asked, brushing off her skirt.

"Slow news day," Mr. Wilkins answered. He placed a hand on each of Elizabeth's shoulders and looked her square in the face. "Are you okay?" he asked.

Elizabeth nodded slowly.

"All right, let me show you to your seat. Now Snow White, do you remember Janette?" he asked as the administrative assistant from his office approached.

"Yeah, sure," Snow White answered, looking confused.

"She'll be sitting with you, okay?"

"We can't sit together?" Elizabeth asked, her face turning pale.

"I promised you I would do everything in my power to keep Snow White safe and out of this. If she's sitting next to you when you get called up, she will draw attention and people may begin to speculate."

Elizabeth glanced around before drawing her daughter in for a tight hug.

"Go get 'em," Snow White whispered before they parted.

Snow White and Janette waited a couple minutes after her mom and Mr. Wilkins disappeared into the courtroom before following. Janette sat them near the back, so Snow White could still see, but not be seen. Snow White glanced at her cell phone and smiled as she read through the encouraging texts from her cousins. She took a deep breath and looked around. She found her mom sitting in an aisle seat near the front of the room. Elizabeth sat wringing her purse in her hands, her eyes darting between doors as she wondered which one he would enter through. How Snow White wished she could be next to her mom, holding her hand for comfort!

She continued to look around the room, her eyes stopping on each of the jurors and wondering about their individual stories. Snow White heard a loud crack as a heavy door was pulled open. Her heart stopped. She turned and stared at the man who entered. No wonder Mr. Wilkins had paused when he first met her. Everything from the bright red, curly hair to the rounded cheeks to the squished, cabbage patch nose were the same. Snow White was the spitting image of her father. He had a thick, red beard which covered much of his face, but there was no mistaking it. Burt Denum and Snow White Princess were definitely related.

Snow White found herself shrinking back as his dark, beady eyes scanned over the room. Her stomach churned and her face flushed with heat. Snow White felt as though the room's temperature were steadily rising, making her chest tighten as she tried to get air. She could feel the beginnings of another panic attack threatening to surface, but thankfully she knew what it was this time. Snow White put her head down between her knees and focused on taking slow, even breaths instead.

"Snow White, are you okay?" Janette asked, her voice thick with concern. "Do we need to leave?"

"No," Snow White gasped, trying to shake her head. "Just give me a minute."

Snow White's breathing became more steady and calm as she regained control. She watched helplessly as Burt Denum's cruel gaze landed on her mother. Their eyes locked for a brief moment before Elizabeth turned away. Burt Denum licked his lips and grinned at Elizabeth, his eyes narrowing in like a hungry wolf. Snow White shuddered. She was very glad he couldn't see her right now.

Soon after his entrance, everyone in the courtroom stood for the judge to enter. Before long, Snow White was extremely aware of just how hard her bench had become. It felt like Mr. Wilkins was interviewing every person who had ever known Burt Denum. If it weren't for the numbness now growing in her thighs, Snow White feared she would have fallen asleep. After what felt like an eternity, Mr. Wilkins called Ms. Elizabeth Princess to the stand. All thoughts of pain gone, Snow White sat up and leaned forward.

Her mom described how she had come to know Burt Denum and then Mr. Wilkins asked questions, in depth, about that awful night. Snow White's eyes stung as she listened to her mom describe every detail. She'd heard most of these words before, but that didn't make them any easier the second time.

After her mom's testimony, Elizabeth climbed down from the stand. As she walked back to her seat, Burt Denum eyed her hungrily, causing Snow White's cheeks to flush with anger. The judge called for a recess and announced they would continue the trial tomorrow. Snow White wanted to rush to her mom's side, but she refrained. She remained quietly in her seat until Burt Denum had been removed from the room. She then stood carefully and stretched her aching legs.

Snow White stepped from the courthouse into the bright California sun. She walked down the steps and found a café nearby. Grabbing herself a drink, she sat at a small table and texted her mom where to meet her. Mr. Wilkins said they needed to talk for a few minutes after court.

"Mind if I join you?"

Snow White looked up and saw a blond young man with large black glasses looking down at her. *Be bold.* Belle's voice echoed through her mind.

"Sure," Snow White tried to smile.

"I saw you in the courtroom today, didn't I?" he asked, taking a sip from his coffee. "Crazy case, isn't it?"

"Are you working on the case?" Snow White asked.

"I wish!" he said, leaning back in his chair. "No, I'm just an intern. I basically get to observe and deliver coffee whenever I'm asked."

Snow White took a sip of her soda and glanced out the window for her mom.

"I'm sorry," he said, sitting upright. "I'm Jeff Davidson, and you are?" he asked, extending his hand.

Snow White shook his hand but didn't offer her name. "I'm not really supposed to say," she said.

Jeff's smile widened. "A mystery woman, huh? I can respect that."

"Mystery woman? I like the sound of that," Snow White smiled. She glanced out the window again and saw her mom waving to her outside. Snow White jumped to her feet. "I gotta go," she said. "We'll be back in the courtroom bright and early tomorrow morning."

Jeff touched her hand, stopping her from leaving. "Well, mystery lady, if you ever change your mind about revealing your true identity, I'd love to take you out for a drink sometime."

Snow White tried to hide her astonishment as she took his card. "Nice meeting you, Jeff," she said, before leaving the café quickly. Snow White couldn't hide the smile on her face. Not only did she just get hit on, but he actually thought she looked old enough to drink!

Once they got back to Belle's house, Snow White couldn't even wrap her mind around the pile of homework stacked neatly on the kitchen table, just waiting to be tackled. All Snow White could think about was going to sleep. Both Mary and Belle asked questions all evening until Lucas finally came to their rescue.

"Can't you see they're exhausted? It's been a very long day for them, I'm sure. Let's just give them some space. I'm sure there will be plenty of time for spewing details after the trial is over."

Snow White smiled at Lucas, offering him a silent thank you. He winked in return, mouthing, "You're welcome."

Snow White and her mom both went to bed early, but they ended up lying awake for a long time, waiting for morning to come.

The second day of trial began similarly, with Elizabeth being questioned by the defense attorney. It seemed to Snow White like they were just asking the same questions that Mr. Wilkins had asked yesterday. It wasn't long before things began to take a turn for the worse. The defense attorney tried to discredit everything her mom was saying. He asked her some difficult questions, making Elizabeth's testimony seem unreliable. Snow White watched as Mr. Wilkins shifted in his seat, his face reddening, and she could feel Janette doing the same beside her. This stupid slime ball was completely turning the case around! Elizabeth looked pained and uncomfortable as the defending lawyer caused her to stumble over her words.

Mr. Wilkins frantically flipped through the papers on the table in front of him. Snow White's palms began to sweat. Was it possible? Were they really going to lose the case now, after everything? Snow White watched her mom, who now appeared to be on the verge of tears. She wanted to scream out. She wanted to jump out of her seat and yell at the jurors, who now wore doubtful expressions, to believe her mom. Her mom was the most honest person on the planet! And why would someone lie about the details surrounding a rape anyway? As if sensing her anger, Janette placed an arm across Snow White's chest, keeping her pinned to her seat. Janette shook her head, encouraging Snow White to calm down.

"And so, Ms. Princess, you don't actually have any proof that Mr. Denum was the one who raped you?"

"Well, no, but..."

"And this happened eighteen years ago?"

"Yes, but...."

"So isn't it possible that the details you remember could have worn over the years? Who's to say the man who attacked you wasn't someone else entirely, but perhaps just reminds you of my client?"

Burt Denum grinned wickedly in Elizabeth's direction.

Snow White couldn't take it any longer. She burst off the hard bench. "Take a paternity test!" she yelled.

The entire room turned and stared, open mouthed at Snow White. The judge banged his gavel and called for order. The defense attorney's jaw dropped the lowest at the sight of Snow White standing there. His eyebrows narrowed together as he glanced between Elizabeth and Snow White. Burt Denum stared hard at her. She could feel his gaze burning through her as she tried to watch the judge. The smug grin on his face quickly faded into surprise, and then anger.

The judge said, "Excuse me, young lady, what did you say?"

Snow White, feeling less brave now, spoke much more quietly this time. "My mom was raped eighteen years ago, and I am the direct result. If you want proof that Burt Denum is the one who did it, then take a paternity test."

The courtroom was in an uproar. Burt Denum jumped from his seat, slamming his fist onto the hard wood table. Mr. Wilkins glanced back at Snow White, looking both relieved and terrified. The judge looked to Mr. Wilkins for verification. The lawyer reluctantly nodded. Janette tugged helplessly on Snow White's sleeve, trying to pull her back down. Snow White caught Jeff's eye from across the room. He stared at her, his mouth agape. Snow White shrugged at him and he smiled.

The courtroom was so loud, no one could hear the judge calling for order. He banged his gavel until the handle broke off. Amid the chaos, Snow White watched her mom to gauge a reaction, but Elizabeth looked unnaturally white. Snow White offered her mom a tiny smile, but Elizabeth wasn't even looking at her anymore. As a bailiff yanked Burt Denum from the courtroom, Snow White watched helplessly as her mom fainted.

Forever After

# Chapter Twenty-One

"So what was it like being in a courtroom?" Ariel asked.

"Hard and uncomfortable. And very boring," Snow White sighed dramatically.

"Except for when you jumped off the bench and made your mom faint!" Cinderella laughed. "I still can't believe you did that, Snow!"

"I can't believe I did that either! But it was all worth it. That horrible man is in prison now, serving two life sentences. I don't think I'll ever have to look at his stupid, smug face ever again."

Snow White glowed as her cousins all gushed over the details from her trial. She debated whether or not to tell them about Jeff, the older boy who'd hit on her in the café, but, smiling, she decided to keep that particular memory to herself. It had been a long week in California, and Snow White was very grateful to be home again. The cousins sat around Cinderella's large, new bedroom. Snow White looked at the familiar furniture and decorations adorning the unfamiliar walls. Her room was basically the same as it had been in the condo, only larger. *Maybe this won't be so terrible*, Snow White thought, stretching her legs along the soft tan carpet.

"Monica, can you come here for a minute, please?" Dana called from down the stairs.

The bedroom door next to Cinderella's opened, Monica's dark head poking out. She shouted for Dana to go someplace that would have gotten the Princesses' mouths washed out with soap if they had used the same foul word when they were her age. Then her door slammed shut again.

Cinderella shook her head and stood to close her own bedroom door more tightly.

"Is she always this rude?" Ariel whispered.

"She wasn't like this when I went to California to meet them last year. Ever since my parents got back together, she's been a real beast to live with. My poor mom! She doesn't know what to do. Actually, my dad doesn't know what to do either."

They heard Dana stomp up the stairs and throw Monica's door open. Dana's voice was surprisingly calm as she spoke to her step-daughter. Monica did not return the courtesy. Dana poked her head in Cinderella's room and asked the girls if they wanted to stay for dinner. Even though she tried to avoid eye contact, Cinderella could tell her mom's eyes were red as she tried to hide the hurt behind them.

"This has got to stop!" Cinderella said when her mom left again. She stood, her fists clenched, and walked next door. Without knocking, she burst through Monica's door. Hands on her hips and eyes like fire, she glared at Monica, who rested on top of her comforter, head cradled on her folded arms. Cinderella softened when she saw Monica wipe a tear from her cheek. "What's going on with you?" she asked, letting her hands drop as she approached her sister's bed.

Monica wiped frantically at her eyes and rolled over so her back faced Cinderella. "Just leave me alone."

Cinderella reached out and gently rubbed Monica's back. "Come on, Mon, remember how much fun we had last year? What happened? Just talk to me."

"I just wish my dad had never married your stupid mom. It's not fair!"

Cinderella had to count to ten before she could open her mouth to respond. "Why do you hate my mom so much?"

Monica began sobbing harder. "I don't...hate your mom..." Her voice faded off.

"Really? Could've fooled me!"

"It's just...my dad and Sophie, they both love Dana so much it's like they completely forgot about my real mom."

Cinderella continued to rub Monica's back while she cried. "I'm sorry," Cinderella whispered. "I know it's been hard on you. Especially because everything happened so fast."

"You just don't even understand!"

"No, you're right, I really have no idea how painful it must have been for you to lose your mom. I know I'd be devastated if I lost my mom. But you have to remember, I didn't even know who my dad was until last year. You had the amazing privilege of growing up with two parents who both loved you."

Monica rolled over and faced Cinderella. Her lip jutted out defiantly, but she said nothing.

Cinderella continued, "My dad never got to hold me as a baby. He wasn't there for my first steps, or my first day of kindergarten, or even my first dance. I can't get any of those memories back. I'm leaving for college in about six months, which means I'll have memories of dad as an adult, and hopefully my children someday will have memories with my dad when they're little, but for me, they never existed and I can't get those back. You had a beautiful, amazing mom who loved you very much. You have memories of her and with her that you can carry with you for the rest of your life. Your mom was taken from you too soon, and that sucks! That really, really, sucks. But she didn't leave you. She loved you and still does. My mom isn't trying to replace her. She lost her dad when she was just a little girl, so I know she would never dream of doing that to you. She wants to love you. She wants to be your friend. And like it or not, she is the one that is here now, and she's the one who will be here for the rest of your life. Do you really want to live the next forty years in misery because you're trying to prove a point? Please just give her a chance. I know she can't replace the mom you lost. I know that! She knows that! But let's cherish your mom's memory by being a real family. Would your mom really want you to be angry and unhappy?"

Monica sat up on her knees and stared at Cinderella, her lip quivering. She fell into Cinderella's arms, almost knocking her over, sobbing into her shoulder. "I just miss her so much!"

"I know." Cinderella brushed her hair with her fingers as she tried to soothe her little sister. "Shhhh. I'm so sorry, Monica," she said quietly.

"You're right," Monica said, pulling back and wiping her nose with the back of her hand. "My mom wouldn't be happy with all the problems I'm causing. She was always a very positive person." Monica sniffed loudly. "But I don't like the way my dad has just forgotten her. It's like he replaced her with your mom and he doesn't even care at all."

"I know that's not true," Cinderella said. "Come here." Cinderella stood from the bed and offered Monica a hand. Monica looked at her reluctantly before finally conceding. She placed her hand in Cinderella's and allowed herself to be led down the stairs.

Steven had just gotten home from work. He and Dana were discussing the events from the day in hushed whispers. Steven looked at Monica sternly as the girls approached.

"Dad, can we talk to you for a second?" Cinderella asked. Monica cowered behind her taller sister.

"Do I need to go?" Dana asked, preparing to stand.

"No, Mom, please stay. We need to work through this. Dad, do you still love Monica's mom?"

"Of course I do," he said, without hesitation.

Monica looked uneasily at Dana. "Really?" she squeaked.

"Yes, baby, I will always love your mom. What's this about?"

"Well..." Monica hesitated.

"Go ahead."

"How can you say that...in front of Dana?" Monica's eyes darted nervously between her dad and step mom.

Dana smiled. "Can I take this one, Steven?"

He nodded.

"Monica, I know how much your dad loved your mom. It's one of the things we talked about before we decided to get married. His love for her will never fade or change, even though he's married to me now."

Monica squeezed her brows together in confusion.

"Let me ask you this," Dana said. "Do you love your dad?"

"Yes."

"Do you love Cinderella?"

"Yes."

"Do you love Sophie?"

"Yeah, I do, most of the time," Monica mumbled, but she began to smile, her face softening as understanding began to sink in.

"Out of your family, who do you love the most? When you love your dad, does that mean you love Cinderella less?"

Monica shook her head.

"Love is not limited," Dana said. She stood, stepped away from the couch, and approached Monica cautiously. "Love is amazing in that it always has room for more. I understand you're feeling upset about your father and me getting married so quickly. But I promise you, I respect your mother very much and I will never try to replace her. You already have one mom, and from everything your dad has said, she sounds like she was an amazing woman! I know you don't need two moms, but I want you to know I'll always be here for you. I love you too, Monica." Dana's eyes watered as she spoke.

Monica rushed forward and flung her arms around Dana's middle, hugging her tight. "I love you, too," she whispered. "I'm sorry I've been so mean to you."

"It's okay," Dana said, kissing the top of her head. "I know all the changes have been hard. Please know your dad and I are both here for you. And please come talk to us."

Monica nodded.

Steven approached and wrapped his arms around Monica from the other side. "Sandwich hug!" he said loudly.

Monica and Dana both laughed as he squeezed them. Sophie ran into the room and launched herself onto the pile. Soon Cinderella joined in. They all stood laughing, their arms entangled around one another.

"Wow, super cheesy," Aurora said from behind them.

Their group hug dissolved quickly. Cinderella looked up and found her cousins staring down at them from the banister with big grins on their faces.

"We didn't know what happened to you," Ariel chimed in.

"Just saving the family is all," Cinderella said. She flexed her muscles and they all laughed.

"Well, we better take off," Aurora said. "I've got a lot of homework."

"Studying This Week doesn't count as homework!" Ariel said.

"It does in my book!" Aurora grinned impishly and headed for the front door.

Snow White waved goodbye before following the twins out the door.

Monica offered to make dinner and she headed for the kitchen, her little helper Sophie skipping at her heels.

"Thank you, Cinderella," Steven said, embracing his oldest daughter again. "I don't know how you did it, but thank you for getting Monica to open up tonight."

Dana nodded. "You were amazing, sweetie," she said.

"I think I've finally decided what I want to study at Utah State," Cinderella said.

"What's that?" Dana asked.

"Family therapy. I think I would be good at it."

Dana smiled at her daughter, wrapping an arm around her shoulder. "You wouldn't just be good at it, you would be amazing!"

# Chapter Twenty-Two

Cinderella rolled out of bed, a huge smile splitting her face. She shuffled into the bathroom and stared at her reflection in the mirror. She wasn't sure what she expected to see, a grey hair? Some wrinkles? But the same old sunflower eyes stared back at her. Yet, something felt different. Today Cinderella was turning eighteen. She wasn't any different than she was yesterday. Same old Cinderella. But, today, if she were to commit a huge crime or something, she would be tried as an adult. It was a silly example, but somehow the word adult made Cinderella suddenly feel much more grownup.

She climbed in the shower and wondered what her cousins had planned for her birthday as she let the hot water run down her back. The best part of the morning had already happened. She slept in! Cinderella loved it when her birthday landed on a Saturday. No alarms, no school, just comfy pillows and a soft comforter. For Belle's eighteenth birthday a few months back, Lucas had rented out her favorite restaurant. It had been an elegant affair, with everyone dressing up in their prom dresses and suits while dining on sushi and tempura vegetables. It was really cool being the only people in the restaurant.

Cinderella's dad wasn't a movie star. She didn't expect anything fancy or over-the-top, yet the anticipation of not knowing was killing her. Her cousins gave her no clues. All they told was she had to be ready to go by 10:00.

Cinderella felt weird not having Belle around for her birthday. The cousins had spent every birthday together since they turned one, where they'd each taken a turn smearing cake all over themselves and each other.

Cinderella realized she'd gotten lost in her thoughts when the water suddenly turned cold, forcing her to jump forward out of the stream. She pulled the curtain aside and glanced at the purple flower clock which hung above the toilet. Her cousins would be there to pick her up in twenty minutes. Yikes! Cinderella shut off the water and got dressed and ready quickly. Just as she was dabbing on a little bit of pink lip gloss across her lips, she heard the doorbell. Cinderella dashed down the stairs, taking them two at a time.

"Bye, Mom! Bye, Dad!" she shouted as she reached for the handle.

"Now wait just a minute," Dana called, coming from the kitchen. "I want to see my girl on her eighteenth birthday. I can't believe this day has come already. I swear I was wiping your bottom and trying desperately to keep you in clothes just yesterday."

"Mom, please!" Cinderella said, rolling her eyes. She sounded embarrassed, but the smile on her face said otherwise. Cinderella opened the door to Ariel, Aurora, and Snow White all with huge grins on their faces. As soon as they stepped inside, they broke into an extremely loud and off-key rendition of *Happy Birthday*.

Their voices alerted the rest of the house, and soon everyone else joined in. Sophie sang the loudest of all. When the song ended, she jumped into Cinderella's arms.

"Happy Birthday, Cinderelly!" she yelled, squeezing tightly around her neck. "I can't wait for your party!"

Everyone exchanged nervous glances. Steven stepped forward and quickly removed Sophie from her arms. "What party?" he asked, laughing nervously.

"The one after..."

Steven placed a hand over Sophie's mouth as he tried not to laugh. "Okay, bye ladies, have a great day!" he said to Cinderella and her cousins.

Cinderella burst out laughing as soon as the front door was closed.

"Darn kid!" Snow White said.

"Who told her anyway?" Aurora asked, looking around.

"It's okay," Cinderella said. "I'll act surprised. Besides, she didn't give me any details at all."

They all piled into the twins' waiting car.

"So what's the plan?" Cinderella asked, clicking her seatbelt.

"Come on, Cindy, you gotta leave us one little secret!" Ariel said. "You'll see soon enough."

Ariel didn't drive far before pulling up in front of a nail salon. "Pedicures!" she said, holding her hands up toward the small building.

"Yay!" Cinderella clapped her hands and climbed out of the car. "This will be the best birthday ever!"

After relaxing pedicures and a trip to the mall, where her cousins let her pick out a new top for her party that night, the girls window shopped and walked around the stores for a couple hours.

"Should we head back now?" Snow White asked, looking at her watch.

"Yeah, I think the guests will all be there by now," Aurora agreed.

Cinderella laughed. They weren't even pretending to surprise her anymore. When they got home, her cousins surrounded her on the porch, making sure she was the first one inside.

"Smooth, guys," Cinderella whispered.

"Oh, come on, you already know what's coming. Just go inside," Ariel said.

Cinderella pulled her house keys out of her purse and unlocked the front door in slow motion, much to the chagrin of her cousins. The lock finally clicked and she twisted the knob gradually.

"Oh, come on!" Aurora muttered. She grabbed Cinderella's hand and threw it aside.

Cinderella laughed loudly. "Okay, okay," she smiled. She grabbed the door handle and pushed the door open. Her eyes were assaulted by a huge crowd of people all yelling happy birthday and jumping up and down. The crowd was framed in a sea of colorful balloons and streamers, running down the walls and hanging from the ceiling above them.

Cinderella didn't have to fake her surprise when she saw the large crowd. She didn't even realize she knew this many people! Her family was all there, of course, along with many faces from school, some she knew well and others she wasn't sure if she knew their names. Cinderella looked back at her cousins, wide-eyed, and they all laughed in response.

"Surprise!" they yelled. Snow White and the twins all threw their arms around her for a large group hug. They pushed her toward the crowd of people full of friends who wanted a turn to say hi and offer birthday wishes.

Cinderella's head began to spin as she hugged and thanked each person she passed. Her mind became a jumble of faces and names. She watched Sophie having the time of her life, running between people's legs and asking them questions like, "Who are you?" and "Those are big teeth — are you a horse?" Sometimes Cinderella wished she could be more outgoing like her baby sister, who didn't seem to have a shy bone in her body.

"I hope she stays that way," Cinderella whispered to herself, smiling. She glanced over and noticed Monica seemed to be enjoying herself, too. Monica was leaning against the far wall of their living room, her face bright red as she spoke to a cute high school boy.

Cinderella's cousins stepped forward, each with an eager grin on their faces. Cinderella reached out and hugged them all with her long arms. "You guys are amazing!" she said.

Ariel smiled. "We're so glad you like it!" she shouted over the crowd.

"How did you get my parents to do this?" Cinderella asked. Her history of birthdays had mostly consisted of small get-togethers with her cousins and her aunts. She'd never been thrown a birthday party even remotely like this.

"It was mostly your dad who helped sell the idea," Aurora said. "He's pretty awesome!"

Cinderella grinned. This party definitely had more of a dad feel than her mom, who preferred small gatherings.

"We invited practically everyone," Snow White added.

"I can tell!" Cinderella said, glancing around. "This is seriously amazing, you guys!"

Her cousins beamed with pride.

Cinderella's face fell for a moment. "It just feels like Belle should be here though, you know? This is definitely her kind of scene."

The twins exchanged a glance. "Funny you should say that," Ariel said. She pulled her hand out from behind her back to reveal the phone she had been hiding. Belle's eager face glowed brightly from the little screen.

"Happy birthday, Cinderella!" she yelled. "Wow, our girls did some awesome work, didn't they?" Belle's beaming face smiled at her through the device.

Cinderella held the phone closer to her face. "They really are amazing!"

"Oh, stop!" Ariel said, grinning.

"Belle helped a little," Snow White admitted, shrugging.

"I only offered ideas. You three carried out the plan perfectly."

"How are you?" Cinderella asked.

"I'm doing really well!" Belle said. Flipping her blonde hair over her shoulder, she added, "California suits me."

"I miss you!" Cinderella said.

"Oh, Cindy, I miss you too! Have the best time tonight and call me with all the juicy details tomorrow, okay?"

"Promise!"

Cinderella handed the phone back to Ariel. Jordan walked over to their small gathering and invited Ariel to dance. Another This Week came over and asked Aurora to do the same. Snow White waved goodbye and excused herself to get a drink. Cinderella watched her walk toward the kitchen and get stopped by a cute boy in their choir class. Cinderella watched as he pulled a blushing Snow White onto the dance floor. "Atta girl," Cinderella whispered.

Dave came swooping past, almost running Cinderella over as he flew Sophie, on her stomach, through the air. Sophie was making loud airplane noises as she zoomed past. "Happy birthday, Cinderella!" Dave yelled over his shoulder.

Cinderella stepped back, laughing. She felt someone touch her elbow and she turned.

Brian stood behind her, smiling nervously, his arm wrapped around the waist of a cute, petite brunette.

"Happy birthday, Cinderella!" he said, releasing the other girl's waist and stepping forward. He gave her a tentative hug, which she returned while trying to avoid eye contact with the other girl. "I hope you've had a great birthday. You really deserve it."

"I'm going to get a drink," the brunette said quietly. "Happy birthday, Cinderella."

"Thank you," Cinderella said. Turning to Brian with raised eyebrows, she asked, "So, who is that?"

When Brian smiled, his entire face lit up. "That's Britney. She's a junior this year."

"She's cute." Cinderella still had no interest in trying to force feelings for Brian, but seeing him here with another girl made her stomach feel funny. She wanted to be happy for him. She really did.

"Thanks," Brian smiled shyly. "I hope it's okay that I brought her here. I wasn't sure, but she really likes you."

Cinderella jerked back in surprise. "She doesn't even know me."

"Oh, come on, Cinderella," Brian said. He seemed to be relaxing now that Britney wasn't by his side. "Everyone in the school knows about you and your cousins. You guys are the famous Princess sisters! The dance stunt you pulled on Cynthia and her friends is still talked about in the halls."

Cinderella was dumbfounded. People actually talked about that two years later?

"Well," Brian said, "I just wanted to thank you. I think we were trying to force more than a friendship and I'm glad you had the courage to speak up. I still really admire you, and I hope we can stay in touch after graduation. You know, as friends." Brian extended his hand toward her.

Cinderella smiled warmly and returned the handshake. "Friends forever," she agreed.

Brian's face then fell. "What's *he* doing here?"

Cinderella turned around in time to see Scott walking through the front door. Brian scowled and walked away, probably to go find Britney. Cinderella didn't really pay attention. Her heart dropped to the floor as she watched Scott scan the crowd. Their eyes met across the room and Scott's smile split his face. "Happy birthday," he mouthed.

"Thank you," she mouthed in return. Cinderella could feel the heat creeping up her neck and wash over her face as she squeezed through the mass of teenagers dancing in her living room.

"Happy birthday, Cinderella!"

She heard the voices around her as she pushed her way through the crowd, but she didn't register any faces. Her eyes were locked onto Scott's soft brown ones and she worried about looking away for fear he might disappear. Scott met Cinderella in the middle of the room. He immediately grabbed her and began to sway with her across the makeshift dance floor.

"I'm sorry," he said. "I stayed away as long as I could."

Cinderella laid her head on his chest. She missed him so much, she wanted to cry. "I'm so glad you're here!"

she said, snuggling deeper into him and soaking up his warmth. He smelled incredible, as usual. Cinderella took a deep breath, bathing her nostrils in his rich cologne musk. "I've missed you so much!" Cinderella felt a drop slide down her cheek and realized she was crying.

Scott gently took her hand in his. "Are you crying?" he whispered. "Oh, Princess, why are you crying?" Scott bent his head down so he could look into Cinderella's eyes.

"I didn't realize how much I missed you until I saw you walk in," Cinderella sniffled as she wiped her wet cheeks with the back of her hand. She laughed at herself. "It's silly, I know."

Scott gently held her chin in his hand. "It's not silly at all. I missed you, too!" Scott looked around and then, standing up straight once again, he grabbed Cinderella's hand and pulled her towards the front door.

The blast of cool air bit their cheeks as they stepped outside.

"I didn't realize how warm it had gotten in there," Cinderella said, shivering. "Brrrrr!"

Scott enveloped Cinderella in his arms. "I'll keep you warm," he promised. He pulled her face up towards his own and kissed her sweetly. Her body tingled as their lips meshed. His hands raced up the length of her back and pulled gently in her long, brown hair. Cinderella brought her hand to his firm chest and felt his heart racing against her palm. Their arms pulled each other closer. They clung to each other until they were both dizzy and out of breath.

When they finally parted, Scott bent over, his hands on his knees for support. "Wow," he whispered. Then standing up straight, he pulled a long white box from his pocket. "Can I give you your birthday present now, before we go back in?"

"Go back in?" It took a moment for the fog to disappear from her fuzzy brain. Cinderella had almost completely forgotten about the party. She lifted the lid from the soft box to discover the most beautiful necklace she had ever seen, laying against a cottony bed. A deep, sapphire blue heart hung from a thin, woven, silver chain. Diamond clusters surrounded the outside of the heart.

Cinderella gasped as she stared at the sparkling beauty before her. "Oh Scott," she whispered, "It's too much!"

"Nothing is too much for my girl."

Cinderella almost dropped the box she held so carefully in her hands and stared at him.

"Cinderella." Scott cleared his throat. "Will you be my girl?"

Cinderella could feel the moisture threaten to break through again. Holding the necklace tightly in one hand, she threw her arms around Scott's neck. "Yes!" she laughed. "A thousand times yes!"

Scott picked up Cinderella around the waist and spun her around. He kissed her soundly as he placed her feet back on the ground. "I love you so much!" he said.

Cinderella wanted to hold onto Scott and never let go. "I love you, too," she choked.

Scott reached for the necklace. "May I?" he asked.

Cinderella turned and held her hair up off of her neck so Scott could secure the beautiful necklace in place. "What about all your rules?" she teased.

"You dated other guys, right?" Scott asked.

"Yes."

"And how did that go?"

"Awful!"

Scott grinned. "You did everything I asked and the best part is, now you're eighteen." He waggled his eyebrows at her, causing Cinderella to laugh. Scott bent down and kissed her again, stopping her mid-laughter. Cinderella melted into his arms. She had been right to think she was done with boys...all boys except for one.

Scott pulled back slowly. "I better get you back inside," he said begrudgingly. "They'll definitely notice you're missing, if they haven't already."

Cinderella groaned. She shuffled her feet forward, barely allowing Scott to guide her back into the house. It felt like walking into a furnace, with all the warm bodies moving around in the confined space. Her mom caught her eye as she stepped through the door.

"Here she is, everybody!" Dana shouted over the voices. Suddenly Cinderella felt herself being pushed up onto a chair as the crowd broke into a boisterous rendition of *Happy Birthday*. Steven appeared from the kitchen carrying a large chocolate cake aglow with the light of eighteen candles. The guests parted, allowing Steven space to get through the sea of bodies and hold the cake up for Cinderella to make a wish.

Cinderella looked out and saw faces of all the people she loved smiling and singing up at her. She caught Scott's eye. He smiled broadly at her, belting every note. His face was the last thing she saw before closing her eyes and making a wish.

# *Chapter Twenty-Three*

Ariel ran her fingers through Jordan's thick hair as he kissed her passionately while the party wound down. Several groups of kids passed by them making out on Cinderella's porch swing as they left the party. The constant traffic of people walking by them did not deter Ariel and Jordan. They continued to kiss, unashamed of their PDA.

"Ariel and Jordan sittin' in a tree! K-I-S-S-I-N-G!" Aurora laughed as This Week followed her down the porch steps.

"Ha ha, super mature," Ariel said, pulling back and sitting up.

"It worked, didn't it?" Aurora asked.

At that moment, Rachel came out of the house and Ariel's breath caught in her throat. Thank goodness for her sister! Not because she was ashamed of kissing Jordan — that's all they were doing — but having her mother witness that would have been embarrassing.

"Can I drive you home?" Jordan asked.

"Sure," Ariel smiled. She tried standing but quickly realized the stupidity of that idea and sat back down. Once her head stopped spinning, Jordan was on his feet, offering her a hand. "Mom, Jordan is taking me home. Is that okay?"

Rachel looked at Ariel with tired eyes. "All right, but nowhere else, please. Just straight home."

Jordan tipped an imaginary hat toward Rachel. "Yes, ma'am."

"Oh, stop that," Rachel grinned, swatting his jeans with her jacket.

Ariel watched the interaction between her mom and boyfriend with a grin plastered to her face. "Mom, stop flirting with my boyfriend," Ariel teased.

Rachel looked up abruptly, mischief twinkling in her eyes. "But you get him all the time."

"Ewww, Mom. Seriously, now you really have to stop."

Both Rachel and Jordan laughed. Rachel walked toward her car with a wave. Aurora said her goodbyes to This Week, blowing kisses and waving as he drove out of sight. Ariel watched her sister and mom leave before Jordan led her over to his truck and they drove home together.

"Jordan?" Ariel whispered his name so quietly that he didn't respond the first time. "Jordan?" she asked again, a little louder.

"What's up?"

"Are you my boyfriend?" She felt silly asking the question, but that word slipped out of her mouth without thinking, and he hadn't corrected her.

Jordan's perfect white teeth shone brightly in the darkness, as oncoming headlights reflected his smile. "Well, I've been calling you my girlfriend to my parents and my friends at work, so I hope you see me as the same."

Ariel shifted in her seat. It seemed like an inappropriate time to fist pump the air, although that's what she wanted to do. Instead, she scooted over to the middle seat of the truck and nuzzled into Jordan's broad shoulder. She rested her left hand on his leg as he drove, giving his thigh a gentle squeeze.

When they pulled into the parking spot in front of Jordan's house, Ariel was about to get out of the car when

Jordan stopped her. He softly placed a large, black hand on her cheek. His fingers went up into her hair while his thumb gently caressed the outline of her lips. He looked intently into Ariel's eyes. She stared back and found they dripped with emotion, like two melting chocolates.

"All right, you're starting to freak me out a little, the way you're staring at me," Ariel said. "Do I have food from the party left on my face?"

Jordan chuckled and shook his head. "You really don't know how incredibly beautiful you are, do you?"

Ariel's cheeks flushed and she looked down at her lap.

"I mean it," Jordan said, coaxing her back into eye contact. "I…I love you Ariel."

Ariel smiled, her emotions pooling in the corner of her eyes. "I love you, too," she whispered.

Jordan let out the huge breath Ariel didn't even notice he was holding. *Wait, did he actually think I wouldn't say it back?* Ariel watched him as he fidgeted with the keys hanging from the ignition. He actually seemed a little nervous, which was starting to make Ariel sweat. "Is there more?" she asked.

"I'm not sure how to bring this up," he said. "But knowing you love me too helps."

Ariel could feel her ears burning. What was he going to say now? He just said the three words she had been longing to hear for so long, and wanted to say herself but didn't have the courage to go first.

"Remember how I told you I was going to open up a garage with a buddy of mine?"

"Yeah," Ariel said slowly.

"Well, we've been looking at places to buy and every time we do, my heart feels sick. If I open up a garage in

Utah, I will have to stay in Utah. The thought of not seeing you every day, well, it just makes my heart ache. I know that sounds really cheesy, but there it is. So, how would you feel if I moved to California with you this summer?"

Ariel launched herself at Jordan, but her seatbelt yanked her back in place. She reached over and unclicked the restraint, yanking it off her chest and shoving it out of the way. She threw her arms around Jordan's neck and began kissing him all over his face, while hot, happy tears rolled down her cheeks. Jordan laughed and pulled her down onto his lap, wrapping his arms around her slender waist. "So will you open the garage in California instead?"

Jordan bit his lip. "Well, that's where the problem lies. I can't afford a shop in California. Land is just too expensive there. I know I could find a job and save up, and then maybe a few more years down the road I'll have enough to look into buying my own garage again."

"Wait, so you're telling me you would come to California with me, but that you'd have to give up your dream first? I don't want you to give up your dream for me!" Ariel said, sliding off his lap. Her elation from moments before deflated as quickly as it began.

"Ariel," Jordan said, holding her hand and intertwining their fingers together. "You are my new dream."

A small cry escaped Ariel's lips and she covered them with her hand. "But…" She tried to think of something else to say but couldn't find any words.

Jordan kissed her on the top of her head and squeezed his arms even more tightly around her middle. "No buts," he said gently. "A garage will still be there five or ten years from now. I'm not giving up that dream. I'm just putting it on hold for a little while. But you, Ariel, you are here and you are now. I'm not willing to give you up for anything!"

Ariel couldn't believe what she was hearing. Was she dreaming? Would Jordan wake up tomorrow, or a month from now, or even a year down the road and regret his decision? Would he end up resenting her for it?

When Ariel remained silent, Jordan whispered her name again. "Are you okay?" he asked.

"I just don't want you to regret this and end up hating me for it," she whispered back.

"Never!" he said, kissing her neck. "There are hundreds, if not thousands of garages in Utah and California alone. But there is only one Ariel Princess."

\*\*\*

The following week, Ariel and Aurora came home from school to find their mother crying at the kitchen table. Ariel carefully set her books on the counter and slid into the seat beside her.

"Mom?" she asked.

Rachel looked up, noticing the girls for the first time. "I'm sorry," she said, frantically swiping at her tears. "I didn't hear you come in."

Aurora sat on the opposite side of Rachel. "What's wrong?"

Rachel tried to wave it off, but the girls would not be deterred. That's when Ariel noticed the crumpled paper Rachel had fisted in her hand.

"What's this, Mom?" Ariel asked, taking the paper from her.

"It's nothing," Rachel said reaching out and trying to grab it back. She was too late—Ariel was already reading the letter.

"This is from USC," she said, glancing at her mom over the top of the paper. Ariel scanned through the letter and realized it was an invoice for her first semester's tuition. Ariel stared at the numbers following the dollar sign. Was that how much every semester was going to cost? Ariel's eyes widened while she stared at the impossibility of her future. All the plans she and Jordan had made over the last several days seemed to suddenly poof away in a cloud of smoke. Ariel knew her mom couldn't afford this. She wasn't even sure she would qualify for student loans of this magnitude.

Rachel shook her head as she wiped her nose with a tissue. "I'm so sorry, Ariel," she whispered.

Ariel wanted to say something to help her mom feel better, like it really isn't that big a deal anyway. Her voice became a huge lump in her throat and she was unable to speak. Ariel simply nodded toward her mom and hoped it was enough. She quietly excused herself and trudged off down the hall. The last thing she wanted to do was make her mom feel bad, yet she couldn't hide her emotions any longer when it felt like her soul was splitting inside.

Ariel slipped out the front door and began walking down the sidewalk. Despite the cold breeze, she felt numb to the frosty air. Without thinking, she found herself on Jordan's front stoop. Her arms folded across her chest after knocking first.

"What's the matter?" Jordan asked, seeing her tear-stained face.

Ariel leaned forward and allowed herself to fall into Jordan's arms. He held her firmly in place until she was ready to talk. After several minutes of standing in the open doorway, Ariel began to shiver. Jordan scooped her up and carried her inside, and then he sat on the couch with her cradled in his lap.

Ariel finally spoke in a quiet voice. "It looks like you might get your garage after all," she said.

"I told you, babe, I choose you first."

"It doesn't look like we're going to be able to come up with the money for me to go away to school after all."

"What?" Jordan couldn't hide the surprise in his voice.

"With the cost of out-of-state tuition, plus housing, plus books, plus the cost of living, like food and other random things, it just all adds up to be more than we can even fathom."

Jordan thought for a moment. "We can't let money get in the way of your future and your dreams. There's gotta be something we can do."

Ariel shrugged. "Like what?"

She could feel Jordan shake beneath her and when he spoke, his voice had a definite tremble. "Like, what if we move in together?" Jordan asked.

"What?" Ariel began to shake herself. It felt like the temperature in the room suddenly shot up twenty degrees. Her head ached.

"Well, I'm going to have to find an apartment anyway. Why don't we just get one together? That way we can share food and you'll still have a roof over your head, but the only thing you'll have to pay for is school."

Ariel sat back, her head resting against the soft cushions behind it and closed her eyes. On the one hand, her heart swelled at the idea of coming home to Jordan. On the other hand, moving in with her boyfriend went against everything she had ever been taught. Her throat became dry and her head spun. "I don't know, Jordan, I…I'll have to think about it."

Jordan seemed disappointed. "Oh, okay," he said sadly. He set Ariel on the couch and rose to his feet. He crossed the room and stood in front of the large window, staring outside.

"Jordan, I love you. I just don't want to ruin the relationship we have now."

"And you think living with me will kill us? Wow, I thought we were on the same page, but I guess maybe not." Jordan walked from the room, his shoulders hunched and his head hung down.

Ariel found herself alone in his living room. When he didn't come back after several minutes, she slid from his couch and slipped out the front door.

\*\*\*

Ariel didn't know what to do. She and Jordan had never really fought before. Now, even days later, they were barely speaking. Jordan suddenly seemed really busy with work. Ariel tried texting him to see if they could talk, but she always got one word responses, or no response at all.

Ariel pushed the door open to her sister's hair school and stepped inside. She didn't really want to be there. She'd rather be wallowing in her jammies in bed, eating a lot of chocolate, and watching Netflix, but she needed a haircut and Aurora begged her to come. She really needed the hours and the practice so she could graduate. Ariel found her sister's chair and plopped down with a huff.

"Still no Jordan?"

Ariel scowled.

"I'll take that as a no," Aurora whispered. She raised her comb and her scissors up for Ariel to see. "So, do you want me to give you a sexy cut and color that will blow

Jordan's mind, so he'll see what he's really missing?" She added a maniacal laugh at the end of her suggestion.

Ariel was half tempted to say yes, out of spite. Jordan was acting like a big baby, but she also still loved him. "No," she finally said. "Something simple. Jordan really likes my hair long."

"What about a long A-line?" Aurora asked.

Ariel thought for a moment. "Yeah, okay. As long as my hair still stays pretty long in the front. It might be fun to try something a little different. I've had the same haircut since like seventh grade."

Aurora crinkled her nose as she raised a chunk of blonde locks. "Yeah, I know."

"Hey!"

"Well, seriously, Ari, try something new and fun once in a while."

"Fine. Just cut a quarter inch all the way around, giving it a nice, even trim." She folded her arms against her chest and glowered at her twin.

Aurora dropped Ariel's hair and looked at her reflection in the mirror. "Seriously?" she asked, eyes wide.

"No, do the A-line. And maybe give me some bangs." Ariel shifted in her seat and picked up a magazine.

"Now you're talkin'!" Aurora got to work. She sprayed and brushed and snipped, all the while Ariel flipped through her magazine without looking up.

Ariel finally got bored with which star wore it best and glanced at her sister's reflection in the mirror. Aurora was pulling on the strands of wet hair behind Ariel's head. She stretched them out to be sure the opposite sides were the same length. The harder Aurora concentrated, Ariel noticed the corner of her mouth would part and she'd poke out her tongue. Ariel snickered. She'd never seen her sister do that before.

"What are you laughing at?" Aurora said, stopping her scissors and straightening up.

"Nothing," Ariel said. "You're just cute. You take this very seriously."

"Well, this is my career and my passion. Would you rather I goof off and just snip in any old place?"

"No," Ariel said, trying to hide her snickering. "I think you're awesome. I've just never seen you concentrate on anything so hard before."

Aurora looked at her sister crossly. "You better watch it," she said. "I'm the one holding scissors and I have access to a lot of dye."

Ariel straightened up and pulled her lips into a serious, straight line. "I'll behave," she promised. "Speaking of dye though," she said, loosening her shoulders again, "where's the mean girl who tried to make you look bad?"

The corners of Aurora's mouth turned up and she glanced around the room. "That's her," she whispered, indicating the girl with a nod of her head. Aurora faked a need for Ariel to be facing the other direction as she spun her chair to face her nemesis. "Sara is the one with the curly brown hair," Aurora whispered. They watched for a moment as Sara nervously snipped an old lady's hair. They continued to watch with amusement as the teacher came over, shook her head, and proceeded to redo everything she had already tried.

Aurora spun Ariel to face the mirror once again. She let out a long, happy sigh. "That feels good," she said. After she finished styling Ariel's hair to accentuate her new cut, Aurora went to find her instructor to come review. The instructor gave Aurora's work nothing but praise. "You are a natural, my dear," she said. "Your sister looks simply stunning!"

Aurora turned to see Sara sneering in her direction. She smiled and waved. Sara turned around in a huff and began cleaning her work station.

"Oh, give it a rest, Sara!" Ruby said as she walked past.

Aurora laughed and turned back to Ariel, removing her cape. "There, now go knock him dead."

Ariel's face fell. "I don't know what else to do," she admitted.

"Walk straight up to him and kiss him," Aurora said. "Then talk to him about how you're feeling. Couples fight. They just do. A fight doesn't mean things are over. It just means you haven't worked it out yet."

"How did you get so smart about relationships?" Ariel asked. She was starting to feel a little better. Maybe a fresh haircut was even better than chocolate and Netflix.

"I'm just brilliant," Aurora said, smiling. "Now go, my next client will be here soon."

Grandma B. walked in the door as Ariel was leaving. "Grandma!" she said, hugging her. "How are you? Is Aurora cutting your hair, too?"

"I'm doing well, sweetie. How are you these days?"

Ariel looked down at her shoes. "I'm okay," she mumbled.

Grandma B. took Ariel's hand and guided her over to some wooden benches, for waiting clients. "Spill everything, girly. A grandma knows when she's not being told the whole truth. Why are you so glum?"

Ariel explained her money worries to Grandma B. as well as Jordan's solution, her uneasiness to his solution, and their fight because of it.

"Oh, darling, I wanted to surprise you with this for graduation, but it seems like now would be better." Grandma B. patted Ariel's hand and continued, "I want to help pay for your college."

Ariel looked at her grandma, unsure. "What?" she said, not allowing herself to believe it.

"I've been saving my money for a lot of years and honestly, I'm old. What am I gonna do with it? I want to see my granddaughters succeed and find happiness in the paths you choose. This way you can still keep your same convictions and go to school without stressing about having leftover money to eat."

"Oh, Grandma, I just don't even know what to say!" Ariel hugged her grandma. "Is this for real?" she asked.

"Yes, dear," Grandma B. laughed, "this is for real. I'll call your mom and talk to her about it tonight. But right now, you need to go have a frank conversation with that boy, and I need to go have my hair trimmed."

Ariel felt better after talking to Aurora and Grandma B. Then she got in the car to drive home. She began to question everything all over again. What would happen if she was completely honest with Jordan? Could she lose him over this? Ariel's mind was so torn, she missed her street and kept on driving. She didn't realize her mistake until several minutes down the road.

She sighed deeply and made a U-turn at the next corner. The lump in Ariel's throat grew bigger as she drove. Her emotions threatened to spill over. If she didn't move in with Jordan, she might actually make the wedge between them even bigger. Could she live without him? On the other hand, if she gave up her beliefs for him, could she live with herself? Ariel's head pounded and her eyes stung. She looked up in time to realize she missed her turn again.

# Chapter Twenty-Four

Ariel found Jordan working on his dad's car outside, in front of their condo. She had him cornered. There was no excuse he could use to get away this time. Ariel sat on the curb beside his car and waited. Jordan slid out from under the hood and stood to get another tool. Ariel held his toolbox on her lap. He saw her and smiled, shaking his head.

"You caught me," he said.

"We need to talk," Ariel said, setting his tools on the curb beside her. She got to her feet and took a few steps toward Jordan until they stood toe to toe. Ariel wove both her hands around Jordan's neck and played with the short hair resting on his nape. Jordan shivered and smiled down at her. Ariel then pulled his face closer and she kissed him.

When she stepped back, she kept her hands around his neck so he couldn't escape again. "I love you, Jordan Johnson," she said, "but I don't appreciate the way you've been treating me lately." She looked at him stubbornly.

Jordan smiled at her, but she could still see the hurt behind his eyes. "I'm sorry, babe. I just didn't know what else to do. I really felt like maybe I was in this more than you were."

Ariel released Jordan and leaned against his dad's car. Jordan placed his hands around her small waist and hoisted her up so she was sitting on the hood. She wrapped her legs around his middle, with Jordan's hands resting on both her thighs. "You know what my mom does for a living, right?" Ariel asked.

"Yeah, isn't she a therapist of some kind?"

"Yes, she specializes in family and couples therapy. She got into it after everything went down with my dad. She wanted to help other women stay out of abusive relationships. And she wanted to see families succeed. My sister and I didn't exactly grow up with an ideal family. I've never known what it's like to have a dad. My mom tries to help couples who are struggling so more families can have the stability of two parents."

"Okay," Jordan said. He looked at Ariel quizzically.

"So one thing my mom has drilled into us, because of sound research," she added, "was that most couples who rush into moving in together end up failing. It's like our relationship is little baby kindling," Ariel said. "If you pour gas on that tiny kindling, just starting out, the gas will engulf it and we'll both burn up." Ariel peeked at Jordan to gauge his reaction. "Does that make sense?" she asked. "Moving in together right now would be too huge a thing for our little relationship to handle."

Jordan cocked his head like he was thinking about her words, but didn't fully grasp them yet. "Okay," he said again slowly.

"And I promised myself and my mom many years ago that the first man I live with will be my husband. It doesn't mean I love you any less," Ariel said, reaching out and stroking his face. "You have no idea how tempting an offer it was for me! I really love you, and I don't want to do anything that might screw this up."

Jordan leaned forward and kissed Ariel's soft pink lips. "I love you, too," he said. "I'm sorry. I don't want to do anything to compromise what you believe. I may not agree with all of it," Jordan said, "but I love you and I want to respect your beliefs."

Ariel smiled. "Does that mean our fight is over?"

Jordan pretended to brush his hands off. "The fight is over," he agreed. "I'm really sorry I didn't understand."

"Now do you want to hear the good news?" Ariel asked.

"Absolutely," Jordan said, squeezing her thighs.

"Grandma B. offered to help pay for school!" she said. "Looks like I'm really going to USC after all."

Jordan hugged her. "Babe, that's great! Now I just need to find an apartment close to campus. And possibly a roommate."

*** 

Ariel sat on Jordan's lap as they scrolled through apartment listings near campus.

"I think you definitely need to be looking for roommates," Ariel said. Her eyes widened as they scanned over another outrageous price.

"Well, it is California. Thankfully I don't need anything very big or fancy."

"A bed, maybe? And preferably a working bathroom?"

"Sounds about right," Jordan said, nodding.

Ariel's phone rang loudly. She and Jordan exchanged a quizzical look. "But I'm right here," Jordan said.

"I know, that's exactly what I was thinking." Ariel scooped her phone off the desk and glanced at the number. Her eyebrows furrowed. "It's Dave," she said, still looking confused. Ariel shrugged and finally pushed the answer button. "Hello?"

Ariel leaned back against Jordan as she listened to Dave's request. Her sudden movement almost tipped the unstable chair over and she sat up quickly, steadying herself. Jordan stifled a laugh and Ariel had to remove the phone from her ear so Dave wouldn't hear her giggles. "Sure Dave, I can help you with that, but listen, I'm at Jordan's house right now. Can I call you back when I get home? Great. Bye."

Ariel dropped her phone on the floor and she and Jordan burst into laughter.

"I thought you were going to tip us for sure!" Jordan chuckled, shaking his head.

"Can you imagine the sound effects Dave would have overheard?"

"So what did Dave want anyway?" Jordan asked.

"He wants to ask Belle to prom and he needs some help with ideas. So, naturally, he came to me." Ariel flipped her shortened blonde hair over one shoulder and waggled her eyebrows at Jordan. He grinned in return.

"Prom, huh? He does realize she lives like 700 miles away, right?"

Ariel shrugged. "I'm guessing he hopes she can fly out for it. Maybe that's part of what he needs help with."

She sighed and took control of the computer. Opening a new tab, she did a google search for "creative ways to ask to prom." She and Jordan spent the next hour reading over people's ideas and responses.

"I can't believe this is really how teenagers date here," Jordan said, scooting back from the computer and, sliding Ariel from his lap, he got to his feet.

"It's so normal to me I can't believe other places don't do it."

"I can't picture anyone from my high school being that cheesy," Jordan stretched. "The whole thing seems really stupid."

Ariel knew she shouldn't be offended. After all, it's not like she was the one who invented this tradition. Jordan's words stung nonetheless. "How did you ask your dates to a dance then?" she asked, trying to hide the hurt in her voice.

"I never went," Jordan said. "Dances really aren't my thing."

Ariel's heart fell.

"I'm going to run downstairs and grab some water. Do you want anything?"

"Sure," Ariel nodded. As soon as Jordan left the room, she opened another tab and did a search for prom dresses. She scrolled through the images, hovering over a particularly beautiful green one. Ariel didn't see when Jordan returned. She stared wistfully at the images on the screen until she heard him walk up behind her. She jumped, closing the dress tab and returned to asking rituals.

"Hey, listen to this one," Ariel said, reading off the first idea her eyes landed on.

Jordan leaned in over her shoulder and smiled.

\*\*\*

"Why is there butter on the floor?" Aurora asked, pushing open the front door after school the next day.

Ariel stopped in her tracks and looked down, barely missing a cube of butter with her shoe. Every few feet and trailing up the stairs, a cube of butter sat. The twins followed the dairy path, which led all the way to their bedroom door. Taped to their door was a message: *Ariel, Just thought I'd "butter" you up before "popping" the question. Will you go to prom with me?*

Ariel pushed the door open and her jaw dropped. Their floor, dresser, bed, and desk were completely covered in a layer of bright, colorful balloons. Ariel dove in, quickly sinking to the floor as a pile of latex overcame her.

Aurora laughed. "Are you in there?"

Ariel reached a hand through the balloons and waved it around. "Still alive!" she sang out.

Ariel's face flushed and her heart began to race. She and Aurora began popping the sea of balloons as quickly as they could. What are the odds anyone else would have asked her the next day? It had to be Jordan, right? After popping what felt like hundreds of balloons, Ariel stuck her pin in a fat blue one. A piece of paper flew through the air. Ariel snatched it up and saw the name *Jordan* looking up at her. Ariel's smile split her face. She felt as though her heart might burst. He really did love her.

# Chapter Twenty-Five

Snow White closed her locker and jumped back in surprise. Dave stood behind the metal door, making a face at her. "Geeze!" she said. "Are you trying to give me a heart attack?"

"Did it work?" Dave's goofy grin lit up his face. "So I have a question for you," he said, placing an arm over Snow White's shoulder as she headed for her next class. "Would you be interested in a blind date?" he asked.

Snow White stuck out her tongue. "Ugh! Why?"

"Because I might know a guy who has a crush on this really cute redhead, but she may not know of his existence."

"What?" Snow White asked.

"I'm serious," Dave said. "One of the guys on my football team thinks you're really cute and he's been wanting to ask you out, but he's kind of shy. And he also is convinced you don't even know he exists."

"Are you sure you have the right Princess?" Snow White asked skeptically. "I think he might be more interested in one of the tall, beautiful ones."

"Come on, Snow White, give yourself a little credit!" Dave said. "You are beautiful. I mean, I totally kissed you once and I'm not into ugly girls."

Snow White shoved him hard. "Yeah, you kissed me to win a bet!" she said.

Dave regained his balance and returned to Snow White's side. "I never would have taken on the bet if you weren't all extremely attractive," he said. "I'm really just that shallow."

Snow White laughed. "Can you at least tell me this mystery boy's name?" she asked.

"Justin Call," Dave said. "Do you know him?"

The name sounded familiar to Snow White, but she couldn't picture a face right away. "I'm not sure," she admitted.

"So, will you have dinner with him tomorrow night?" Dave asked.

Snow White stared hard at Dave. She kept waiting for him to laugh and say just kidding, but he didn't even crack a smile. "You're sure he said my name?"

"Oh my gosh, Snow White. Here," Dave said. He pulled her over in front of a mirror and made her look into it. "What do you see?" he asked.

"I see the chubby, awkward version of my cousins," Snow White said.

Dave rolled his eyes. "Do you wanna know what I see? I see a girl with beautiful red hair, amazingly intense green eyes, full kissable lips, gorgeous skin, and curves that most guys dream about. The only thing wrong with this picture is her confidence needs a little bit of work. Guys don't like girls who dig on themselves. So think about that and let me know about tomorrow night." Dave walked toward his own class and left Snow White standing in front of the mirror.

During English, Snow White carefully pulled out her cell phone and quickly typed 'I'm in.' She put her phone away and tried to concentrate on her work.

***

"What did I get myself into?" Snow White paced back and forth in her small room. "Why am I doing this?"

Cinderella started getting dizzy just watching her constant movement. "Snow, sit!" she commanded. "I can't finish your makeup if you don't hold still!"

Snow White sat in her desk chair but continued to fidget. Cinderella rubbed her arms from her shoulders down to her wrists. "Deep breaths," she said. "You're doing this because a boy likes you, and why wouldn't he?"

Snow White opened her mouth to speak but Cinderella cut her off and put up a finger. "Don't answer that," she said. Cinderella carefully outlined Snow White's green eyes with a dark purple eyeliner. She then put the finishing touches on her smoky eyes and took a step back to admire her work. "Here," she said, handing Snow White a tube of lipstick. "I think this color will look best with your fair skin."

Snow White leaned toward her mirror and swiped the tube across each of her lips. She rubbed them together and puckered for Cinderella. "What do you think?" she asked.

Cinderella smiled. "I think you're ready," she said.

Snow White's heart raced. Her palms were already starting to sweat and he wasn't even here yet! She shook her head. "I'm not sure I can do this," she said.

"You can and you will." Cinderella tried to offer her encouragement.

"But the only other dates I've been on have been dances, with you guys. There was always a conversation going. What if neither of us can think of things to say? What if we both just stare at each other all night and we can't find anything to talk about?"

"Then you'll chalk it up to experience," Cinderella said. "Not all dates are going to be amazing. Some will be good and some will be bad. In the end, at least you get free dinner."

Snow White forced a smile. She tried taking deep breaths but she couldn't help worry. The doorbell downstairs rang and she was suddenly out of time.

"He's here!" Cinderella squealed. She gave Snow White a quick hug. "Have so much fun! Be yourself and just relax," she said. "I'll stay up here and then slip out after you leave."

Snow White nodded and waved goodbye. She forced her heavy feet to move down each stair. She took another deep breath and opened the door.

"Hi, Snow White, I'm Justin."

Justin was shorter than Snow White guessed he would be, but he was still taller than she was, which really wasn't a difficult feat. Broad-shouldered and stocky, he had the build of a football player. He had a sweet, genuine smile which Snow White returned. She was immediately drawn to his eyes. They weren't really blue. They seemed almost grey. Whatever color they were, Snow White knew she would be just fine looking into those eyes for the evening.

He led her toward a waiting beige sedan. Snow White stood by the passenger door while Justin walked around to the driver's side. He was about to climb in when he noticed her still standing there. "Oh!" he said, running back around the car. Justin quickly opened her door. He blushed and apologized. "Sorry," he kept saying over and over again.

"Don't worry about it," Snow White tried to calm his nerves. "Dave and his brother sort of spoiled me into expecting it, but I know a lot of guys don't open doors anymore."

"But my mom taught me to. I just don't go out very often and I forget," he stammered.

"Why don't you go out very often?" Snow White asked as he climbed into his own seat.

"I'm not really sure how to talk to girls," he said. He looked ahead at the road as he spoke. Snow White noticed his ears turned pink.

"You're the first guy to ever ask me out," Snow White admitted. She could tell Justin had turned to look at her, but she stared out her window at the passing cars rather than see his reaction.

"Really?" he asked. "I have a hard time believing that. What about Dave?"

"What do you mean?" Snow White asked.

"Well, I thought maybe you and Dave had a thing going at some point. I've seen you guys together a lot at school. It took me a long time to get the nerve to ask Dave about you guys. He assured me you weren't dating."

Snow White laughed. Is that why she never got asked out? Because of her friendship with Dave? "Dave is like a brother to me. He's actually the only guy I can really talk to and I think that's because he's more like family than a guy. I'm not intimidated by him."

"Really?" Justin's voice sounded hopeful.

"Yes, really," Snow White said. "In fact, he's like crazy madly in love with my cousin Belle. So no, there's definitely nothing between the two of us."

Justin glanced at Snow White and they exchanged a small smile. "Do you like Olive Garden?" he asked, pulling into the parking lot.

"Love it," Snow White said.

Justin parked and climbed out of the car. He almost made it to the door when he turned and realized Snow

White wasn't behind him. Snow White realized she liked to watch his ears turn pink when he realized he'd forgotten her door again.

"Sorry," he mumbled as he opened her door.

Snow White smiled. "It's okay," she said. "If you want me to, I can just open my own doors."

"No, I want to do it for you," Justin assured her. He stepped ahead and held the door to the restaurant open. "After you," he said.

Snow White stepped inside. Her stomach rumbled at the smell of garlic and bread and cheese mingled together. She flushed. "Sorry," she said, "I guess I'm hungry."

Justin put his name on the waiting list and they sat side-by-side on the bench. Snow White wasn't sure what to say next. Why was her brain suddenly completely blank? She couldn't think of a single question she wanted to ask him. Justin appeared to be having the same problem. He glanced around the restaurant, but never at Snow White. The more time that passed, the more awkward Snow White felt. After ten minutes of waiting, Snow White felt like she'd missed her chance. *Now if I say anything, it will just seem forced because so much time has passed*, she thought. She was tempted to pull out her cell phone, but she didn't want to be rude to her date.

After what felt like an eternity of sitting, Justin turned to her. "So what do you like to do?" he asked.

"I love movies," Snow White said. "My cousins and I watch movies all the time. What about you? Do you have a favorite movie?"

"I actually don't watch a lot of movies," Justin said, shaking his head. "But I love watching sports, especially football. If the TV is on at my house, it's because there's a game on."

"Wow," Snow White said. "Do you have any brothers or sisters?"

"I have five brothers."

"Five? Wow!" Snow White was starting to wonder if they were going to have anything in common.

"Yeah, and we all love sports. Especially my dad. Well, I guess he's probably the reason we love them so much. My dad started teaching us how to throw and catch a ball from the time we could walk. Maybe before. Does your dad like football?"

Snow White pictured the man with the large red, bushy beard and the dark, beady little eyes. Her mind flashed to the way he had stared at her with pure hatred in his eyes. She shivered at the unexpected memory. "No, it's just me and my mom," she said.

"No brothers or sisters? Wow, Must be quiet."

"Yeah," Snow White said, still trying to shake his dark image from her mind. "It's usually pretty quiet."

They still had lulls in the conversation throughout dinner, but overall Snow White felt like they got along pretty well, especially considering they were both introverts. After Justin paid the check, he made sure to hold open the restaurant door for Snow White. He remembered to open her car door first before climbing in himself. He beamed as he got behind the wheel again. "I remembered!" he said proudly.

Snow White congratulated him. "See, you can do it. All it takes is a little practice."

Justin began driving her home when he suddenly swerved into another parking lot.

"Whoa!"

"Sorry!" he said. "But do you want ice cream?"

Snow White looked up and noticed the little ice cream shop in front of them. *Teenage boys sure can eat!* She thought. She still felt completely full from the dinner she didn't even finish, but she also didn't want to end the night quite yet. "Sure," she said, trying to imagine how she could possibly fit more food into her stomach.

Justin jumped out and opened her door. "See!" he proudly claimed.

Snow White laughed. He was getting more comfortable with her, but she kinda missed seeing his cute pink ears when he blushed. They walked inside and after ordering a triple scoop for himself, Justin stepped aside. Snow White approached the counter and asked for a small chocolate cone.

"That's all you want?" Justin asked.

"Yeah, I'm not a big football player like you," she said. "I know it's boring, but simple chocolate is my favorite."

Justin shrugged and paid while the teenage girl behind the counter made their orders. When the girl was done, Snow White with her small cone and Justin with his monstrous one stepped outside. It was a warm night. The air was still and quiet. "Do you want to go for a walk?" Justin asked.

Snow White shrugged. "Sure," she said, taking another lick. They walked along the sidewalk, past several store fronts. Justin told Snow White about his hopes of playing college football while they walked. As he spoke, their hands accidentally bumped. "Sorry," Snow White said as warm tingles shot up her arm.

Justin asked Snow White about her plans for next year as he took another giant bite of ice cream. Snow White couldn't believe it! He was almost done with his large, triple-scoop cone and she was still licking hers, which didn't even look much smaller. Their fingers brushed again as Snow White told him how she was still unsure, but trying to decide between a couple options.

Justin popped the final piece of cone into his mouth and stopped Snow White. His voice shook as he spoke. "Can I, ummm...can I hold your hand?" he asked. His ears turned fuchsia and Snow White smiled.

"Yes," she said, reaching out to him.

Justin took her hand, interlocking their fingers and they walked back toward the car. Snow White knew her face must be beet red from all the heat she felt in her cheeks. Her hand and arm tingled from his touch. He paused beside Snow White's door and looked straight into her eyes. For a moment, Snow White thought he might kiss her and her heart began to race. This was the closest she had gotten to his face all night and upon closer look, his eyes were definitely grey. Grey with flecks of blue.

Justin reached around her and opened the door, helping Snow White inside. When he got behind the wheel, he reached for her hand, which she willingly gave. They talked about music as he drove her the short distance home. He walked Snow White up to her front door. She was happy for another opportunity to look into his beautiful eyes. She noticed the tips of his ears flush pink and wondered what he was thinking. Then he leaned in and gave her a quick hug.

"Goodnight, Snow White, thank you for going with me tonight," Justin said.

"Thank you. I had a great time," she replied.

He jumped from her porch and got in his car. Snow White watched him drive to the end of the street, and her heart skipped as she watched him turn around and head back to her. Justin climbed from his car and walked back to the porch. "Snow White, will you go to prom with me?" he asked. "I know it's not cute and original, but there it is. I'm not good at being creative."

Snow White's heart began to race, her face felt consumed with heat. "Sure," she said nodding.

"Okay." Justin backed up and returned to his car. Waving, he pulled away again. Snow White sighed happily and went inside.

# Chapter Twenty-Six

Aurora kissed This Week goodbye and walked into her beauty school for another day of work. Sara stood by the entrance, her nostrils flaring as she watched the exchange.

"Do you even know his name?" she asked snidely. "I heard you just call all the boys you date This Week," she said, using exaggerated air quotes. "Is that so you don't get their names all mixed up?" Sara stamped her tiny little foot as she spoke, making Aurora want to laugh, but she refrained. She remembered what Grandma B. had said about mean girls.

"Yes," Aurora said through gritted teeth, "I know Charlie's name. And no, I don't call any of the boys I choose to date This Week. That's an inside joke my sister and cousins came up with." Aurora was tempted to add another snide remark in return, but she balled her thought up into tight fists and walked inside the building.

They had a busy day ahead of them. They were nearing graduation, which meant more customers were willing to let the students cut their hair. Aurora got her station organized and soon found her chair filled with one client after another. Saturdays were always the busiest, but today was even busier than any of the previous weekends.

Aurora chatted happily with a little girl and her mom, an older gentleman, and then two preteen girls who giggled way too much. Aurora remembered being that age and she smiled patiently at them as she styled their hair in the same fashion as their favorite stars.

Aurora's hands were beginning to cramp, so she took a moment and shook them out after the giggly girls left. She grabbed her water bottle and took a long, slow swig before the next client plunked down in her chair and she was off again.

Aurora jerked up when she heard yelling from across the salon. A middle-aged woman with too-short hair was irate and yelling in Sara's face, who looked like she might burst into tears at any moment. Aurora wanted to feel smug, but she couldn't. Not after seeing the look on Sara's face. She just felt bad for her. The teacher came over and tried to smooth things over, even stepping in and trying to fix the cut herself.

Aurora smiled down at her client, a boy of about eleven, and began asking him questions about school. She tried to distract both him and herself from the embarrassing incident. The boy wasn't interested in talking much, but he smiled politely until Aurora was finished.

She looked at the clock and saw it was almost noon, her stopping time for lunch. Her instructor came over and Aurora breathed a sigh of relief. Her stomach rumbled, her back ached, and her fingers were starting to go numb. She began untying her apron. "Thank goodness!" she said. "I need a break!"

"Oh, shoot," her instructor said, grimacing. "I wasn't coming over here to relieve you. I was going to ask if you could go for another hour. I think Sara needs a break, and we have clients lined up outside the door.

Aurora stole a glance at Sara and found her sitting in a salon chair, with her head in her hands. "All right," Aurora nodded, "I guess I can go longer."

"Thank you, Aurora!" her teacher enthused. "I'd much rather have my best out on the floor during a busy day than my, well, anyway…" Her voice trailed off, and then she ran across the room to relieve Sara for lunch.

Aurora found a new sense of energy. Did her teacher really think she was the best? She beamed as she welcomed another client and chatted happily through the next hour.

Ruby came into the salon and waved at Aurora as she walked past. "Did you know people are asking for you?" she said.

"What?" Aurora was stunned. Usually the people who came to the school were looking for a good deal, which also meant they usually wanted to be done quickly, too.

Ruby nodded and gave her two thumbs up. "I could hear them as I walked past the front desk. 'I want the girl with the pink hair. How long is the wait for the girl with the pink hair?'"

Aurora glanced around to see if anyone else was listening. She happened to look up in time to see Sara, who was back from lunch, drop the razor she had been working with. It crashed to the floor with a thud, then continued to buzz in a circle before Sara bent down and grabbed it.

"Be more careful!" the instructor snapped.

Aurora felt a pit in her stomach as their teacher's scowl turned to a smile when she approached Aurora. "Looking fabulous," she said, touching the lady on her shoulder. "You can go to lunch when you're done here."

Aurora nodded and finished up with her client's bob before spinning her around and removing the cloak. "You're all set," Aurora smiled.

The woman stood inches from the mirror and examined her new cut. "That girl wasn't kidding," she said, handing Aurora a business card. "People are asking for you and I can see why. You have a natural talent for hair. I own a high-end salon in Salt Lake. I'd love to have you come work for me after graduation," she said.

Aurora's eyes widened as she examined the card. She wanted to jump up and down and scream with excitement. It took every ounce of self-control not to hug this strange woman. Instead she thanked her politely and put the card in her pocket. She couldn't wait to graduate!

After a short break, Aurora returned to her work station and was immediately given one client after another. She stole glances at Sara whenever she could to see how she was doing. A cute young girl bounded into the room and into Sara's chair. She looked over at Aurora and began crying. "No, I want her to do my hair! I want the pink lady!" She pointed as she wailed, so pretty soon the entire salon knew what she wanted. Aurora stared down at her own client's hair and tried to not look up. She was trying hard not to let Sara, or anyone else, see her smile. She wasn't trying to gloat, but her lip muscles were betraying her.

The mother of the little girl desperately tried to soothe her daughter. Her face looked strained and her eyes were tired. Both she and Sara were trying to get her to sit still in the chair, but she slid down so she lay on her back, with her legs flailing in the air. Aurora couldn't take it any longer. She grabbed something from her cupboard said, "I'll be right back," to her own client and calmly walked across the room.

Without looking at Sara or the mom, she approached the little girl and knelt down beside her chair. Upon seeing the pink lady, the little girl popped up in her seat and stared. Aurora looked the little girl straight in the eyes and said, "What's your name, sweetie?"

"Eliza," the girl mumbled with her fingers in front of her mouth.

"Did you know we have special treats here for big girls, Eliza?" She pulled a pink sucker out from behind her back and held it up. "We don't allow baby tantrums in the salon," she said, carefully holding the precious sucker over the garbage can.

"No!" the little girl reached a hand out to try and rescue it.

Aurora held the sucker inches from the girl's face. "Now, do you want this?"

"Yes!" the girl giggled eagerly, swinging her legs back and forth.

"Then you need to sit up and act like a super big girl while Miss Sara cuts your hair, okay?"

The girl made a pouty lip. "But why can't you cut it?"

"Because it's not my turn. Right now it's Miss Sara's turn. But I'll make you a deal. If you can be so super good and hold still for Miss Sara, when she's done cutting your hair, you can come over to my chair and I'll put a little bit of pink in your hair, okay?"

The mom's eyes widened and Aurora stood. "It washes right out," she whispered. The mom looked relieved and nodded. Aurora knelt back down, holding the sucker in front of her face again. "So Eliza, do we have a deal?"

Eliza snatched the sucker and giggled eagerly as she sat back in her chair. Sara put the cape over her and looked at Aurora with widened eyes. Aurora patted her on the back and returned to her own work station.

Aurora glanced up a few minutes later and was happy to see the little girl was calmly sucking on her pink sucker and acting like a little angel for Sara. Aurora smiled to herself. A few minutes later, when Aurora had finished with the lady she had been working on, Eliza came skipping over to her. She climbed up into the high chair and proclaimed, "I want my pink now."

"Please?" Aurora said.

The girl looked at her like she'd spoken a foreign word. Aurora continued to watch her, one eyebrow raised. When the little girl realized she wasn't backing down, she sighed and conceded. "Please?" she finally asked.

Aurora nodded and wrapped the cape around her neck again. After a couple quick sprays she held up a small mirror for the girl to look in. "See?" she said. "You and I are like twins now."

The little girl squealed in delight as she looked at her own reflection. She jumped from the chair and climbed into her mother's arms. "Mommy, look! Look it! I'm just like the pink lady now!"

The mother thanked Aurora profusely before leading her precocious daughter out of the salon. Aurora straightened her apron and cleaned up her work area to prepare for the next customer.

Ruby stopped by her station for a quick break. "That was awfully nice of you," she said, nodding her head in Sara's direction. Aurora looked up in time to see Sara scowling at her. She shrugged.

"I'm not going to waste my energy holding a grudge."

"I don't think I could be that nice to someone who was so mean to me," Ruby said in a low whisper.

Aurora glanced at Sara again. She looked frazzled and stressed. As much as she wanted to, Aurora couldn't stay angry with her. She just felt sorry for her. "I truly hope she finds a way to be happy."

Ruby laughed. "I think she just enjoys being miserable."

"That's what I mean," Aurora said. "I hope she can learn how to be happy, because what she's doing so far isn't working. It's sad."

"Are we taking a break, ladies?" the instructor said in passing.

"Sorry," Ruby mumbled. She exchanged a smile with Aurora and went back to her own station.

Aurora called for her next client and was surprised to see This Week, who'd given her a ride to the salon earlier in the morning, walking toward her with flowers in his hand.

He approached Aurora carefully, a half grin on his eager face. He stepped forward and kissed Aurora's cheek before handing her the small bouquet of daisies. He climbed into her chair and smiled at her through the mirror.

"Just a trim, please," he said.

Aurora set the daisies down and looked at him quizzically. "What are you doing here, Charlie?" she asked.

"I wanted to see you and I wanted to run an idea past you," he said. "I know you don't normally date guys for more than a week or two, but I'm having fun with you and I don't want to stop. So I have a proposition for you. Will you go with me to prom? It's our last big dance of high school, and I don't want to go with anyone but you."

Aurora began squirting Charlie's hair and running a comb through it while she thought. In all her dates throughout high school, no one had ever asked her to stay with him. Several of them had mentioned it, but then when the week was actually up, they had all parted ways without much fuss. Aurora was completely shocked. "You won't be sick of me after three weeks?" she asked.

Charlie's eyes lit up. "Not a chance."

Aurora smiled shyly at him and began buzzing the nape of his neck with the razor. "Okay," she said, nodding. "Let's go to prom."

Charlie's smile stretched across his entire face. "Can I take you to a movie tonight after work?"

"I don't know. That might be pushing it." She winked at him.

# Chapter Twenty-Seven

As Belle walked through the halls of her new school, a huge pink banner which hung from the ceiling caught her attention. The words Senior Prom splashed across it.

She thought of all her cousins going to their own prom back in Layton in just a couple weeks and her stomach tightened. The last big dance of their high school career and she wouldn't even be going with her cousins. They'd spent every other dance for the last three years together. And for the last two years, her date had consistently been Craig. Her heart still stung a little at the thought of him. Belle looked up at the banner again, overwhelmed by the sudden urge to tear it down. She wanted to be excited for it, she really did, but the word prom only made her think of all the people she missed.

As Belle walked down the cement steps after school, she glanced across the street. Her eyes caught sight of something and she had to do a double take. No, Dave couldn't be in California. Her eyes must be playing tricks on her. Belle glanced around again but there was no sign of the cute guy in a blue baseball cap. She shook her head and turned the corner to where her car was parked.

After she arrived home, Belle tossed her backpack onto a kitchen chair and plopped down. She flipped through the stack of auditions her father had left on the kitchen table. He was working hard to try and find her an agent. The idea equally scared and excited her. Did she really want to be an actress, like her parents? Belle pushed the papers aside and reached into her backpack so she could start on homework. Along with her math book came a flyer they had passed out at school. More information about prom night.

Belle climbed out of her seat and walked over to the refrigerator. She pulled the door open and stared at the contents inside without really seeing anything. She finally grabbed a can of Dr. Pepper and returned to her table.

Belle thought she could hear some faint music playing. She stood once more to investigate. Walking through the house, Belle couldn't find the source of the music anywhere. As she passed by the heavy front door, Belle decided to open it, and she found the music was louder outside. She walked to the end of the driveway, following the sound of music, where two large, iron gates stood guard in front of the house. Belle approached the gate and squinted into the bright sun. She stopped in her tracks and froze mid-step.

Dave stood on the other side of the heavy gates, holding his iPod in an outstretched palm and a small speaker in the other. Belle couldn't quite tell what song he was playing. Just like the mystery guy she saw earlier, Dave wore a blue baseball cap. He smiled eagerly as Belle approached him. She typed in a code and stood back as the iron gates creaked open. Dave stepped forward. He paused the music, setting his device on the grass. He shoved his hands into his pockets and kicked at the ground. "I hope it's okay that I'm here," he said.

Belle rushed forward and threw her arms around his neck, almost knocking Dave off balance. He wrapped his arms around her waist and held her tightly against him. "Well, in that case, I better head home," he said, pretending to leave.

Belle held onto him even tighter. "Don't ever leave me again," she whispered.

Dave clung to her and closed his eyes. "Done," he whispered.

When she finally took a step back, Belle realized her eyes were moist. "How did you know?" she asked.

"Know what?"

"That I was feeling homesick and really needed a friend right now," Belle said. Dave deflated a little at her use of the word friend.

"I'm just amazing, I guess," Dave grinned. "Actually, I wish I could take all the credit, but I'm here with my mom. She's helping me look at the campus and housing for next semester. She wanted to run a few errands, so I asked her to drop me off on her way."

"So was that you I saw at my school, too?"

Dave looked embarrassed. "I wanted to come say hi, but then I decided we could probably talk easier if I just followed you home."

"Oh, so you were stalking me?" Belle asked with a glint in her eye.

"Yeah, basically," Dave said.

Belle led Dave into her house as they spoke.

"Wow, this place is huge!" Dave said, looking around from the vaulted ceilings to the vast staircase that greeted them in the entryway.

"Yeah," Belle said. "It's a big adjustment from the condo, that's for sure." She led the way through the entrance into the kitchen, where she reached in the fridge and pulled out a soda for Dave.

Dave sat beside her at the tall kitchen table and took a swig from his cold drink. "I have to admit something," he said. "I had ulterior motives for coming to California.

Finding housing was how I convinced my mom to let me come, but I really just wanted to see you."

Belle felt her heart quicken. "Oh yeah?" She tried to act casual.

Dave placed one of his large, warm hands over Belle's. "Belle, do you think we could ever be a couple?"

Belle looked into his face. She had forgotten how easy it was to drown in his blue eyes. "I'm not sure, Dave," she admitted. "You shattered my heart once, so how can I trust you with it?"

"Time?" Dave answered her question with a question. "I'll spend months, years even, trying to make it up to you. I want you to trust me again. I'll do everything I can to protect your heart." Dave eyed Belle's lips eagerly as he leaned closer and closer toward her face. When she didn't push him away, Dave closed the gap and kissed her gently. Belle returned his kiss with force. She grabbed the back of his head, running her fingers over his hair as their lips met. Dave raised his right hand and cupped the side of Belle's face in it.

They only stopped kissing when the front door opened and they heard Mary's voice float in from the entrance. "Hello? Belle?"

Belle sat back, breathing heavily. "We're in here, Mom!"

"We?" Mary appeared a moment later. "Dave!" she said, unable to keep the surprise from her voice. She walked over to the table and took a long drink from Belle's Dr. Pepper.

"Hey!" Belle said, but Mary ignored her.

"So, to what do we owe this honor?" she asked.

"I'm in town looking at housing for next year," he said. "And, of course, to see Belle."

Mary looked from Belle to Dave and broke into laughter. "You two are back together, aren't you?"

"What?" Belle asked, fidgeting. "How could you possibly know that?"

Mary smiled. "Your messy hair is a dead giveaway that you two were kissing before I came in here."

As they exchanged a look of disbelief, Mary laughed even harder. Belle wished her chair would open up and swallow her. Dave looked like he was thinking about something similar.

"I'm sorry," Mary put her hands up in defense. "I'll leave you guys alone."

Belle picked up her drink and moved over to the couch. "I'm sorry," she said. "My mom can be so embarrassing!"

Dave followed suit and sat down right beside her. "I'm just glad she didn't up and slap me for kissing her daughter," he replied.

Belle smiled. "That would have been awesome to see, though," she said, her eyes lighting up with mischief.

"Gee, thanks," Dave grinned. "It probably would have been worse if we'd gotten caught by your dad. I still don't think he likes me much."

"Do you blame the guy? You did punch him in the face once," Belle teased.

"Oh, you had to bring that up," Dave moaned. "Do you think he'll ever come around to me?"

"Well, it depends on how trustworthy you remain," Belle said. "I don't think he would hold back his bodyguard from finding you if you ever break my heart again."

"Duly noted," he gulped.

"Oh, hi dad!" Belle waived over Dave's head.

Dave jumped and turned around to nothing. Belle burst into laughter. "You really are afraid of him, aren't you?" She doubled over on the couch.

"I am not," Dave grumbled. "You just surprised me, that's all."

Belle laughed until Dave grabbed her middle and began tickling her. "Oh, that's it!" he said. Belle squirmed and screamed as she tried to escape. Dave's phone began ringing in his pocket. Belle used the distraction to slide out from under Dave's hands and slip off the couch. He watched her through narrowed eyes as he answered his phone. "Hi, Mom."

Belle wandered away to give Dave some space. He found her a few minutes later in the den, scanning over the bookshelves that lined the room. "My mom is on her way back to pick me up," he said. "Can I see you again tomorrow?" he asked.

Belle smiled. "Probably," she said.

"Just probably?" Dave asked.

"Well, that depends on if my dad permits it. He'll find out tonight that you're in town. So we'll see how that goes first." Belle batted her eyelashes playfully at Dave.

Dave watched the corners of her mouth twitch and he realized she was teasing him. "You're such a brat!" he laughed.

Belle's smile widened. "Come on, my spunk is one of the reasons you love me so much."

Dave wrapped his arms around her waist from behind and hooked his chin over her shoulder. "It really is true," he said in a husky voice.

Belle could feel tingles creeping up her neck from Dave's voice. She closed her eyes and soaked in the moment. After tomorrow, Dave would return home and she would be all alone again. Mary appeared in the doorway. "Dave, your mom's here," she said.

Dave reluctantly let go of Belle. She turned and faced him. Dave glanced at Mary, who rolled her eyes. "Oh, for heaven's sake," she said, covering her eyes. Dave kissed Belle goodbye and then told Mary the coast was clear.

"See you tomorrow, Belle," Dave said. He turned to Mary. "Will you walk me out?"

Mary looked at him quizzically, but followed him out the front door. When she came back inside, Belle pounced. "What was that all about?" she asked.

"Oh, don't worry about it," Mary said. "You'll find out soon enough."

"But I want to know!" Belle protested.

"Oh, come on, let the boy have his secrets," Mary said.

The next day school seemed to drag for Belle. She wanted nothing more than to see Dave again. She couldn't wait to feel his muscular arms wrapped around her and his firm lips pressed against her own. Belle grinned when she came out of the school and found Dave leaning against her car. "Stalking me again today, huh?"

"Yes, but today is different because I'm not trying to pretend like I wasn't here."

Belle laughed. "Good plan."

Dave handed her a folded up map. "Do you mind if I drive and you can play navigator?"

Belle took the map and handed him her keys. "Be my guest."

"Thanks!" Dave said. He opened her door before climbing in himself.

Belle opened the map. "How do I look at this thing, anyway? Why don't you just use the GPS on your phone?"

"You'll see," Dave said.

Belle wrestled with the paper as she unfolded it. To her surprise, she found a homemade map inside, complete with little pictures that Dave had drawn and a squiggly line connecting the pictures until it ended with a large red X.

"Where do we go first?" Dave asked.

Belle glanced at the first picture, squinting her eyes to read what he'd written beside it. "Looks like we're going to the grocery store," she said.

"All right, navigator, get me there."

Belle guided Dave through the streets of her neighborhood until they pulled into the parking lot. Once inside the store, Dave gave Belle clues until they ended up in the bakery. When they came upon the brownies, Dave handed her a puzzle piece. Belle held it up and examined both sides. There were letters on the puzzle piece, but the letters weren't complete so it was too hard to read.

"The first time I met you, you were standing on my porch with a plate of delicious chocolatey brownies. I couldn't believe my luck! I had moved in across the street from five beautiful girls, but one of the girls really stuck out to me over the others. She had gorgeous blonde hair, beautiful tan skin, and wouldn't take crap from anyone. She was spunky and completely full of life."

"Oh! Oh!" Belle raised her hand eagerly. "Was it me?"

Dave smiled and kissed her.

"It was me," Belle grinned.

"Well, come on. We better go to the next stop if you're going to finish this puzzle."

Next, Belle guided them down the road to a McDonalds. They climbed out of the car and Dave walked around to the Redbox. He handed her another puzzle piece, which was indecipherable. "One day, a few weeks after I met the most amazing girl I'd ever known, I had the luck of spending a whole afternoon with her. We ended up outside a McDonalds to choose a movie, and we shared our first kiss."

"Me again?" Belle asked excitedly. She leaned in and kissed Dave.

Once they were back in the car, looking over Dave's map, Belle guided him back to her high school. She looked at him quizzically. "I know we never did anything here," she said.

"Work with me," Dave said. He guided her up the cement steps where they stopped and sat on the top one, looking down. He handed Belle a third puzzle piece. "I can't really bring you to Layton High right now, so just use your imagination," he explained. "At a high school dance, I chose the worst time possible to blurt out my feelings for you. I wish I could change the way I first said I love you, but I can't so..." Dave shrugged. "It will forever be a part of our history together."

She helped Belle back into the car, where she guided them both to a big iron fence. "Hey, this is my house," she said.

"Yup!" Dave smiled. After Belle opened the gate, they pulled up the long driveway and walked inside. Dave guided her to the kitchen table and handed her the final puzzle piece. "Yesterday was the best day of my life. The girl of my dreams, the girl I've loved for years, decided to give me a second chance. I know I did some stupid things in our past, but I hope our future will last forever."

Belle laid the puzzle pieces on her table and moved them around until they spelled out a message: 'Will you go to prom with me?' Belle stepped back and looked up at

Dave, who waited expectantly. "But I live in California now," Belle said, the hurt etched in her face. "Are you talking about your prom or mine?"

Dave took her hands and walked her over to the couch. "I talked to your mom yesterday," he said, grinning. "I offered to pay for part of your ticket, but she told me your dad would cover the plane ride. You can come back for the last dance and say a real goodbye to all your friends. Plus you can see your cousins all again, too."

Belle squealed and bounced on the couch. "Are you serious?"

"Well, it's not like I'm going to take someone else!" Dave exclaimed. "But as student body president, I kind of have to be there. I presented my case to your mom, possibly begged a little, and she agreed to make it happen."

Belle grabbed Dave's face and kissed him passionately.

"Wow! I'll take that as a yes."

"Take it, mister!" Belle smiled so wide, her cheeks began to hurt. She was going home.

# Chapter Twenty-Eight

Cinderella drove through Sardine Canyon just as the sun began to set. The sky was lined with an amazing blend of pink and orange. With the beautiful green mountains against the sunset backdrop, it looked like an incredible piece of artwork. Cinderella's cell rang as she rounded the final corner and saw the stretch of fields in front of her.

"Hello?" she said through the speakerphone.

"Are you here yet?"

Cinderella laughed. "Is someone getting a little anxious?"

"Yes!" Scott said. "It's been forever since you visited me in Logan. I can't wait to start our date."

Cinderella smiled. "I'm about ten minutes outside of Logan. Just hold your horses. I'll be there soon."

Scott sighed dramatically. "Fine! But drive faster!"

Cinderella laughed again. He was acting like a little kid waiting for Christmas morning. "Wouldn't you rather I get there safely?"

"Yeah, I guess."

Cinderella could picture Scott pacing around his apartment, watching out the windows for her car even though he knew she wasn't there yet. "Okay, well I'm going to hang up now so I can drive. I love you."

"I love you, too. See you soon."

Exactly ten minutes later, Cinderella pulled up to Scott's apartment. He came running out of the building toward her. He grabbed her bag off her shoulder and threw it down on the grass, and then he picked her up in a huge bear hug. As he brought her back down, their lips found each other. "I love you, Princess!"

Cinderella rubbed her nose against his. She would never get enough of hearing him say that. "I love you, too!" Scott picked her bag up off the grass and swung it easily over his shoulder. He took her by the hand and walked inside. "So who am I rooming with tonight?" Cinderella asked.

"The girls next door. They're awesome—you're going to love them." Cinderella followed Scott up a flight of stairs to the second floor. He pulled out his key and unlocked the first door they reached. "I still can't believe your parents let you come visit me without a chaperone!" Scott said, dropping her bag in the kitchen and hugging her again.

"I know!" Cinderella laughed. Her mom had relaxed so much these last couple years, it felt like a miracle. "I think a lot of it has to do with you being my chaperone to California last year. They trust you," she said, placing a hand on Scott's chest. "And they know I'm staying the night with your neighbors, which helps immensely. Speaking of my parents," Cinderella pulled out her phone and called them. "I just got here, I'm safe," she said. "Thanks, Mom, I will." Cinderella listened for a minute then handed the phone to Scott. "She wants to talk to you."

Scott took the phone. "Hey, Dana!" He nodded and agreed to several things before a serious expression crossed his face. "I promise," he said before hanging up.

"What was that about?" Cinderella asked.

"I think your mom just threatened to kill me if I don't take good care of you and return you safely," he said.

"What?" Cinderella laughed.

"Seriously. She said your dad bought a gun…just for me."

They both broke into laughter. "So what's the plan tonight?" Cinderella asked.

"Dinner and dancing," Scott said.

Cinderella bounced on her toes. "I can't wait!"

"Are you hungry now?" Scott asked.

"Ravenous!" Cinderella said.

"Well, then, we better get you some food." Scott retrieved his wallet and keys from his bedroom, and then they left. "I better introduce you to the girls next door," Scott said. "That way when I bring you in really late, you won't feel awkward just meeting them."

Cinderella nodded. "Lead the way."

Scott knocked on the door and introduced Cinderella to three of the girls she would be bunking with. They gave Cinderella a spare key in case they were in bed when she needed to crash. Cinderella thanked them and waved goodbye. "They do seem really nice!" Cinderella said as they left. Scott took Cinderella by the hand and guided her to his car. He opened her door and bowed. "Your chariot awaits, your highness."

Cinderella laughed and curtsied before climbing in. Scott flashed her his cheesiest grin before walking around the car and climbing in himself.

"We're such dorks," Cinderella laughed.

"Speak for yourself. I'm nothing but a charming Prince."

They both laughed again.

Cinderella reached for his hand and rested her head on Scott's shoulder, sighing contentedly. After a few minutes of happy silence, Cinderella sat up. "This is weird," she said as Scott drove them to the restaurant.

"What's weird?"

"So far tonight has just seemed so quiet. Last time I visited you at Utah State, you had a dance party going on in your living room. Your door was open and you had tons of people in and out of your apartment all night long."

Scott nodded. "Last time you visited me, I was trying to show you and Dave a good time. So I invited a bunch of friends to hang out with us. But this time, I want to keep you all to myself. I hope that's okay."

Cinderella leaned against Scott's shoulder and took a deep breath of his amazing cologne. "It's more than okay," she sighed happily.

Scott pulled up in front of a Mexican restaurant. "I hope you're in the mood for tacos," he said.

Cinderella nodded. "I like food."

As soon as they were seated, Cinderella began inhaling the chips and salsa.

"Geeze, do I get any?" Scott teased.

"Sorry!" Cinderella said. "I didn't get lunch today and I'm starving."

Scott pushed the chips closer to her. "Have at it," he said, leaning back and watching her with amusement.

After the waiter took their orders, Cinderella paused from eating. "I'm moving here in like four months. Can you believe it?"

"Wow, you're going to smell like beans all the time," Scott said with a serious expression.

Cinderella gave him in exasperated look. "Not here," she said, pointing to their surroundings in the restaurant. "I'll be in Logan! With you! It's like a dream."

Scott reached across the table and took her hand. "I can't wait! We're going to have so much fun!"

"You'll have to help me figure out my first semester of classes and then show me where to go to those classes," she said.

"First class we're signing you up for is beginners Western Swing," Scott said.

"Beginners? Don't I know all the beginners stuff already?"

"Yes, but the class is being taught by yours truly next semester."

"No way!" Cinderella yelled louder than she intended to. Several people in the restaurant turned in their direction. She covered her mouth with her hand before whispering, "No way. Babe, that's amazing!"

"Yeah, I just got the job. I'm so excited! I'll get to dance every single day. And if you take the class, I'll be able to use you as my assistant, so I won't have to dance with anyone else." He waggled his eyebrows, causing Cinderella to laugh.

"I'm getting so anxious. I'm just ready for graduation now!"

"It's called senioritis," Scott told her, "and everyone gets it. Only two more months. Hang in there."

The waiter brought out their food and then dropped a huge sombrero on Cinderella's head. Scott tried not to laugh, but he failed miserably.

"Ummm, what's this?" Cinderella asked.

"For your birthday!" the waiter announced. He and several others, including Scott, broke into the birthday song. Scott pulled out his phone and began snapping pictures. Cinderella made several faces at him before pulling her cheesiest grin. When they finished singing, the waiter took the sombrero back and they were left to eat in peace.

"What was that all about?" Cinderella asked, leaning across the table toward Scott. "My birthday was several weeks ago."

Scott grinned mischievously. "I know, but I thought it would be funny. And it totally was!" He held up his phone to show off the pictures he took.

Cinderella tried to snatch the phone away, but Scott pulled it just out of reach. "Come now, Princess, eat your dinner so we can go dancing." He bounced his shoulders to the music, imitating some dance moves in a seated position.

Cinderella shook her head. "You're such a nerd."

Scott winked at her and continued to stationary dance.

Cinderella moved the food around on her plate and kept glancing at Scott as they ate.

"Out with it," Scott said.

"What?"

"Don't play coy. I know you want to ask me something, so what's up?"

Cinderella sighed and put down her fork. "Will you take me to my prom?" she asked. "I know you're done with high school and everything, but it's my last dance and I really want to go." Cinderella blew out a deep breath.

Scott smiled. "Of course I will, Princess. I'd love to!"

Cinderella smiled. "Really?"

"Yes, really. You don't need to be scared to ask me questions," Scott said. "I am your boyfriend, after all. Prom is one of my duties."

Cinderella's cheeks flushed. Boyfriend. She just loved hearing that word! She ate until her stomach was happy, and then she had the waiter box the rest so she wouldn't feel too full to dance. Scott, on the other hand, cleaned his plate. Cinderella watched him through widened eyes. "I don't know how you can do that," she said, sticking out her tongue. "I didn't even eat half my food and I'm full."

Scott rubbed his belly. "It's because I have a lot more storage space." After paying the check, Scott stood and offered Cinderella his arm. "Shall we?"

She stood and grabbed onto his firm bicep. "This right here is one of my favorite things," Cinderella said, rubbing his arm up and down.

"In that case, I will not stop working out."

"Please don't!"

Scott grinned and leaned over, kissing her on top of her hair. "Every time I see you, I can't believe you're actually here! And I can't believe you're mine." Scott stopped walking and turned Cinderella toward him so he could kiss her. Their lips touched softly at first, but as they continued, their kiss became more firm and frantic. Scott's hands ran through Cinderella's hair and down the length of her body, and back up again until he wrapped them tightly around her waist. Cinderella finally broke the kiss and they both gasped.

"Wow," Cinderella breathed, bringing a hand to her dizzying head. "We better be careful."

"Yeah," Scott said, shaking his own mind clear. "Too much of that can be intoxicating." Taking a deep breath, Scott reached for Cinderella's hand and they walked the rest of the way to his waiting car.

Cinderella squirmed in her seat on the drive over to the dance club. She was so excited, she couldn't even sit still. "And this time I have a driver's license with my birthday on it," she said excitedly. "I'm legit."

Scott shook his head. "I can't even believe what a bad example I was for you. I never should have snuck you guys in."

"No, we shouldn't have," Cinderella agreed. "But we learned our lesson and this time you won't have to."

Cinderella jumped from the car as soon as Scott parked. He got out and stared at her in shock. "Excuse me, young lady, but what do you think you're doing?"

Cinderella looked down and jumped back in the car, pulling the door shut behind her. "Oops!"

Scott opened her door and offered her a hand to climb out. He placed a hand over his heart and pretended to be wounded. "I can't believe you denied me the honor of getting your door." He sniffed.

"Oh, stop." Cinderella patted his arm. "It was one time and I'm just really excited!"

Scott grabbed her hand and pulled her toward the club's entrance. "Well, let's go then!"

It took a moment for Cinderella's eyes to adjust to the darkness and the black lights inside. Scott led her past the pool tables and through a door to the main dance floor, where country music blared so loudly, she could feel it vibrating in her bones.

"Do you want to practice first, or do you just wanna go for it?" Scott yelled above the music.

"You are great at leading, and I know how to follow. Let's just go!"

Scott smiled broadly and he took off, twirling Cinderella through several complicated moves. He lifted her above his head, spinning around in circles. He flipped her over his shoulder and she found her feet once again. Scott called out instructions when he needed to, but most of the time, Cinderella followed his arms and went wherever he guided her. The music faded into a slow song and Cinderella was grateful for the chance to catch her breath. Scott wrapped his arms around her, pressing his body up against hers from behind, and they gently swayed to the music together. Cinderella's heart raced and her already red face grew even hotter. The thought of going home tomorrow caused a stabbing pain in her heart. She wanted to be with Scott forever.

The slow dance ended abruptly and a line dance took over the floor. Cinderella backed into line beside Scott and, taking her by the hand, he led her through the steps. By the end of the line dance, she could do them all on her own. When another fast-paced song blared right after the line dance, Cinderella motioned to Scott that she was thirsty. They stepped into the cool air of the hallway. She bent down to take a drink from the fountain. Scott lifted her long hair from her hot, sweaty neck and blew a nice cool breeze along her collar, sending chills down her back.

Cinderella stood up straight and shivered. "Oooh, that feels good!" she said. Scott smiled down at her, giving her a peck on the lips before taking a long, slow drink himself. They went back out onto the dance floor and discovered it had become twice as busy. People were almost body to body as they tried to maneuver their way around the cramped room. Scott led Cinderella over to a corner where they had a tiny bit of extra space. He spun her around quickly, and then lifted her off her feet, dipping her low over his bent leg. Cinderella pointed her toe in the air, as she had been taught. "You're such a natural!" Scott said, beaming. "I can't believe how much you remember from last time!"

Cinderella tried to shrug it off, but she was glowing inside. "I had a good teacher," she said.

After they finished several more dances, a girl in tiny short shorts and a tube top approached Scott, rubbing a slender hand along his bicep. "Hey, there," she said in a breathy voice. "Wanna take me for a spin around the dance floor?"

Scott removed her hand from his arm casually and said, "No thanks. I'm here with my girlfriend." He pulled Cinderella closer and together they moved and spun under the dim lights. Cinderella smiled up at him. She was his girlfriend. She loved the sound of that even more than when he called her Princess.

After an hour of dancing, Cinderella decided the club didn't play enough slow songs. As much as she loved having Scott pull and twirl her around the room, nothing compared to when he held her close and their bodies swayed as one to the music. The chance for her heartrate to slow down once in a while was a nice break, too.

After two hours of dancing, both Scott and Cinderella were dripping with sweat and completely exhausted. "Are you ready to go?" Scott shouted over the booming bass of another line dance.

Cinderella pushed her hair out of her eyes. "I'm done," she said, nodding.

Cinderella wrapped an arm around Scott's waist and he put an arm over her shoulder. Together they stumbled out to his car. Their tired, aching feet could barely keep them standing anymore. "How many classes a day will you be teaching of that?" Cinderella asked as she reached over and blasted Scott's AC. The cool air against her hot, sticky body caused goosebumps to pop up all down her arms and legs.

"Two to three," Scott said.

"How are you going to do that for two to three hours every day?" she asked.

"Well, it's the beginners' class, so we'll be going much more slowly than you and I just did. I'll teach a move, and then we'll pair off and practice, teach a move, and then pair off and practice again. It won't be the same as constant movement on a hot, crowded dance floor."

Cinderella's body was exhausted but her mind still felt wide awake. "I'm not tired," she announced as they reached Scott's apartment.

"Neither am I," Scott said. "Do you wanna watch a movie?"

"Let's see, sitting still and cuddling with you? This seems like a win-win! Yeah, let's watch a movie."

Scott grinned at her as he put the car into park. This time he didn't have to remind Cinderella to sit still. He walked around and opened her door, offering a hand as she climbed out.

"My feet hurt," Cinderella whined.

"Come on," Scott coaxed her. "I'll rub them for you when we get inside."

Cinderella's ears perked. "I think I'm okay with this plan."

After looking through Scott's small assortment of movies, they chose a comedy they'd both seen before. Scott turned on the movie and sat against the couch cushions on one side, indicating to Cinderella to sit on the opposite side and place her feet in his lap. He slipped off one shoe and peeled her sock off.

Cinderella cringed. "Are you sure you want to touch my gross, sweaty feet?"

"Your feet are not gross. They're actually rather cute," Scott said, holding her foot up and examining it more closely.

"Whatever you say," Cinderella shrugged. She sunk back into the cushions and turned toward the movie while Scott rubbed her feet, one at a time.

"Don't fall asleep on me," Scott said, squeezing her second foot.

Cinderella popped her eyes open. "I'm not," she yawned.

"Yeah, I believe that," he teased. "Do you want to turn the movie off and call it a night?"

"No!" Cinderella sat straight up, holding her eyes open wide.

Scott laughed. "Come here," he said. He pulled Cinderella into his arms. She lay her head against his chest, his muscular arms encircling her middle.

"Where are all your roommates?" Cinderella asked, suddenly looking around. "I just realized I haven't seen any of them tonight."

"They went out of town for the weekend," Scott said. He stretched his legs out along either side of Cinderella. "I've got the place to myself."

Cinderella felt heat tickling up her spine. She and Scott were completely alone in an empty apartment. She brushed the thoughts aside and snuggled deeper into Scott's embrace. Cinderella began to feel her eyelids droop about halfway through the movie.

Then she felt Scott's hot breath against the back of her hairline. He moved forward and began kissing her neck. Cinderella leaned against him as he made his way down her throat. Each kiss left her skin tingling. Scott made his way over to her ear, where he gently began to nibble. Chills surged down Cinderella's spine. She tried to shift in her seat, but a fire had been ignited within. Cinderella couldn't take it any longer. She turned her body toward Scott and found his lips. He met hers with hunger, and soon they were kissing passionately. The movie was long forgotten. Scott's hands moved up and down Cinderella's back, lingering on her soft, warm stomach, where her shirt had gotten pushed up a little when she turned. His thumb ran along the length of her silky soft skin.

Cinderella pushed against Scott, kissing him with force. Her thoughts became a blur. Her body ached and pleaded for more. Scott moaned softly, and then he reached up and grabbed the corners of Cinderella's shirt and pulled it back down. He gently pushed Cinderella off of him and they both sat up, panting. She put her head in her hands. She couldn't believe she had just done that!

Scott looked at her timidly. "I'm so sorry!" he said. "I can't believe I just let that happen."

"It takes two to tango," Cinderella said mournfully. "I was at fault just as much as you were." She gathered her long brown hair behind her head. "Thank you," she whispered, a tear silently rolled down her cheek and Scott scooted closer, brushing it away with his finger. "Thank you for stopping us."

"Please don't cry," Scott said. He ached to pull her in close and protect her from the pain he had caused.

"Have you ever…gone that far with another girl before?" Cinderella was embarrassed to be asking the question, but she just had to know.

"No," Scott said, without hesitation. "Never."

Cinderella's face lit up. "Really? Not even with Jenny?"

"Never with Jenny, or anyone else," he said. "I'm saving myself for marriage. I know it sounds old fashioned, but that's the way my parents raised me, and it always made sense. Why would I give away a piece of myself to another person unless I knew that person was going to be my partner for life?"

Cinderella cried out and covered her face with her hands.

"I'm sorry, what's wrong?" Scott asked, scooting forward.

Cinderella chuckled softly. "Nothing's wrong. In fact, I've never been happier than I am right now."

Scott furrowed his brow and looked at her, trying to decipher if she was laughing her crying.

"That's the way I've always felt, too," Cinderella admitted. "I just never thought I'd find a man who agreed with me. A man I love with all my heart!" Cinderella was so happy she felt her heart might burst.

"So you never did…with Brian or anyone else?" he asked.

Cinderella shook her head fiercely. "Not even close!"

Scott's smile brightened the whole room. The relief on his face shone like a flashlight.

"I want you to be my first one and my only one," Cinderella smiled shyly.

Scott stood from the couch and lifted Cinderella onto her feet. He pulled her into a big hug and held her close. "First one, only one," he whispered in her ear. "But for right now, I can't trust myself around you. I better take you next door."

"You don't want to finish the movie?" Cinderella asked.

Scott shook his head. "You better go."

He guided Cinderella through the kitchen and picked up her bag. He walked her next door, where he slipped the key into the lock and pushed it open. Cinderella stood on her toes to kiss him goodnight, but Scott put up a hand to stop her. "Goodnight, Cinderella," he said. His face looked pained. Cinderella closed the door behind him and fell against the wood. She cried silently into the doorframe. What just happened? Did she blow it again for good?

# Chapter Twenty-Nine

Belle stood in front of Cinderella's full length mirror, examining her long yellow gown front and back. She smoothed down the material of her dress and turned side to side. The gown swished around her ankles as she moved.

"This really is a great room," Belle said when her cousins slipped in the door.

"Oh, Belle, you look amazing!"

"I love that dress!"

"My turn!" Aurora shrieked, running into the large, walk-in closet with her pink gown in hand.

Cinderella hugged Belle from behind. "I'm so glad you came back for this!"

Belle laughed. "Down, girl. It's just a dance."

"I know, but it's our last dance and we all have dates. This is just so fun!" Cinderella bounced on her heels. "Okay, I can't wait for Aurora. I'm changing in the bathroom." She grabbed her sparkly blue dress from off the bed and left the room.

"Boy, she's happy," Belle remarked.

"Yeah, she's been giddy like this since she and Scott finally became official. If she weren't so cute, it would be nauseating."

Aurora emerged from the closet and strutted around the room. "So what do you think? Does the dress clash with my hair, or accentuate it?"

"I think you look like a beautiful wad of cotton candy," Ariel said.

Aurora stuck out her tongue at her sister. "Super helpful, thanks."

"You look gorgeous, Rora," Snow White said.

"Thank you. At least someone here has good taste," Aurora said, shooting her sister a dirty look.

Ariel laughed. "I'm teasing you, you know that. You look phenomenal! No one else could pull off that much pink, but you make it glamorous. This Week will love it."

Aurora cleared her throat while she primped her hair in the mirror behind Belle. "His name is Charlie."

Ariel glanced at her sister in astonishment. She'd never been corrected before. Could this mean something? "I'm sorry," Ariel said, glancing at Snow White and exchanging a shrug, "Charlie will love it."

Aurora nodded.

Cinderella came back in the room, wearing her floor length, sparkly blue gown. It had a wide neck, without being completely off the shoulders. "What do you think?" Cinderella asked.

Her cousins oohed and aahhed appropriately.

"All you need are glass slippers to complete the look," Belle said.

"How about these?" Cinderella held out a pair of beautiful, silver heels, which wrapped around the ankle.

"I love that we're doing this," Ariel said, emerging from the closet in her skin tight, jade mermaid gown. "Brian really said people still talk about that Homecoming?"

"Yeah," Cinderella nodded. "If it's true, people are really going to get a kick out of us recreating that dance tonight."

Belle smiled. "I don't know about you guys, but I can totally pull off the yellow ball gown better than the animated Belle."

Her cousins all laughed as they continued to primp and prep for the dance.

"Aren't you going to get dressed, Snow?" Cinderella asked, looking over her shoulder. Snow White sat on her bed watching the others get ready. She jumped up when Cinderella said her name.

"Oh yeah! I got so lost in watching you guys, I almost forgot!" Snow White grabbed her dress and dashed into the closet, leaving it open a crack so she could hear. "So Belle, how are things going with Dave?" her muffled voice asked through the closet.

Belle couldn't hide her grin as she smeared some lipstick across her lips. "Pretty well," she said. "I'm sure things will be even easier when he moves to California. Right now, we just text a lot and sometimes talk on the phone. The long distance thing isn't so bad, though, really. I still can't believe Craig wasn't even willing to try it."

"Do you realize if things work out between you and Dave, and things work out between Cinderella and Scott, that the two of you could become sisters-in-law?" Snow White emerged from behind the cracked door to see Cinderella and Belle exchange a startled look.

"I don't know why I hadn't really thought of that," Cinderella said.

"Wouldn't that be weird?" Belle asked. "Your kids would know me as Aunt Belle instead of Cousin Belle."

"Really weird," Cinderella admitted.

They both returned their gaze to Snow White, as she approached the mirror, grinning ear to ear.

"Wow," Cinderella breathed.

"You look incredible, Snow!" Belle's eyes popped when she spoke.

Snow White continued to grin in return. The navy blue and gold gown hugged her in all the right places, accentuating her curves. The color was a perfect contrast for her fair skin and bright red hair.

"Hurry and sit down here so I can do your hair," Aurora urged. "The guys will be here soon."

Snow White did as she was told. Aurora pulled most of her hair up, leaving some down to form ringlets around her face. While she worked, Belle applied finishing touchups on makeup for all the girls.

"Maybe if things don't pan out as an actress, I should become a makeup artist instead. That way I can still rub shoulders with all the stars, but have less pressure. I really do love doing makeup on other people. This is really fun!"

"You do the makeup, Aurora will do hair, and I'll direct the films. Then we can all work together!" Ariel said.

"And Snow White can star in the film; check her out!" Belle said, spinning Snow White around for all to see.

Snow White looked like a regular movie star. She felt like one, too. Prom night would definitely be a night to remember!

"Are Dave and Scott taking you guys together?" Aurora asked, puckering her lips in the mirror and applying a coat of shimmery pink lipstick.

"Actually," Belle said, smiling, "we're all going together."

Aurora and Snow White both turned and stared at Belle. "Even us?"

"Yes. As a present to me, Dave secured all your dates to be a part of our group tonight. Our stretch limo should be here any minute." Belle squealed.

Ariel coughed. "Stretch limo? Even Jordan? Seriously?"

"Yes, even Jordan. Actually, I think he's the one who secured the car."

Ariel ran to the window and looked down. "Oh my gosh, here it comes! I can see it!"

The others flew to Cinderella's window.

"Is that thing going to fit in my driveway?" Cinderella asked."

"No way. I'm sure they'll park on the street," Belle said. "Well, come on, what are we waiting for?" She picked up the bottom of her gown and ran down the stairs, her cousins following close behind.

*\*\**

Scott led Cinderella out onto the dance floor as they entered the decorated conference center.

"How can you be ready to dance?" Cinderella moaned. "I'm so stuffed!"

Scott pulled her close. "We'll just start with a slow dance and work our way up. You didn't have to finish your entire steak, ya know," he teased.

"Yes, I did," Cinderella grinned, swaying along with him. "My mom took so many pictures! By the time we got to the restaurant, I was starving to death!"

Scott chuckled. "Your mom does like the camera."

"I especially liked the shot she got of Sophie kissing you on the cheek. I think that girl has a mad crush. I'd be worried, except I know you have a thing about ages."

Scott tickled Cinderella playfully and she giggled. Things had been a little weird between them since the incident in Logan. Scott seemed more nervous around her than usual. It was nice to have him teasing her again.

"You guys are nuts," Belle whispered as she walked past, holding her stomach.

"Let me get us some drinks," Dave offered.

Belle sat down near the refreshment table and watched Dave. "Uh-oh," she whispered.

"What's up?" Ariel asked, sitting in the chair beside her.

Belle nodded toward the table with her chin. Craig was approaching Dave with a scowl on his face. Jordan watched the interaction, confused.

"They have a history, so-to-speak," Ariel explained.

Belle casually leaned closer to see if she could catch a snippet of their conversation.

"I see you swooped right in," Craig said.

"Finders keepers," Dave shrugged with a smile.

"Go for it, man," Craig said shaking his head. "That girl is crazy! She was already talking about having kids and stuff."

"You're the crazy one," Dave said casually, taking a sip from his punch. "That's Belle Princess you're talking about! If she told me she wanted a hundred kids, I'd marry her tomorrow and get started. You don't let a girl like that go for anything."

"Whatever, man." Craig shook his head again and walked away.

Dave scooped up a second cup of punch and walked back over to Belle. "Here you go," he said, handing her one.

Belle took the offered cup and set it down on the table. She stood and grabbed Dave's face, kissing him hard and long. "I love you, David Prince," she said when she released him.

Dave wrapped his arms around Belle and hugged her tight. "I love you, too, Belle." He smiled and led her out onto the dance floor.

"Awww," Jordan mocked, "that was so cute."

Ariel gave his shoulder a shove. "It's about time, that's what it is!" she said. "Those two have been on a freaking roller coaster ride of romance since they met."

Jordan laughed. "Well, glad I missed the drama then."

"Is this anything like your prom in Oregon?" she asked.

"I don't know. I didn't go. Jordan shrugged.

"What? Why not?"

"It wasn't really my thing. Besides, I had no one I wanted to go with." Jordan leaned in and kissed Ariel lightly on the lips.

"Awww," Ariel said, mimicking Jordan's voice. Then she smiled at him and batted her eyes.

"It's a good thing you're so cute," Jordan said, grabbing her chin and kissing her again. "Come on." He stood and extended his hand to her. "You better show me what these high school dances are all about."

Ariel was amazed to see that Jordan could really move on the dance floor. She was used to seeing him covered in grease and motor oil. She knew he was great with his hands, but she was blown away to see how smooth he was on his feet as well. She moved alongside him, swaying and shaking to the beat. Ariel saw Aurora and Charlie walking towards them, and she reached up and gave her sister a high five as they passed.

Aurora let Charlie wrap his arms around her as they snuggled at the table, watching dancers move past them. Aurora was good at flirting. She felt she had obtained champion status in this department, but she had been with Charlie for three weeks. They had moved past the flirting stage. They were actually starting to have real, meaningful conversations and Aurora felt lost. She didn't know how to act in this situation. How did her sister and cousins keep their relationships going?

Charlie began tracing lines on the back of Aurora's hand with his finger.

"You ready to keep dancing, or do you need more of a breather?" he asked.

Aurora snuggled into him and sighed. "I'm actually just enjoying this right now."

Charlie smiled and squeezed his arms tighter. "Me too," he whispered.

Aurora grabbed Charlie's wrist to look at his watch. "We have to meet my cousins in twenty minutes for our group picture. After that, let's get out there and show them how it's done."

Charlie sighed deeply and kissed the top of Aurora's head. She closed her eyes and sank into the warmth of his protective arms around her. Maybe she didn't need to worry so much. Charlie, his arms, and that moment felt pretty nice.

When the song changed and the room quieted, Aurora peeked her eyes open and looked out across the dance floor. She noticed Snow White and Justin, moving closer for the slow dance, but still looking stiff. "Oh, I hope she's having a good time," Aurora whispered.

"Who?" Charlie asked.

Aurora stared ahead. "Snow White."

Snow White's arm ached with stiffness. She looked around the dance floor at Cinderella and Scott, Belle and Dave, and even Ariel and Jordan. They all looked so natural and calm the way they held onto each other while slow dancing. So why did this feel so awkward? Snow White watched her cousins, and then looked at Justin and herself to compare. Justin held his frame stiffly, like he was trying to win an award for ballroom dance or something. The others seemed looser, like their arms were an extension of each other.

Snow White was glad when the song ended and noticed it was time to go get pictures taken. She and Justin hurried over to where they all gathered, just outside the door.

"What are we going to do, guys?" Belle asked. "Last dance picture ever. Let's make it memorable!"

"Don't we just stand stiffly and smile?" Jordan asked.

"Only if you're completely lame!" Aurora said, shooting him a funny look.

"I don't know what they did at your school," Cinderella added, "but it's kinda the thing here to be as creative as possible."

Scott started chuckling. Everyone looked at him. "I've got it," he said, his eyes shining with excitement. "You all wore dresses to match your names and characters tonight, right?" He glanced at the girls.

"Right," Belle said, nodding. "Our last show to the school that we love who we are and no bully will ever change that."

The other girls nodded proudly.

Scott's smile widened. "So to top off your night, what if we all posed as the characters for your final picture? I mean, you're already wearing the dresses. Why not take it all the way? It just seems too perfect."

"What do you mean, babe?" Cinderella asked.

"Like you will be sitting and I'll be kneeling in front of you, putting on your shoe. Aurora can be laying down in front and Charlie can be kissing her awake."

"I'm in!" Charlie yelled, raising his hand.

Everyone laughed.

"I've got it!" Justin snapped his fingers and ran back into the dance hall.

"What was that about?" Cinderella asked.

Snow White shrugged. "Beats me." She watched nervously while the line in front of them got smaller but Justin had not returned yet. Her cousins were all talking frantically and over each other about how they each should pose. Justin popped his head around the corner just in time. He held up an apple.

"Where'd you get that?" Snow White asked.

"Centerpiece decoration from the refreshment table," he said, tossing the apple up into the air and catching it again.

Snow White smiled warmly at him. Justin reached out and squeezed her hand.

"All right, you're up," the photographer called to their group. Dave handed him their ticket and everyone moved into place excitedly. They had to create layers in their small space so they could all fit into one picture. Aurora lay on the floor in her pink gown, with Charlie bending over her and kissing her lightly on the lips. Jordan lay on the ground on the opposite side with Ariel, in her green silky dress kneeling beside him as though she had just pulled him from the water. Cinderella sat with her blue gown draped around her, in the center of the picture, as Scott knelt in front of her, slipping her shoe back on her foot. Belle stood behind them to one side, in her full yellow dress, holding up a mirror. Dave stood directly behind the mirror, holding his hands up in the shape of claws and growling like a beast. Next to them, Justin dipped Snow White low in her dark blue gown with golden accents, the apple dangling from her hand.

The photographer laughed and shook his head. A crowd of students, waiting for their own turns, all stopped their conversations and watched the masterpiece take place. When the photographer snapped several pictures and announced he got it, the other students began to laugh and cheer.

"Looks like the Princess sisters have done it again," Scott said.

# Chapter Thirty

Cinderella looked up into the stands and watched her family. Some guy was talking to Monica, whose face looked flushed. Cinderella smiled. She remembered when Scott, or any boy for that matter, had made her nervous too. Sophie sat on Steven's lap, waving frantically in Cinderella's direction. She snuck a tiny wave at her little sister in return, and Sophie squealed. Grinning, she glanced at her mom, whose eyes were shining as she listened to the principal speak.

A little further down the aisle, Belle sat sandwiched between her parents. When Cinderella's eyes met hers, Belle pulled a face. Cinderella had to stifle her giggle. Belle had graduated the week before and made sure to rub it in to the rest of her cousins that once again, being the oldest, she had beaten them to something.

"I still can't believe Lucas came with them," Snow White whispered from behind her.

Cinderella turned. "I know! He's always so busy with the show. But I'm really glad he's here. It's nice to have the whole family together like this."

Snow White adjusted her graduation cap and nodded. "Gosh, these things itch. Is yours bothering you?"

Cinderella smiled. "No, I'm okay. But I have such a thick coat of hairspray on, it's probably preventing this cap from actually touching my head." She reached up and touched her own cap before turning back around.

The line began to move forward. Cinderella nudged Aurora, who stood directly in front of her. Aurora was busy waving animatedly up at her mom and grandma. "I'm going, I'm going." She turned and smiled at Cinderella. "This is it!"

As the procession moved forward, toward their seats, Cinderella looked up into the bleachers again. Her eyes scanned the crowd until they fell, disappointed, on the empty seat beside her mom. Her shoulders slumped and she sighed.

"Don't worry," Snow White said, touching her elbow. "He'll be here."

Cinderella offered her a weak smile.

They walked down the aisle and brushed past another line of students. Snow White's steps quickened when they saw Justin ahead. He reached out a hand as they passed and gave Snow White's fingers a squeeze.

"You guys are so cute that it's gross," Cinderella whispered.

Snow White laughed. "I know," she smiled, her head held high. "But we're nothing compared to you and Scott." She made a gagging noise.

Cinderella forced a smile. "Yeah…" she said. She wasn't so sure. Scott took her to prom, like he'd promised, but the weeks since, he'd been acting really strange. She could never get ahold of him. All he was good for was a quick text now and then. She didn't know if this was his way of breaking up with her.

"So tell me, has Justin kissed you yet?" Cinderella asked, trying to take her mind off Scott. The line turned down their row. Cinderella and Snow White were finally able to sit.

Snow White quirked her mouth. "No," she sighed. "I'm starting to think I'm just un-kissable."

"That's the dumbest thing I've ever heard," Aurora interrupted. "Maybe you should just make the first move."

Snow White put her hands up. "Absolutely not! I could never do that. Way too scary!"

"So maybe he's just as shy as you are," Ariel whispered.

"I think he just knows what you went through with Dave and he's being a gentleman by waiting. He wants you to know he's not just using you," Cinderella mused, offering her own thoughts.

Snow White shrugged. "I'm sure you're right. Justin is super sweet that way. But sometimes I wonder if it's just me."

Aurora, Ariel, and Cinderella all sighed loudly. "Oh, Snow."

All the graduates were now seated and the crowd hushed as the program began. Cinderella found herself paying more attention to an empty seat in the bleachers than the speakers up front, who were mostly boring anyway. She couldn't wait to move up to Logan. She only hoped their relationship would still be alive by the time she did.

When Belle's gaze turned to the podium, Cinderella followed. Dave was the elected speaker for graduation. No surprise there. She turned her attention to him. Cinderella felt the tears welling up as Dave spoke of moving on and chasing their dreams. It was no wonder he was going into marketing. The boy definitely knew how to sell something! Cinderella cheered loudly and whistled along with the rest of the student body when Dave finished speaking.

The next speaker, some state official, droned on in a monotone voice. He single-handedly killed the buzz and motivation Dave had inspired among the crowd. Cinderella folded her program into a fan and began waving it in front of her face. The room grew hotter with every moment they were forced to sit tightly together. Finally, after what felt like hours, Cinderella's row stood to receive their diplomas.

Cinderella walked forward slowly. They stopped right before they reached the stairs to the stage, waiting for their names to be called. Cinderella rested her head on Aurora's shoulder. "I'm ready for a nap," she whispered.

"No way!" Aurora hissed. "Tonight is the all-night grad party! You can't crap out on us now. You still have at least ten hours to go!"

Cinderella moaned. "After this hot room, with all those long speakers, I'm going to need a gallon of Vanilla Coke to get me going again."

"I can make that happen," Aurora said.

"Ariel Princess," the principal read.

Ariel walked across the stage, smiling up at her mom, her grandma, and Jordan. With the bright lights shining down on them, it was hard to make out specific faces in the crowd. Ariel moved her tassel across her hat, took her diploma, and shook hands with several people standing in line.

"Aurora Princess."

Cinderella felt her cheeks warm as she awaited her turn. This time, it wasn't from the overcrowded room. This was really it—the end of her childhood and the start of adulthood. She took a deep breath and stepped onto the stage as the principal called out, "Cinderella Princess."

She walked across the stage and tried to look up, but was blinded by the lights. She smiled anyway, knowing her mom would be taking a million pictures. As the principal handed her the diploma, something shiny caught her eye.

Cinderella glanced down and noticed a diamond ring, sparkling brightly in the stage lights, was tied to the ribbon around her diploma. Cinderella looked up in shock. There, at the bottom of the stage, knelt Scott on one knee.

Cinderella looked up at the bleachers and squinted. Her parents and sisters were all cheering loudly. How had he gotten to the stage without her noticing? Cinderella moved toward him slowly, her legs shaking like jelly. She noticed her image being displayed on the big screen overhead. Scott stared at her, his smile bright, his eyes shining. Cinderella reached him and almost stumbled over. Was this real?

She stared at the ring again and held it up in front of her as she approached Scott. He took the diploma from her hands and slid the ring off. Then he held it out to her.

"Cinderella, I know we've had our ups and downs. I know we're both still young and have a lot of growing up to do, but there is no one else I'd rather grow up with than you. My life isn't complete without you in it. You've owned my heart since the day we met. I'm here. I'm yours. You have my heart from here until eternity. I love you! Will you marry me and continue life's journey together?"

Tears slipped from the corner of Cinderella's eyes. She stood frozen, staring at Scott. She couldn't imagine a day without Scott, let alone a lifetime. "Yes!" she nodded.

Scott slipped the sparkling princess cut onto her finger with trembling hands. He stood and kissed her deeply. The crowd cheered loudly. Scott took Cinderella's hand and walked her off the stage. The principal tried to quiet the screaming students and their families, but they continued to clap and cheer. He put up his hands and finally hushed the crowd. "Let's keep things rolling," he said.

Scott walked Cinderella back to her seat. He hugged her and kissed her again lightly. "I love you so much," he whispered.

"I love you, too," Cinderella said.

"I'll see you outside."

Reluctantly, Cinderella released his hand and returned to her seat to cheer on Snow White as she walked across the stage. Aurora and Ariel both threw their arms around her and tried to ask questions in excited whispers.

"Were you expecting that?"

"Did you know?"

Cinderella's could feel her heart thumping all the way up to her throat. Dazed, she stared down at her left hand and admired the diamond that now rested there. She shook her head, glancing up at her family, who welcomed Scott back to the bleacher with hugs. "I had no idea."

\*\*\*

Snow White looked up as Justin offered her a hand. She took it and he helped her up and out of her go kart. She laughed. "That was so fun!"

"I can't believe you've never driven a go kart before!" he exclaimed.

"I've never had the chance," Snow White said. "That was so fun! Can we do it again?"

Justin laughed. "Of course! We've got all night." He reached out and held Snow White's hand, causing her to blush.

"You're cute when you blush," he said.

Snow White went from pink to crimson. Justin's smile grew wider. "What should we do next?"

Snow White glanced around and noticed the twins standing outside the miniature golf course. They waved her over. She pulled Justin toward them. "Hey, guys."

Ariel and Aurora stood amidst Charlie and a group of previous This Weeks. How they could all date Aurora and then still hang out and be friends was beyond Snow White. "We're all going over to play laser tag next. Do you guys want to join us?"

Snow White looked at Justin, who shrugged and nodded. She turned to Ariel. "Sure! Lead the way."

"We're just waiting for Cinderella."

"Where is she?" Snow White asked.

"Guess," Ariel said, pointing.

Cinderella stood near the bumper boats, her phone up to her ear, a finger plugging her other ear as she attempted to have a conversation over the sounds of the fun center.

Snow White rolled her eyes. "How many times has she called him?"

"I lost count," Ariel said.

"Oh, that's it." Aurora threw her hands up and marched over to Cinderella. Snow White watched as Aurora grabbed the cell phone out of her hands. "Hi, Scott. It's Aurora. Look, I know you guys just got engaged and want to be all lovey dovey, but you get to be with her forever now. We only get one grad night. All I'm asking is that you let us borrow Cindy for this one night. She needs to have some fun before she's an old, married lady. Thanks, Scott, you're the best." Aurora made a kissy noise and hung up. "There," she said, sliding the phone into her back pocket. "I promise he won't change his mind in the next few hours. Now let's go play!"

Snow White and Justin laughed as they watched the drama unfold.

"Hey!" Cinderella said indignantly. Aurora ignored her and walked back inside. Cinderella gave up and followed her cousins to the laser tag arena, where they got in line.

"I can't believe she's engaged," Justin whispered, looking at Cinderella.

"I know, it seems weird," Snow White nodded. "But at the same time, for Cinderella, it fits. She's one of the only eighteen-year-olds I know who is mature enough for marriage."

Justin nodded. "Yeah, I guess I can see that."

Once inside the dark maze, Snow White ran around, trying to tag people with her laser gun. She giggled every time she got tagged and her pack would vibrate. She turned down a long tunnel and screamed when someone grabbed her arm.

"Sorry," Justin said.

Snow White laughed. "You startled me."

"I can't wait anymore."

"What?" Snow White asked.

Justin leaned forward and kissed Snow White softly on her lips. He looked up into her face and when she didn't object, he kissed her again.

Snow White was surprised, but she closed her eyes and kissed him back. Suddenly she and Justin both jumped back when their packs vibrated. A group of boys from the other team laughed as they ran away.

Justin smiled tentatively at Snow White, his teeth glowing green in the black light. Snow White giggled. He took her by the hand and led her after their attackers. "Let's go get them," he said. She couldn't wipe the smile from her face as she allowed him to pull her around the maze.

After the game ended, they joined her cousins and some other friends in the café for pizza. Snow White listened as they all shared their plans for college and the years ahead. She couldn't believe graduation was over and she actually made it. A few short months ago, the thought of life after high school was terrifying. Now, Snow White actually looked forward to the months and years ahead.

In discovering where she came from, Snow White had learned who she wanted to be. For the first time in her life, she actually had dreams of college and a career. She wanted to go into therapy and help women who had suffered like her mother learn to cope with and overcome their trauma. She wanted to help others so they wouldn't have to live in pained silence like she and her mother did. As she looked around the table at her cousins, her sisters really, she knew even though they were each taking their own paths, nothing would ever tear them apart. They would remain the Princess sisters from now until forever after.

.

Forever After

# *Epilogue*

## Five Years Later

Cinderella looked down at the tiny little bundle she cradled in her arms. Scott wrapped his arm around her shoulders and lay his head on top of hers.

"You sure there's a baby in there?"

Cinderella pushed the layers of pink blankets away from her tiny pink face. "There," she said, beaming with pride.

Scott leaned over and stared into her perfectly round face. "Dang, we do good work."

Cinderella looked up at him and they exchanged a smile. Scott leaned down and kissed her sweetly on the lips. "I love you more than anything, even more so now than the day I married you."

The baby began to squirm and fuss a little, so Cinderella bounced her up and down. "And I love you! From the moment our lips first touched while standing on that stone A, I knew we were meant to be."

Scott kissed her again just as someone knocked on the door. "Get a room!" Aurora teased, pushing the heavy hospital door open and entering.

"No, that's how they got here in the first place!" Ariel added.

The twins and Snow White all piled into Cinderella's cramped hospital room and gathered around her bed.

"She's perfect!"

"She's beautiful!"

"Are you ready?" Cinderella asked, reaching out and placing a hand on Ariel's protruding belly.

"I don't know," Ariel said, hugging her middle. Her wedding ring sparkled under the bright hospital lights. "Were you ready?"

"Fair enough," Cinderella smiled. "In just one more month, you'll be in the hospital bed and we'll all be surrounding you to meet that little boy of yours."

Jordan came up behind Ariel and placed his hands on her stomach. "We can't wait!" he beamed with pride.

Snow White approached the bed. "Can I hold her?"

"Of course!" Cinderella said. She carefully lifted the baby and placed her in Snow White's arms.

"So how are things going with Grey?" Cinderella asked.

"Oh, we actually broke up last week," Snow White said, shrugging. She continued to stare into the baby's perfectly round sleeping face.

"Oh, Snow, I'm so sorry to hear that!" Cinderella said.

"Don't be," Snow White answered casually. "He actually wanted to get more serious and talk about marriage and our future. He was a really nice guy, but I just couldn't picture our 'Forever After' together. You know?" Snow White gently rocked back and forth as she spoke.

"Any new prospects on the horizon?" Ariel asked.

"Not yet, but I'm really okay right now." Snow White suddenly jumped, causing the baby to fuss. "Oh my gosh, I forgot to tell you guys! Have you heard my mom's news yet?

Cinderella took the baby back and bounced her gently, soothing her back to sleep. "What?" she asked.

"My mom is getting married! Remember Mr. Wilkins from the rape case?" Snow White moved across the room and sat on the bench which connected below the window.

Ariel reached her hands out and took a turn holding the baby in her arms. "You mean the guy who put your dad in prison?" she asked, her mouth agape.

"The very same one!" Snow White said, beaming. "I've never seen her this happy before. It's pretty awesome."

"Wow!" Aurora said. "I didn't even know they were dating!" She reached for the baby, but Ariel turned away, shaking her head.

"They've been in touch all these years but never really dated until the last few months. It's crazy how things work out sometimes."

"Tell her congratulations!" Cinderella said, adjusting her position on the stiff hospital bed. "That's so great!"

"Your turn, Aurora," Snow White said. "How is This Week doing?" she teased.

"Actually," Aurora said, straightening up, "I have been dating a wonderful man. His name is Ryan. We met when he came into the salon to have his hair cut, and we just celebrated our six month anniversary yesterday."

Cinderella, Snow White, Scott, and Jordan all applauded her. Ariel's hands were filled with baby or she would have joined in. Aurora played along and took a deep bow. "Thank you, thank you," she said. "I know this is pretty amazing. I may have finally found the right guy for me."

"He's really great," Jordan piped in. "You guys will all love him. Aurora is not allowed to break up with this one, or I might be heartbroken."

Ariel giggled. "He's really into cars, too," she explained.

"So has anyone heard from the newlyweds?" Scott asked.

With another light tapping on the door, Belle and Dave came walking in, hand in hand.

"Speak of the devil," Scott said. He crossed the room and patted his younger brother on the back. "How was the honeymoon?"

"Hawaii was incredible!" Belle said. She approached the bed and gave Cinderella a big hug. "I can't believe I'm an aunt," she said, stealing the baby away from Ariel.

"Hey!" Aurora said. "I was next!"

"Sorry, I get dibs 'cause I'm the oldest," Belle added, smiling. "So, did you finally decide on a name?" she asked, looking from Scott to Cinderella.

"Do you remember how much we all used to hate our princess names growing up?"

"Ummm, yeah," Snow White said.

"Absolutely," Ariel said.

"Definitely," Aurora added.

"But they're not so bad anymore," Belle added. "It took a while, but I wouldn't change my name for anything now."

The other Princess sisters agreed.

"That's what Scott and I were talking about," Cinderella said. "We all grew to love our names. So it turns out maybe our moms knew what they were doing after all." She looked around the small, white hospital room at each of her cousin's happy faces. "So we decided to carry on the tradition. Everyone, meet Jasmine."

If you enjoyed The Princess Sisters trilogy, check out another one of Stacy's books: My Name is Bryan:

# CHAPTER ONE
"Hardships often prepare ordinary people for an extraordinary destiny."
-C.S. Lewis

June 1979

"Cliff jumping. You in?" Bryan's smile widened as he watched his best friend's eyes light up.

"Absolutely! When?" Greg asked.

Bryan threw his large duffel bag into the opening under the bus. "I don't remember. I think my dad said it's toward the end of the trip. But apparently we get to conquer some pretty big rapids first."

"Sweet! This trip totally beats what we did last year."

"Yeah, no kidding."

Bryan and Greg stepped away from the bus, wandering across the parking lot to settle under a large oak tree.

"Hey, man, you ready?" Another lanky teenage boy came up to the pair.

"Yeah, my dad was telling me about some cliffs we can jump off during the rafting trip." Bryan could hardly contain his excitement.

"Oh yeah? How high?"

"Not sure," Bryan said, looking around as some other guys approached. "But it sounds awesome."

"What sounds awesome?" one of them asked.

"Cliff jumping," Greg chimed in.

"Seriously? Sweet!"

"Are the leaders going to let us?"

"Yeah, Duane is the one who told my dad about them," Bryan said.

"Hey, looks like we're loading now." Greg pointed at the line of teenagers snaking their way through the parking lot and onto the bus.

Bryan and his friends were the last to get in line.

"Oh, man, that means we're probably sitting up front."

"Loser seats. Right behind the…" Bryan trailed off as they climbed the three steps and found the last two empty rows were directly behind the chaperones, just as he had feared. "Parents," he sighed.

Carol Jean turned around in her seat and flashed her son a huge smile. Bryan tried to return the grin, but it came across as more of a grimace. It was bad enough his parents were on the trip, but now he had to sit by them?

"Oh, Bryan," Carol Jean laughed. She rolled her eyes and turned to her husband, Glenn. "Have you ever seen a more sullen teenager?" she asked.

Glenn turned in his seat and smiled. "Well, he is stuck with all us old fogies. Poor kid can't catch a break. First his boss doesn't want him to come, then he has to travel on his last youth conference trip with both his parents and his sister. Maybe we should start planning his pity party now."

"Okay, thank you," Bryan waved his parents off and turned to Greg.

"Your boss didn't want you to come?" Greg asked, putting on his black aviators and leaning back in his seat. "How come?"

"Summer is the busiest season for pouring concrete, as I'm sure you can imagine," Bryan explained. "My boss couldn't find a replacement so he didn't want me to come." Bryan shrugged. "I was able to talk him into it eventually though."

Greg nodded.

Bryan lay his head back against the soft, grey headrest and closed his eyes. He wasn't tired enough to sleep, but after working hard labor outside every day, it felt nice to just sit and relax with his eyes closed. His thoughts traveled to Jana and he wondered what she was doing at that moment.

As if reading his thoughts, Greg asked, "So how are things going with Jana?"

Bryan opened his eyes and smiled. "Really great! She's amazing and lots of fun."

"So what're your plans? You gonna keep pouring concrete?"

"For now. At least until I can get a job at a garage somewhere."

"Still no college?" Carol Jean asked, trying to hide the disappointment in her voice. She had been eavesdropping from the row in front of them.

"What would I do with college? If I'm going to be a mechanic, the best schooling I can get is in a garage."

"Have you found a garage to take you on as an intern yet?" Glenn asked, trying to turn around in his seat.

"No. I thought it would be better to start applying after this trip. I didn't want to get on somewhere only to tell them I needed a week off."

Glenn nodded his head in agreement. Bryan watched as his dad quickly put his focus back on the driver and the road. His dad had a map in his head and could get anywhere without a problem. He always preferred the scenic route to reaching his destination quickly. Bryan knew it drove him crazy to just sit back and watch as the driver sped past several attractive pullouts. His dad constantly said, "Life is about the journey," before turning down a dusty little side road. But they always ended up right where they needed to be. Bryan smiled as he watched Glenn's lip twitch. He knew it was killing him not to say anything.

Bryan looked down the long row of seats toward the back of the bus, catching his sister's eye. He smiled, but Becky returned to her conversation without acknowledging him. The game was on. Bryan stared, unblinking at the side of Becky's face. His eyes bore into her cheek until it started to turn pink. His eyes narrowed, but still he didn't blink. Becky's mouth twitched at the corners, until she finally broke into a smile. Bryan laughed and turned around in his chair. He had won.

The drive was peaceful, especially compared to family vacations. With four younger sisters, road trips were anything but quiet. There was always fighting over seats or music or screaming at each other to stop touching.

"If both your parents are here, who has your other sisters?" Greg asked.

"Brenda is at a junior rangers camp, and both Glenda and Jenny are staying with a cousin."

"So this must be a nice week off for you, huh, Mrs. C?" Greg asked, leaning forward.

"I'm not sure I'd call rafting through rapids a relaxing week off, but I'm sure we'll have fun."

Several hours later, the bus jostled Bryan awake as they drove over loose gravel, nearing the San Juan River. He hadn't even realized he'd fallen asleep. Once they reached the river and everyone climbed off the bus, they split into smaller groups of ten or so to a raft, and each raft had a chaperone in charge. Duane walked to the front of the group and welcomed them enthusiastically.

"How's everyone doing this morning?" he asked.

"Fabulous, marvelous, and wonderful!" Glenn's response was louder than any of the kids in the group. Several of them turned toward him and smiled. His enthusiasm increased the excitement around them.

Once everyone was quiet again, Duane gave a small lesson on rowing and had the kids all practice smooth, strong strokes together. Once food and supplies were safely loaded, the kids climbed aboard the big yellow rafts and pushed off.

They spent the first two days on the water for a good portion of the day. They pulled off occasionally to eat or explore but spent most of their time working together to row through the brownish green water. They had little time for floating, as the water moved quickly over the large rapids. When they did get moments of calm, the kids got in water fights with the other rafts or jumped in the water to swim and cool off. They had to travel so many miles each day to ensure they'd make it to the next camp site and that the trip would end on time.

Having already turned eighteen, Bryan was one of the oldest kids in the group. He was even in charge of his own raft since there weren't enough adults to go around. He took this charge seriously and watched over his group as he guided them down the smooth river.

On day three, some of his group began to get restless so Bryan devised a plan. They slowed down and waited for Becky's raft to come into view, and then they pulled up alongside it to ambush her and her friends. Several boys jumped aboard, grabbing the screaming girls and throwing them into the water. The girls squealed and tried to get away, but the ambush worked in the end. They not only emptied their opponent's raft, but they were saved from boredom as well. Becky grabbed onto the side of her brother's raft, gasping, and asked Bryan for help. He grabbed her by the lifejacket to pull her aboard, when two other girls popped up from the water and grabbed Bryan, yanking him in. The cold water rushed into his face, burning his nose and eyes. He sputtered and coughed, and then broke his head through the waves, chuckling.

On the last night of the trip, as their raft neared Slickhorn Canyon, Bryan and his friends began talking excitedly about the anticipated cliffs.

"Did Duane say how tall the cliffs are?"

"No. You wanna take bets?"

"Twenty feet."

"Fifty feet."

"One hundred feet!"

Bryan and his friends laughed as two of them jumped into the waist-high water to help pull their raft ashore. Bryan slowly got to his feet and wiped the sweat from his brow. Leaping from the raft and pulling it the rest of the way up the bank, he held the yellow beast steady so his passengers could climb out. Duane appeared at their sides, a glint in his eye as he whispered, "You boys ready?"

They nodded enthusiastically. "Let's do it!"

They hoisted the raft further up the bank. Dinner was underway and several groups of teenagers relaxed around the bank where they had made camp. Excited at the aspect of exploring the canyon and finding the cliffs to jump from, Bryan definitely wasn't ready to be done for the day. A stream flowed into the canyon, forming several smaller ponds. Duane led the way, following this stream past the surrounding area.

"I'll catch up to you guys in a minute," Bryan called. Duane nodded. The boys hooted in excitement as they followed closely behind him, making their way up the steep, red rocks. Bryan had to get his raft secure for the night before he could go. Since he was in charge, it was his duty every night to make sure the raft was tied down and their supplies were safe. Once everything was carefully placed in the shade of some nearby trees, Bryan ran to join the others.

He began hiking in the direction the other guys had gone. He hiked nearly a mile and was about to turn back when he saw them jumping off a ledge that overlooked the water. The crimson cliff stood before him like a towering giant, with arms stretched up toward heaven. A smile spread across his face and he lunged at the overhang; David was ready to take on the mighty Goliath. Bryan could hear laughter growing closer as he climbed higher and higher. His long legs made the ascent easy, and as he grabbed the last dusty ledge, he heaved himself up and over the top. Spending the last couple months working hard outdoors had seriously increased Bryan's muscle mass, so he was able to climb up to the rocky ledge with relative ease. As he watched the other jumpers, some hit the water with pencil-straight legs while others bent their knees, looking as though they were sitting mid-air. A couple of the guys started doing flips off the cliff edge into the water. It seems inevitable that when a large group of guys get together, they try to outdo one another. Bryan watched another buddy flip off the ledge and land feet first in the water below, and then jump up out of the ripples and shake the water from his hair, laughing as he made his way back to the shore to try it again.

Bryan didn't want to do a flip. That just seemed stupid. It's harder to control the way you land, and he was nervous about clearing enough space to keep his head from hitting rocks. He couldn't really just jump either. After the flippers, that would make him look like a pansy. Bryan spent the majority of his life living near a pool, and he spent a large number of weekends on a lake with his family's boat. He was a seasoned swimmer. He had no doubt in his mind that he could show up these boys.

Bryan stepped closer to the edge and looked down, waiting for the others to clear out of his way. With perfectly straight arms raised above his head, he bent his knees slightly for momentum and jumped. A huge smile spread across his face as he sailed through the air, the wind caressing his cheeks as the water neared. Bryan knew he had done a perfect swan dive. He only wished he could have seen how beautiful it must have been to the onlookers. His fingertips touched the cool liquid first, his body forming a flawless straight line behind them. But something was wrong. He was sailing through the water, and the river floor was coming too fast. His hands hit the sand hard. His elbows buckled. Bryan's head smashed into the bottom and with a loud POP, he knew his life would be changed forever.

# About the Author

Stacy Lynn Carroll has always loved telling stories. She started out at Utah State University where she pursued a degree in English, learned how to western swing, and watched as many of her fellow students became 'True Aggies'. She then finished her BA at the University of Utah where she got an emphasis in creative writing. After college she worked as an administrative assistant, where she continued to write stories for the amusement of her co-workers. When her first daughter was born, and with the encouragement of a fortune cookie, she quit her job and became a full-time mommy and writer. She and her husband have three children, two Corgis, and a fish named Don.

If you enjoyed this book, Stacy would love and appreciate your reviews on Amazon and Goodreads! She also loves to make new friends! Follow her on Facebook: https://www.facebook.com/authorstacylynncarroll
Twitter: @StacyLCarroll
Or visit her website: www.stacylynncarroll.com

www.ingramcontent.com/pod-product-compliance
Lightning Source LLC
Chambersburg PA
CBHW070304260626
47160CB00003B/704